BEAUTIFUL BROKEN MESS

ALSO BY KIMBERLY LAUREN

Beautiful Broken Rules

Beautiful Broken Promises

BEAUTIFUL BROKEN MESS

KIMBERLY LAUREN

This is a work of fiction. Names, characters, organizations, places, events, and incidents are either products of the author's imagination or are used fictitiously.

Published by Montlake Romance, Seattle

www.apub.com

ISBN-13: 9781477827802
ISBN-10: 1477827803

Cover design by Mumtaz Mustafa

Library of Congress Control Number: 2014955025

Printed in the United States of America

For all the amazing bloggers, readers, and authors who have loved these characters just as much as I do. You've surprised the hell out of me. I'm eternally grateful.

BEAUTIFUL BROKEN MESS

- ONE -

AUDREY -

To say it simply, my life is a broken mess. In the back of my mind, I often wonder if people are given a set number of obstacles they have to overcome before they die. If that's the case, then hopefully I've already hit my limit for this lifetime. Because no matter what I do or how I try to live my life, everything seems to come out wrong.

This catastrophe of a life was inevitable, though. My parents began the cycle when they decided that getting high and not using condoms would be a stellar idea. As if that wasn't bad enough, my mom made sure that it stayed a mess when she decided to resume her life of boozing and drugging while pregnant. Luckily, the only side effect resulting from her recklessness was that I was born with a low birth weight. Her worst decision of all was deciding to keep me when she very well could have given me to a deserving couple who would have actually wanted me.

I often find myself daydreaming about what my life would be like now if she had just given me up, like her labor-and-delivery nurse quietly suggested. Would I live in an actual house? Would I have normal parents who go to normal nine-to-five jobs? Would I have siblings? Or my favorite one of all, would I have a real bed?

Because of her suspicion that my mom would be a horrifying parent, a nurse actually advised her to look into adoption within the first twenty-four hours of delivery. I'm still baffled that they even let her leave with me. She loves to tell me that story too; only she revises it every once in a while by saying I was actually the horrible one, and that it was no wonder the nurse suggested it. But apparently, the enticement of a welfare check convinced my parents to keep me, regardless of the fact that neither of them cared anything about me.

When I was four I realized that food costs money, and I couldn't wait for the day when I could leave the house and earn some of my own. From time to time I caught a glimpse of what money looked like, but it was usually in a back-alley exchange or over the counter of a liquor store. When I was ten, I started mowing lawns; when I was fourteen, people in our trailer park allowed me to babysit their children. I knew by then that if I earned my own money I could use it to buy food, which was hard to find at our house. I loved going to school because it was usually the only time I got a real meal.

I'll never forget the first time I stepped into a grocery store with a pocketful of my own cash. I didn't realize how the exchange worked, or how much food actually cost. I ended up walking out with only a bag of apples. I loved apples, and the only time I had ever had them was when they served them on occasion with lunch at school.

When the grocery checker informed me I couldn't afford the apples *and* the loaf of bread, my decision was easy. I wanted the apples. I was so proud of myself for actually being able to buy food to take home to my parents. I just knew they would smile and maybe . . . just maybe they would finally praise me.

As I proudly walked through our old, creaky front door, my dad took one look at the bag and asked, "What the hell are those?" At that moment, I should have noticed the slurring of his words or the wobble in his walk, but I didn't.

So I smiled and replied enthusiastically, "They're apples. I bought them all by myself." An intense rage shot across his face and my smile plummeted. Maybe he had misunderstood me.

"You spent money on some damn fruit? How the fuck could you be such an idiot? We don't need any shitty fruit," he screamed at me, while ripping the bag from my shaking hands.

Every once in a while I think back on that day, and every time it plays like a slow-motion horror movie in my head. I remember watching the bag come toward my face and thinking, when the first apple hit, that it wasn't any worse than his fist felt. Then the force of four more apples followed behind, pounding against my flesh, and it was worse—much, much worse. *Whack, whack, whack. Whack.*

I also remember that I didn't scream or make a sound. I had learned early on that screaming only made the punishment last longer and he was going to do this regardless of my distress. I slumped down into my protective position on the floor and tucked in my legs, while trying as best I could to cover my face. When the fruit wasn't doing anything besides becoming a sopping wet mess against my body, he then switched over to his fists. I recall him screaming about wasting money and throwing in a few other unpleasant terms he had created for me.

I lay on the ground and waited for the punishment to end, while fist after fist and a couple of feet continued their assault. I knew he wouldn't stop until he'd worn himself out. *Wham* . . . my face, *wham* . . . broken rib, *wham* . . . my stomach.

Mercifully, once the pain reached an all-time high, the blackness engulfed me. The blackness was safe. Sometimes I wished I could just stay there.

When I finally came to, Mrs. Thomas, the next-door neighbor, was hovering over me, trying to get the swelling down by placing bags of frozen vegetables across various parts of my body. I didn't even want to know the extent of my injuries. The bruises took months to heal. I wasn't allowed outside of the trailer, and my mom pulled me from school, informing them that I would be homeschooled. Yeah, right. Unless watching her down an entire forty constituted homeschooling, I wasn't learning much.

Mrs. Thomas helped me heal every day, but she didn't want the authorities coming around any more than my parents did. So she never called for help. She had her own secrets to hide, only one of them being her drug-abusing husband. I never ate an apple again.

~

Shortly after my seventeenth birthday, I was hired to work in the kitchen of an Italian restaurant on the nicer side of town. For me, working in a restaurant was a dream. The hours were long and required me to stay late into the night. Perfect. The less time I had to spend at home, the better. Another bonus was that Chef Moretti, or Nico, as he let me call him, favored me above the other employees. I think it's probably because I worked the hardest, never wanting to go home.

Some nights when the restaurant was slow, he taught me how to cook a few of the dishes we served. I was constantly fantasizing about one day living on my own and being able to prepare authentic meals for myself at home. Food from plastic bags or cardboard boxes wouldn't be allowed. I was excited at the idea of being able to bring home fresh fruits and vegetables. Except apples—never apples.

Nico didn't know how abusive my parents actually were, but I think he understood to an extent why I had to hide from them.

When I started working there, I asked him if it would be possible to keep half of my earnings saved on the side, my reason being that my dad required me to bring home a pay stub so that he would always know how much I made, and how much he could take from me. I was allowed to buy groceries and a bus pass, but any remaining balance went directly into his hands.

Thankfully, one look into my pleading eyes and Nico had agreed. I didn't know much about the tax system, but I knew enough to know that what he was doing could have gotten him into trouble. I lost track of how much Nico put away for me, but I knew my balance was slowly building. One day, it would help me escape this town.

~

One Friday, after cashing my paycheck, I head to the grocery store and buy all of the items my dad had preapproved. My list mostly consists of ramen, peanut butter, and spaghetti. I also purchase the one item that will hopefully keep my dad's hands off me—a bottle of whiskey. While sometimes this backfires, typically it keeps him in a better mood. It's a risky line I walk every day.

I recently made friends with a grocery checker named Oliver, who sells me the alcohol even though I'm underage by a few years. His smile creeps me out a little bit, but if a smile is all that he's offering, I can return that. I always ask for paper instead of plastic. It's harder to swing a paper bag around as a weapon, like you can with a plastic bag. I'm a fast learner.

After making my purchases, I walk down the sidewalk toward the bus stop, gazing inside the shop windows as I go by. I love admiring all of the items I can never afford to have, like books, new clothes, or even jewelry. Just as I pass by my favorite bookstore, a large figure carrying a giant box steps out of the door and slams right into me before I can get out of the way. I watch in horror as my bag of groceries crashes to the ground. My stomach plummets when I hear the worst sound of all . . . the whiskey bottle shattering inside the bag.

I suck in an enormous lungful of air and fall to my knees. "No, no, no . . ." I whisper through a sob. Tears well up in my eyes at the idea of going home empty-handed.

"Shit, I'm so sorry!" I hear the stranger say, as he sets his box on the ground and kneels down in front of me. "Let me help you clean this up."

"No, no, no . . ." I repeat, lost in the idea of how my father will react to this. I'm still not looking up at whoever just signed my death warrant, but I watch his strong hands as he scoops the shattered glass and the soaking wet boxes back into the torn paper bag. The spilled milk mixed with the smell of whiskey is nauseating.

"Damn, I think all of this is ruined. I'm really sorry," he continues, with a hopeless apology that won't keep the bruises at bay.

All I can do is stare at my shaking hands. *Maybe I can go ask Nico for money from my side account to buy more groceries*, I think. *Surely he can help me.* But then I remember he left this afternoon to go up north for a visit with his mother, who has fallen ill. I don't have a phone number to reach him, and I'm sure he won't be able to help from long distance anyway. *This is it, then. I have to face the music and go home empty-handed. I'll survive. I always survive. I have only one more year until I can get out of this town.*

A warm hand reaches out and forces my chin up. "Look at me," a stern voice commands gently.

His glacial blue eyes dominate all other thoughts at the moment. The way he looks at me, I realize he must have been trying to grab my attention for a while. I slowly come back down from my panic.

"There you are . . ." he says softly, sounding a bit relieved. With one hand still holding my chin up, he wipes the tears out of my eyes with his other hand. I clear my throat, but I'm still unable to speak to this stunningly attractive person. Now that my vision isn't clouded, I can fully take him in. His entire demeanor commands my complete attention. I don't know why, but I suddenly crave the idea of *allowing* someone to have that control over me, to *actually trust* another person. I've never fully trusted anyone. I've never been given the *opportunity* to fully trust anyone.

Even though he's crouching down in front of me, I can tell this guy has long, muscular legs. I'm five foot ten, so it's hard to come across people who are much taller than I am. I like the idea of being able to look up into his eyes. He's also fit. If the polo shirt he's wearing with the logo of the local hotshot football team didn't give it away, his large shoulders and wide chest would have.

Looking beyond his intense blue eyes, I notice the warm, dark brown color of his hair, and I'm surprised to see natural highlights scattered throughout. With his free hand, he reaches up and threads his fingers through the strands and lets them fall haphazardly back down. The way the pieces fall perfectly into place makes it seem as if even his hair knows how to submit to his strong will. I begin to wonder how my body would feel under those fingers. Would it submit as easily as his hair?

He clears his throat, which pulls my attention back from the unexpectedly sensual thoughts I'm having. "You realize these are just groceries, right?" He slyly grins at me in question. I nod my head but still can't reply. "I'll replace them for you. It's the least I can do for knocking you over."

As he helps me up to a standing position, I think about rejecting his offer. It's not like he knew I was going to be walking in front of the door at that exact moment. Just because a measly bag of groceries brings me to my knees in a pathetic crying pile, that doesn't mean he should have to buy anything for me. On the other hand, I'm not in any position to decline help. My choice is either to save my pride and deal with my dad's wrath or to let this stranger, whom I'll never see again, assist me. I choose the stranger.

"Thank you." I meekly smile while wiping the last of the moisture from my eyes.

When we finally extend to our full heights, I am excited to see that he's at least four or five inches taller than me. Seeing the full package standing in front of me doesn't hurt either. He's gorgeous. I watch as he reaches down to grab the box he almost mauled me with and sets it into the back of a giant, four-door, black pickup truck. I don't know much about cars, because I ride the bus, but this truck has to be expensive. There aren't any scratches on the paint and not a speck of rust on the rims.

Unlike me, he actually belongs on this side of town. I just work here. Our city is divided into two vastly different areas, based on economic status, and I've never understood why they didn't just separate into two different cities. This side of town has the golden-child high school that receives all the funding for their state-championship-winning football team and award-winning academic decathlon team. My school had ten girls get pregnant last year instead of twelve, which was the total from the previous year. I call that progress.

The beautiful stranger comes over and scoops up my pitiful, ruined bag of groceries and begins to rifle through it before tossing it into a nearby trash can.

"My brother is actually at the store right now, picking up groceries for my mom. Mind if I just text him a list of everything you had? That way you don't have to go shopping again, and we can just go grab some coffee instead." He nods his head toward the chic little café across the street.

"Uh . . . sure. I can tell you what I need," I reply.

"No worries, I remember everything you had." He shrugs his shoulders while quickly typing out a list on his expensive-looking, touch-screen phone.

I nervously bounce on my feet, feeling uncomfortable with this favor. "Can you ask him to put my groceries in a paper bag, please?"

"Of course. They always put them in bags," he says, only half paying attention to me.

"No, it needs to be a paper bag, not plastic," I state adamantly, causing him to look up from his phone.

"Okay . . . no plastic, understood." He eyes me curiously, but there is no way I'll be explaining that one. As he slides his phone into his back pocket, he looks down into my eyes. "I'm Jace, by the way. Sorry about my earlier introduction," he says apologetically.

When he wraps his arm around my shoulders, I smile inwardly at his forwardness. "I'm Audrey . . . Audrey Mills," I reply. As we walk toward the café, I tease, "Are we getting coffee just so you can get out of shopping?"

He dramatically brings his free hand up to his chest and gasps, "Whatever do you mean? Me? A guy? Get out of shopping? Never!" He's the one teasing me now.

A laugh bubbles up out of my throat. "All right, all right, I get it. Guys don't like shopping."

When we approach the door, he reaches out and opens it for me. I've never been around someone who acts like a gentleman before. I didn't know guys like this really existed. When I smile up at him on my way through the door, I silently thank him.

"If you want to go shopping, babe, I'll take you right now. I figured I just met this beautiful girl and I'd rather get to know her instead of shopping at a lame grocery store," he responds with a sly grin on his face.

I point my finger at his chest. "You're a charmer, you know that? I should watch myself around you." He winks at me and continues to pull us along toward the counter. This is another thing on my long list of Never Have I Evers. I've never been in a café. There doesn't seem to be a point in going inside when you can't afford anything. I understand that a café sells coffee, but the menu board seems to have a thousand different drinks that I have never even heard of. I'm seeing words like "Frappuccino," "Macchiato," and "Americano," all of which are lost on me. I was already starting to doubt that I fit in here, but this just confirms it. Quickly, I scan the board so I can just order something, anything.

As I stand, lost and confused, I feel his warmth as he comes up behind me. "Let me pick your drink. I see an open leather chair over there you should go and snag," he says, as he points over to the crowded seating area.

"Am I that easy to read?"

"I've got you covered. Now go grab that seat," he says with a wink, avoiding my question. It's embarrassing that he can tell how out of place I am here, but I delight in the idea of him taking control of the situation. I can let him do that.

I sidestep through the crowded café. A study group takes up the only section of tables and chairs. The rest of the room is filled with leather chairs for lounging. I assume that all of these people attend the local community college because they have advanced textbooks and laptops out, and the high schools aren't back in session yet.

When I get to the leather seat Jace had pointed out for me, I realize it's the only seat available. I stare down at it, wondering if I should sit in it or let him have it. I mean, he's already paying for my mystery drink *and* groceries.

"You realize that's just a chair, right?" he whispers into my ear from behind, mimicking his earlier comment about my groceries.

"You should have it." I gesture toward it. "I'm all right standing."

"Sit," he softly commands and I obey, slightly bemused by this hold he has on me.

He pulls the wooden coffee table across the tile floor to the front of my chair and sits on it, facing me. I'm surprised the small table can handle his large frame, but it seems to be holding up well.

I'm keenly aware of how close he's sitting, and even though this place is packed with chatting people, I feel as though it's only him and me. His knees brush the outside of mine and he squeezes my legs together between his. When I look up, I see he's watching me as I observe our legs. Don't get me wrong: I'm not new to this flirting game, but with him it's actually exciting.

We sit there staring at each other, and shockingly, it isn't uncomfortable or awkward. It's as if we're having a silent conversation, getting to know each other in this intimate, inaudible way. His eyes seem as if they're peering into mine, trying to discover all of my secrets that are hidden in the darkest of depths. I hope he never has to know those secrets, although I would love to be comfortable enough with someone to finally divulge all of my thoughts. It sounds quite freeing, to be honest.

Jace smiles perceptively, and when the waitress brings our drinks out, his eyes finally leave my face. He reaches up to her tray and brings a mug and a water bottle down in between us. When he hands me the mug, I stare at the caramel-colored drink that has a frothy white top. It still feels a bit too warm to drink, so I place it on the table next to Jace to allow it to cool down. I look up when I can practically feel him laughing at me.

"It's a chai tea latte."

"I know," I lie to him.

"No you don't." He laughs again. "You're a coffeehouse virgin, aren't you?" When I don't respond, he gives me a sweet smile. Not one that is meant to ridicule, but just one that shows he's trying to figure me out. "That's cool. I'm glad I could be your first."

My eyes bug out at his innuendo and I finally begin to laugh at myself. "I'm pathetic, aren't I? I mean, who has never been to a coffeehouse?"

"Not at all; I'm finding you refreshing."

His comment makes me blush, so I decide to change the subject. "How old are you?" I'm assuming he's in high school because of the shirt he's wearing, but it could just be from a past year. I watch as he takes a long pull from his water bottle, and for some reason, the up-and-down movement of his throat as he swallows continuously mesmerizes me. Would it be weird to put my lips on his neck right now?

"Eighteen," he replies. "You?"

I nod my head. "Just turned eighteen last week."

"No shit? So did I. What day?"

"The fourteenth."

He points to himself and says, "The thirteenth—beat you by a day!" His smile is infectious. "So what's a gorgeous, *eighteen*-year-old girl like you doing buying whiskey?" he asks, smirking.

I make a disgusted face. "I don't drink; it's for my dad." I resolve to leave it at that. The fact that I buy my dad liquor in the hopes that he won't beat the crap out of me is not something I plan on sharing.

"You don't drink? Seems like every high school kid around here does. I like that. I don't touch the stuff either," he says with a smile.

I'm assuming that we don't indulge for vastly different reasons. I don't drink because I've seen what it can do to a person and I've smelled the horror on my dad's breath one too many times.

Fortunately, he doesn't dig any deeper, instead asking, "So, did you just pay Oliver off like everyone else?"

"Pay him off? No, he doesn't ask me to pay him," I reply, confused.

If I had to pay the guy any more than what I already spend there, I wouldn't be able to afford anything besides the whiskey. Without thinking, I reach into my purse, grab my cherry-vanilla lip balm, and spin the bottom. As I slide the balm against my lips, Jace's eyes follow the trail.

"That jackass makes everybody pay him . . ." I watch him pause as I rub my lips together and he begins to study me. "Well . . . I guess you *would* be an exception." His legs squeeze mine a little tighter.

Together we sit and talk for what seems like hours. We talk about future college plans and how boring high school is. We even have a debate over whether reading an actual book is better than reading from a device. I root for the actual paper-and-spine book, but he trumps me by pulling out his smart phone and showing me how he has over two hundred books right in his back pocket.

Who would have thought a guy in high school would actually enjoy talking about books? I almost reach to grab his face in that moment, so I grab my drink instead and take the first sip.

Oh, that's nice. I've never tasted anything like this before. It's definitely not that black sludge my dad brews every morning. Although it's long since cooled to a tepid temperature, the flavor is sweet and slightly spicy at the same time. Now I wish Jace hadn't introduced this to me, because I'll be lusting after this drink every time I pass this place in the future.

"This is fantastic!" I think I'm a little too excited over a drink, so I try to tone down the enthusiasm. "Great choice," I say and smile up at him.

He watches me intently again. "Must be a chick thing. My mom always gets me to pick that up for her when I'm down here. I'm sure she'll be proud to know it helped me pick up a girl."

"Oh, is that what this is—a pick-up?" I ask, while trying to tamp down my obnoxious smile.

"Damn straight." He leans down so our faces are only inches apart, and I can feel his breath lightly teasing my lips. In a low but firm whisper, he says, "I like you, Audrey. I plan to take you out and kiss you good night over and over until you agree to let me do it all again the next night."

Floor. Puddle. Me. *Holy hell.*

I stay there, not daring to move an inch, in hopes that he'll lean in and put me out of my misery, because his lips are entirely too tempting to be that close. I silently implore him to show me just one of those kisses he's talking about. As if on cue, a loud buzzing begins to vibrate between us and I jump back, startled.

"Easy, gorgeous . . ." he says, his voice sounding a bit breathless. Maybe I'm not the only one affected here. "It's just my phone." He pulls it out and I watch as his fingers slide and tap continuously on the screen. "My brother put your groceries in the truck. He had to go into the bookstore."

"I should really get going anyway. My parents are expecting me, and I don't want the milk to get warm . . ." I trail off because I can feel the start of my nervous rambling, and let's be honest, my parents are never expecting me.

JACE -

I nod my head and stand. Will I ever see her again? Does she want to see me again? Hell, I already sound like a whimpering, lovesick puppy. *You would wreck this girl, Jace.* She just seems so fragile, yet deep in her eyes I can see fierceness, and damn if I don't want to unleash that.

When I grab her hand and lace my fingers through hers, she stands without hesitation and allows me to lead the way. I can't even remember the last time I held hands with a girl. She seems to like when I take control, though. I walk her back out to my truck, quicker than I mean to. I need to drag out this time I have with her.

"Do you need a ride home?" *Please say yes.* I click the key fob and open the back passenger door, and then she reaches in to grab her *paper* sack. I want to ask her so many questions, like why paper?

Is she an environmentalist? Does she not want to clog our landfills with more plastic? Because she seemed so adamant about it, almost as if she was frightened, and that's the only conclusion I can come to right now.

"No, I'm just around the corner."

I have to keep touching her, and I am *not* a touchy-feely guy. Who the hell is this girl? She has to be a witch. That has to be it. She must have cast a spell on me, because it's the only way I can explain my actions around her. *Christ, stop touching the poor girl!* I can't help myself, so I place my hands on her shoulders to keep her from leaving just yet. Shoulders are a safe zone, right? I'm pretty sure I can still touch her there and it isn't inappropriate.

"Can I have your number?" I ask, trying to recall the last time I actually had to ask a girl. Probably never, and even if I did, I sure as hell never called them. But she's leaving and I'm panicking.

"No, but can I have yours?" she counters and smiles confidently up at me. Fuck, I'll bet that smile gets her anything she wants.

I'm puzzled as to why she won't give up her number, but I realize I have to go slowly with this one. "Approach with Caution" should be taped across her chest. Wait . . . screw that. Nobody'd better be touching that chest, except for me.

She continues smiling at me while I give her a half-cocked, questioning look as if to say *What are you up to?* I decide to let her have her way, reaching behind her into the truck to grab my notebook with a pen tucked inside the metal spiral. She watches as I write my ten digits onto the lined paper and then tear it from the binding.

After I fold it into a small square, I think of another way I can touch her. Pathetic, I know. She's still glancing at my hands holding the paper when I reach down and slowly slide it into her front jeans pocket, feeling the heat of her skin through the fabric. *Damn, so close yet so far away.* When my hand slips from the confines of the pocket, she releases a trapped breath. I'm willing to bet she liked that about as much as I did.

I instantly cup her face firmly in between my hands, because I need her full attention. "You don't get to ditch me. I want to see you again." I hope that the sincerity of my statement is getting to her through those beautiful brown eyes.

"I won't," she whispers back.

I know that I must have a cocky grin on my face, but damn, it's nice to know how much I seem to affect her. "Well, I guess I'll be the pitiful guy at home, waiting for a girl to call him," I say, winking. "Bye, Audrey."

She needs to walk away now before I kiss her. If I do, I'll kiss her so hard her lips will bruise. She needs to walk away, but instead, she's just staring at me with that hopeful look on her face. Then all at once the look dies, and she says, "Bye, Jace."

Was she hoping that I would kiss her too? Before she can get out of arm's reach, I pull her back in front of me. I need to know that I'll see her again. "You know that party Cole West throws every year before school starts?" I ask, throwing out the first thing I can think of.

She doesn't say anything for a long time, and I start to think about what I asked. It doesn't seem like a hard question. Everyone knows about Cole's parties. I know she doesn't go to my school, but people in town gossip about them for weeks afterward. Every August around this time, his parents fly up to DC for business purposes, and that giant house of his just begs for a party. I can picture Audrey now, wearing a bikini and all wet from swimming. Shit, she needs to answer me so I can divert my attention away from thoughts of tiny bikinis, water, and her body. She nods her head.

"You'll be there tonight, right?"

"Uh . . . if you want me to," she replies.

"I want you . . . there." I mostly just want her, but I also want her at that party with me.

"Okay, I'll come. Where is it?"

This girl is hard to comprehend. Cole's parties never change their venue. I cock my eyebrow up at her and ask, "You've never been?" When she shakes her head, I'm floored. Cole is everybody's friend; he knows no stranger. How has he missed this one? And thank God he has, because she might have been the one exception to the bro-code of not hooking up with your buddies' girls, current or past. "It's at Cole's house, which is the biggest one on Lincoln Court. You can't miss it." It's a monstrosity. Way too big for three people.

For a fraction of a second, I see her face fall, but she quickly picks it back up and says, "Wow, okay . . . I'll be there tonight."

I can tell she's uncomfortable about something and that she's only agreeing to go because I want her to. Problem is, this girl looks cute even when she's uncomfortable. I can't hold out any longer. I reach out and situate her bag of groceries on the passenger seat again. Then before she even realizes what's happening, I grab her arms and pin her against the side of the truck.

I can feel her heart beating wildly against my chest, so I lean down and press my lips against hers. Damn, she's sweet. I shouldn't have started this, because how the hell can I stop kissing a mouth that tastes like honey? With a little bit of persuasion, I coax her lips open and instantly my tongue is slowly dancing with hers. I still have her arms in a tight grasp against the truck, but she doesn't seem to mind. She's letting me control this.

My right hand slides away from her arm and over her waist, and I have to hold on tightly, afraid this enchantress will disappear. When my other hand leaves her arm, she instantly laces her fingers through my hair, which pulls a moan from my mouth. Our kiss deepens, both of us needing more. Then, *damn it all* . . . she lifts one of her legs and wraps it around my waist. I can't stop myself from shoving her back farther into the truck and grabbing the warm skin on her thigh to hold it in place. She fits me perfectly.

After a couple of heated beats, I realize that I'm about to rip this girl's clothes off in the middle of the parking lot. My mom might be the coolest parent ever, but she would kill me if she heard about this from the old lady gossip in this town. So reluctantly, I break the kiss. Her eyes remain closed and she's trying to catch her breath, as am I. Who knew making out could be so damn hot?

"Holy hell . . ." I breathe.

"Wow . . ." she says in the same moment.

"You'll be there tonight." It's not a question anymore.

She nods her head and I hand her back the groceries. Without another word, I watch as she walks away carrying her paper bag, even though everything within me is saying she shouldn't go. Call it the White Knight Syndrome, but there's just something about a beautiful damsel in distress, and I sure as hell want to be the one to save her.

- TWO -

AUDREY -

When I sit down on the city bus—the stop was just around the corner, so not a total lie—I finally get a chance to breathe in and out. How did a simple trip to the grocery store just rock my world off its axis? Did Jace really exist, or was he purely made up of too many library-loaned romance novels?

If I had a best friend, I would be running to her right now to tell her everything. But I don't, so I'll just have to replay that make-out scene over and over in my head. Lord knows it'll never get old. Maybe I'll sneak over to Mrs. Thomas's to call my cousin, Kennedy, who lives in Connecticut. We've been getting closer the past couple of years, and she always tells me she can't wait until I get my own phone so she can call whenever she wants.

I could use another girl's perspective, since I'm still really confused about the whole incident. One minute he's taking me to coffee because he feels bad about ruining my groceries, and the next he's pinning me up against his truck and owning me. I've kissed plenty of guys. It's what you do when you're bored out here: you mess around and get into trouble. But I can definitely say that I have never been kissed like *that.*

I can't even call that a kiss, because it was on a whole other level. He made me forget about everything . . . where I was, where I'm from, and even where he's from. It was just my lips and his, dueling for more. I don't know what came over me when I lifted my leg, but that moan he made spurred me on.

At the thought of my groceries, I quickly grab the bag from the seat next to me and glance inside. Shit! No! Damn, why hadn't I been more specific? First of all, the whiskey is some top-shelf brand that I know cost about seven times more than the cheap one I always buy my dad. The milk is organic, the spaghetti is whole-wheat, the peanut butter has added omega-3, and to make matters even worse, the ramen is the low-sodium kind. This grocery bill had to have been way more than mine typically costs because all of this stuff is the freaking healthier version! My dad is going to murder me and I'll never make it to the party now.

A few weeks ago, I caught the tail end of my mom packing up all of her things and throwing them quickly into a beat-up old suitcase. A fancy black car pulled up out front, and my mom rushed to step in it without even a second glace my way. I don't care where she went or even why she left, but I do care that I'm getting the short end of the stick yet again. Ever since that day, my dad has been strung tighter than usual and flying off the handle in the blink of an eye.

My walk home from the bus stop doesn't take long, and when I open the door, I quietly step into the house. I'm relieved to see he isn't home yet from the farm that he works on when he's sober enough to show up. I might actually have a chance to get out of here unscathed. My dog, Chuck, saunters over with his tail wagging to greet me. Chuck, who we think is some kind of cattle dog, is the only loved member in this house. Everybody loves Chuck. He found us last year and never left, thankfully, because he's my only saving grace in this godforsaken house.

"Hey, buddy," I say while scratching behind his ear. "I gotta leave again soon, but I'll be back later."

I rush through my shower and put on the makeup Mrs. Thomas passed down to me a while back. Right as I'm slipping my feet into a pair of sandals, I hear my dad's truck backfire out front. Quickly, I open the window in the bathroom and slip out into the knee-high grass. I can't let him see me right now. Once he gets a look at those groceries, he will blow a gasket from the amount of money I "wasted."

Just as I'm rounding the corner, I hear the old screen door slam open, loudly crashing into the metal siding. Before I can hide somewhere, he's grabbing me by the arms. Coincidentally, he's holding me in the same exact way Jace did not even two hours ago, except this is nothing like how Jace touched me. This is malicious and meant to leave a mark. *Well it was nice knowing you, Audrey.*

"Just who do you think you are, and why the hell do I see a bottle of whiskey on my damn counter that cost more than I make in a month?" I have no words; they've all dried up. "You think you're better than me, girl? You're too fucking good to buy the cheap one? You gotta go and waste my money?"

His money? I'm pretty sure *I'm* the one working fifty hours a week in the back of a hot kitchen. Not that it matters to him, though.

"The store was having a sale," I manage to squeak out, without looking up at him.

"You think I'm some kind of idiot?" *Yes, yes I do*, I think. But I don't say that because I'm kind of attached to my face.

Just then, Mrs. Thomas steps out of her trailer with a broom in hand. "Knock it off, Lee!" she hollers over at him.

Mrs. Thomas is about sixty years old, but I wouldn't underestimate her and what she can do with a broom. When my dad hears her, his grip loosens a fraction, and he turns to glare at her for interrupting.

"You're out there on your damn porch with that nonsense. I haven't called the cops on your shit yet, but that don't mean these other people won't," she says, pointing out our inquisitive neighbors.

When he realizes we have an audience, he reluctantly releases me. All the blood rushes back to my upper arms, and they begin to tingle from the return of blood flow. I immediately step away from him and head toward the bus stop at a clipped pace.

As I'm walking away, I hear his deep baritone say, "You can bet your ass we'll talk later."

I have roughly 283 days until I graduate. On day 284, I hope to have at least a thousand miles between us.

JACE -

"Dude, did I just see you molesting some chick on the side of the truck?" Jaxon asks with an irritating laugh, as he climbs up into the passenger seat.

"I don't think you can call it assault when she's a willing participant," I retort.

"Damn, man, you had Mrs. Jones blushing. I had to distract her on the other side of the store to get her away from the window. Looked like you were into her, whoever she was."

"She was hot, right?" I ask, as I pull the truck out of the parking lot.

"I couldn't see her since you were too far down her throat. I did see her leg hiked up though . . . whoo . . . wait until Mom hears."

"Don't," I growl.

He holds his hands up in surrender. "Hey, she won't be hearing it from me."

Shit, the last thing I need is someone hounding me about the mystery girl I was practically screwing up against my truck. Mom will be the worst. I typically never show interest in girls, at least not publicly. So far, every girl I've come across has been . . . dull, unyielding, or just plain pushy. I don't have the patience for that crap.

Holy hell, though—Audrey made the blood begin pumping in my veins again. She lit me up the way a defibrillator restarts a heart, providing a much-needed shock to my system.

"I want to meet this chick. She has to have a golden pu—"

Instantly, my fist slams into his bicep before he can finish that statement, and I watch victoriously as he sucks in a harsh breath of air and grabs his arm. I know it wasn't my hardest blow because it wasn't coming from a decent angle, but I'm glad it inflicted pain.

I point right at him and say, "You'll stay away from her, and shut the hell up about her body." *End of story.*

I hear him whistle while shaking his head. "Man . . . I need to meet this girl. I mean, you don't hook up with chicks ever, and this one had you practically marking your territory for all to see."

"You make me sound like a damn virgin," I complain.

"Might as well be," he responds drily.

"Just because I don't screw every girl that walks past me, and in public, I might add, doesn't mean anything."

"That chick last weekend was fine as hell and you know it," he says, grinning.

I don't even answer. Sometimes I feel that if I respond in any way at all, he thinks it justifies his actions. Ever since Dad died last year, Jax has been uncontrollable. Mom says he's going through his own grieving process, but in my opinion, it's getting out of hand.

Last weekend, he hooked up with a girl from our school at a party, right outside on one of the pool loungers for everyone to see. Granted, it was pitch-black outside and most of the party was inside, but they still gained a small audience. The weekend before, he got in a fight when Grayson Jones accidently bumped into him at a party and spilled his beer. A couple of days later, he beat Kyle Martin's face in when he thought the dude had touched his Camaro, although it turned out he hadn't. Jax has just become a loose cannon.

"So, on a scale of one-to-getting-arrested, how crazy are you going to be tonight?" I ask as I pull into Cole's driveway. He called earlier asking for help with setup, so I'm dropping Jaxon off to pull our share of friend-duty.

He tugs the door handle and scoots out of the truck. "Hmmm . . ." He rubs the scruff on his chin, being his typical asshole self as of late. I put the engine into reverse because I don't have time for his bullshit, and I hear him respond, "Chill, dude. I'll be good tonight."

I have no idea what his idea of "good" is anymore. "I'll be back later. I need to run all this stuff back to Mom."

~

I arrive at the party later than I wanted to, because Mom had me running around doing all the errands Jax was supposed to do weeks ago. I should have just told her I met a girl and I needed to leave to be here before she arrived, but I didn't feel like playing twenty questions with her tonight.

The street around Cole's house is packed, so I have to park on the next block over. There's no way Audrey could miss this place, and I can feel my blood pumping faster in anticipation of seeing her again. Now I just need to locate her, but it shouldn't be hard to find a stunning, long-legged brunette with the biggest brown eyes I've ever seen.

When I walk in the door, I immediately spot my idiot brother standing toe-to-toe with Mike Bailey and see that they've drawn a crowd around them. I already know what this is about. Jaxon slept with Mike's girlfriend yesterday at the lake and he must have found out; girls talk too damn much. And did I mention Jax has been an asshole lately? I'm sure he can handle himself with Mike, but I decide to stay in close proximity in case I need to break it up. There aren't many guys here big enough to pull my brother away from a fight.

Jaxon appears pissed at having to discuss his actions, but it serves him right. I'd try to go a few rounds with the dude too if he'd slept with my girl. Right as the situation starts to get heated, I watch as *my* stunning, long-legged brunette jumps up into Jaxon's arms. Across the room from them, I freeze, my feet rooted to the floor. When Audrey grabs his face and starts kissing him, my fists open and clench shut with each movement of their lips together. *What. The. Fuck?*

They break the kiss after an eternity, and all I can see is the back of her head and Jaxon's surprised, cheesy grin. "Hey, baby," he says, while gripping her ass. This cannot be happening.

I take a few determined steps forward and then notice the bruises on her arms and immediately retreat back. Shit, I must have hurt her today. How the hell did that happen? I know I was caught up in the moment, but I never realized I was hurting her.

She's probably fucking pissed so she's trying to get back at me. Girls do shit like that. I'm trapped in this strange bubble of wanting to go and rip her from my brother's arms and wanting to leave, because I'm undoubtedly the last person she wants to see right now. My mind is made up for me when I see Jax lean in and take her mouth again. I've never hated him before, but right now it's really damn close. I almost knock over three different people in my hasty departure out the door.

AUDREY -

I gasp awake as a heavy weight lies across my chest. My eyes spring open and I realize the heavy weight is actually an arm, and attached to that arm is a gorgeous, dark-haired, and tanned Jace.

Last night did not go as I had intended it to go. When I arrived at the house that could only be described as a mansion, I waited outside the front door for a solid fifteen minutes. I was hoping I'd run into Jace, so I wouldn't have to walk in alone. Even with all the awkward stares I received and remarks wondering who I was, I still waited.

When I realized he must have already been inside, I decided to approach the ominous, twenty-foot wooden double doors. As I tried to slip inside unnoticed, I instantly focused on the marble entryway tiles and the ornate, metal balustrade alongside the massive staircase. The place was pretentious, and I assumed that the guy who lived here was a privileged douchebag. Usually they're the only kind of people who live in places like that.

The house was packed to the brim and loud. Plastic cups littered the expensive flooring and people were already stumbling about everywhere. It was just another reason why drinking has never appealed to me. Why would you want to lose control of your capability to function?

I saw that there was a crowd gathering around two guys, and the spectators seemed to be spurring them on. With a closer look, I realized I knew the taller of the two. Jace didn't look the same as he did earlier that afternoon, though. He wore a scowl that I never imagined could cross a face like his. Earlier, he seemed so light and playful, as if he didn't have a care in the world.

I began to push my way through the crowd, despite the ugly looks girls were giving me. When I approached the center, I noticed Jace's fists were tightening, his jaw was tense, and he was more than likely about to get into a fight with the person in front of him. I didn't have time to stop and listen to what they were arguing about, although I did notice his adversary looked to be the angrier one. Before either of them could take a swing, I took matters into my own hands.

I squeezed in between the two boys and jumped into Jace's arms. While it was certainly bolder than I would typically ever have been, I didn't want to ruin my first night with him by having to nurse his fat lip or black eye. I got enough of those at home for the both of us.

Proudly, I got the reaction I intended as he took three steps backward and looked into my eyes. Before he could think about setting me down and returning to his altercation, I grabbed his face and tried to continue what we had earlier up against the side of his truck. There was something different about the kiss, though. It wasn't bad, but it didn't have the same effect on me as it had before.

When I pulled back, I saw him grinning from ear to ear and looking pretty pleased with himself. I smiled sheepishly at him, and I knew that my face was turning red from embarrassment. He definitely wasn't expecting a move like that from me, a girl who was crying about spilled groceries only a couple of hours ago.

As he grabbed on to my behind, he grinned and said, "Hey, baby." There's that cockiness I got a glimpse of at the coffee shop earlier that day. Although his voice seemed deeper, I liked the smooth, light drawl I had heard earlier outside of the bookstore.

Before I could let myself down, he leaned in and took my mouth hungrily against his and began to walk through the crowd. As we made our way past, I heard groans of disappointment, probably from the loss of a good fight. Mission accomplished, though. I was just glad to have found Jace in the chaos.

As we wove in and out of the crowd, I was still gripping his strong shoulders and my legs were wrapped around his waist. I caught a few dirty looks along the way and it began to make me feel self-conscious. I've never been the type to cause a scene or be the center of attention, and this was the last place I wanted to start. This crowd could rip me apart.

Jace carried me effortlessly down a flight of stairs to what appeared to be a basement, although it was just as loud and lively down there as it was upstairs. He finally set me down, and I felt the familiar smooth surface of a pool table and the smooth billiard balls knocking against my thighs. Pool is one game I know well. When you spend at least three days a week picking your drunken father up from a bar, you learn how to have some fun in the process.

A tall, lanky blond guy rounded the side of the table and slammed his cue stick down bitterly. "You're an asshole, Riley. I was so damn close to sinking that eight ball. Next time, set your flavor-of-the-week down on a chair." The angry stranger stalked away to a fridge full of beer.

"Riley?" I questioned.

"Last name," he replied roughly with a cocky grin and I nodded.

"Flavor-of-the-week?" I couldn't help asking.

I'm not naive, but I also hadn't pegged Jace for the type of guy to just kiss every girl he comes across. Before he could answer, another blond-headed stranger walked up, interrupting us.

"J, what the hell? You seriously need to knock it off," he growled.

The guy was almost the same height as Jace and was extremely handsome with messy blond hair. I took a second to drink him in because he had an amazing body, not to mention lips that movie stars would pay thousands for.

"Chill out, Cole. You know how Mike overreacts," he laughed, not taking the situation as seriously as his friend seemed to be.

So *this* was Mr. Richie Rich. Well, maybe he had paid thousands for those lips, then, although I doubted it. He probably had been unfairly blessed with them.

Cole stepped forward, ready to retaliate, when he spotted me and seemed to swallow his retort. "Are you dating anybody right now?" he questioned. When I shook my head, he continued, "That's good to hear. And we'll talk later, J."

When he stomped away, Jace leaned in and took my mouth again with his lips. I wrapped my hands around his neck, trying to ignore the fact that we were in a room full of strangers and something appeared to be off with him. The rest of the night continued this way, with random make-out sessions between shots and me defeating him in pool.

That's how I ended up the next morning in what seemed to be a media room, on a huge sectional couch between the softest sheets imaginable. Seriously, if I thought there was any way I could stuff these in my purse and walk out unnoticed, I would. As I'm coveting the fabric in an embarrassing manner, Jace rolls over and smiles at me with tired blue eyes.

I follow his every movement, watching his delicious muscles move beneath the skin as he stretches out his arms. My eyes immediately zero in on the black ink and intricate patterns wrapped around one of his shoulders and sweeping down to his bicep. I've always found tattoos fascinating, and I can't wait until I can get one of my own. I can tell the ink is new because there are some areas still healing, so he must have gotten it last week for his birthday.

"I don't remember much from last night, but I'm pretty sure we never swapped names," he says through a gravelly voice, and I'm instantly confused. "I'm Jaxon."

I spring forward, clutching the top sheet to my bare breasts. "What? Jaxon? I thought you said your name was Jace!"

"Oh, shit. I didn't tell you that was my name last night, did I? The last time I pretended to be him, he kicked my ass."

"No . . . not last night . . ." I say, still not understanding.

"Nah, you got the wrong twin, sweetheart." He shakes his head. "Well, on second thought, I guess you got the right twin. Jace is the dull one." When he winks at me, I feel like I'm about to be sick.

Twins? Jace is an identical twin? This has to be a monumental misunderstanding. First of all, there should never be two guys who look like this set free to roam the female population. Second of all, that should be the first thing that comes out of their mouths! *"Hi, I'm Jace and I have an identical twin brother, so don't accidently kiss him."* Anything to help us poor, confused girls out.

I start to scan through memories of last night, trying to reassure myself that he's wrong. Jace is just messing with me; he has to be. I didn't hear anyone call him Jaxon last night, but then again, I didn't hear anyone call him Jace either. Well this is fantastic. Just add one more point to the never-ending total on the scoreboard that is the mess of my life. I sit up and begin searching for my clothes. While pulling on my shirt and shorts, I look over to see *Jaxon* eyeing me with curiosity.

"I'm Audrey," I stammered.

"You're just gonna leave, Audrey?" he asks, still looking perplexed.

"Yes."

"Most girls want either my number, breakfast, or to date me after a night together," he says arrogantly.

"I don't."

I know I'm being unnecessarily harsh, but right now my stomach is on the floor and I want to leave before I get any queasier. Last night, I thought I was with the charming, authoritative guy who made my toes tingle and the hair on the back of my neck stick up. I thought I was kissing the same guy who took charge in the parking lot and who rescued me from spilled groceries.

How could I have not taken more seriously the strange feelings I had throughout the night? I remember thinking that his voice sounded off, and then there were the kisses that felt different. *Idiot, idiot, idiot, Audrey!*

Jaxon sits up with a smile on his face, looking like he has an idea. "Audrey, let's hang out today. I want to talk to you about some things." I try to ignore him and continue for the door. "My mom makes the best French toast . . ." he trails off enticingly.

I can see the victory on his face when I misstep. Because seriously? French toast just *sounds* delicious, and I've never had a homemade breakfast before. But I can't go back to his house where Jace obviously lives. Oh no, what if he saw me kissing Jaxon last night and that's why I never saw him? Maybe I *should* go over to his house so I can find Jace and explain.

"Just breakfast, then I'm going home." I give him a stern look.

"Yes, ma'am," he teases. Then he pulls out his phone and begins tapping the screen. "Let me text Jace, so he can come pick us up. I didn't drive." *Oh, this won't be awkward at all . . .* When his phone beeps, signaling an incoming message, Jaxon laughs. "Damn, he's in a bad mood. His chick . . ." He pauses and then looks at me. "Sorry, that's rude. The girl he was interested in must not have shown up last night." I try to hide my grimace at the mention of "the girl he *was* interested in."

He motions for the door and we walk down the grand staircase. I cringe at the mess scattered throughout the house. There are tables dispersed in the living room, some with red plastic cups lined up in triangle formations and little plastic balls floating in the alcohol. Beer cans have been tossed in the corners and on luxurious couches. There's even a pair of dirty socks hanging from a silver chandelier and a broken vase on the fireplace mantel. I don't know Cole's parents, but I can only assume they will be livid if they could see the state of their beautiful home.

"Wait right here; I'll grab Cole," Jaxon says, as he walks down the hallway.

I make my way into the kitchen to find the trash bags. I decide to begin in here and start by tossing all of the cans, bottles, and paper plates into the bag. I have almost filled the second bag when they both walk into the kitchen. I can't help noticing that the boys on this side of town are achingly handsome. It must be good breeding. I can understand why girls were giving me dirty looks last night for kissing Jaxon. They wanted their turn with him.

Cole grins at me while grabbing a set of car keys from a nearby cabinet drawer and says, "Don't worry about that, pretty girl. All of this will be taken care of later." He shoves Jaxon on our way out the door and says, "Now *this* one is a keeper." Jaxon looks back and gives me a playful grin.

~

Cole drops us off in front of an attractive two-story farmhouse. While this house is also quite massive, it isn't pretentious like Cole's. It's sophisticated yet charming and has a beautiful wraparound porch. This house is perfect. I could live happily on the front porch alone. In my head, I picture myself lazing around on the outdoor sectional, reading book after book all day with a glass of sweet tea. Hey, a girl can dream every once in a while.

Jaxon leads me inside the heavy, wooden front door, and before I can fully take in my surroundings, I ask for the bathroom. I need to take a second to compose myself before seeing Jace again.

JACE -

I hear Cole's Porsche 911 pull away, and I get up to confront my brother about last night. After I left the party, I spent the remainder of the night in the barn, pounding the heavy bag my dad installed for me two summers ago. I tried to let all of my aggression loose, and was doing a good job of it until I split the leather and had to step away, somewhere around two in the morning. I'm pretty sure I can keep myself in check with Jax now.

As soon as I round the corner near the kitchen, I see a familiar set of beautiful brown eyes looking around, as if she doesn't know which door to approach first. She's wearing the same clothes I saw her in last night, and damn if that doesn't make me grind my molars together in frustration.

I watch as her eyes grow wide the second she realizes it's me standing in front of her. "Jace?" she breathes out.

"Well, I see that you *didn't* forget who I am," I reply. I know I sound like an asshole, but I can't help myself so I add, "Have fun with my brother last night?"

She frowns and rushes toward me, grabbing my biceps. "You never told me you had a twin."

"What does that have to do with anything, Audrey?"

"Jace, I thought Jaxon was you. I didn't realize my mistake till this morning." Her eyes fill up with tears and as they threaten to spill over, my gut clenches. She thought *I* was arguing with Mike last night, that *I* was the one kissing her while holding her legs around my waist? Shit.

Instantly, I stalk forward, backing her up against the wall and completely surrounding her with my body, not letting her escape. Lifting her chin, I look down into her eyes and seconds later, I devour her lips with mine.

She lets out a long sigh in between our lips and threads her fingers through my hair while grasping it roughly. My tongue flicks into her mouth and her tongue begins to flirt with mine. It takes me a solid minute to come back down from the high of having her mouth on mine again, and that's when I think about why she's here now and where she's been all night.

"You slept with Jax?" I whisper, while firmly holding her face between my hands. She looks surprised, and when her bottom lip begins to quiver, I know what her answer is. I step away, conscious of the fact that I can't hold her any longer, but I need to hear her reply. "Answer me," I growl.

I shouldn't have kissed her, because I can tell by the shock on her face she thought that I would get over that little part. Only focused on her, I just hadn't fully comprehended it yet.

"Jace . . ." she whispers, "I thought I was with you."

"Did you call out my name?" I ask tensely.

She shakes her head from side to side and shocks me by adding, "I didn't call out anything."

I step forward, lower my forehead to her shoulder, and groan. This only makes me want her more. She should have been with me. Audrey deserves for someone to make their name rip from her mouth, to drive her so absolutely insane it would be impossible for her to hold it in. What a fucking shame.

"Please . . ." she whispers, begging me with her glistening eyes to let this go. But all I can see now is that my brother has been here.

"The fact that he even brought you here says that you mean something to him," I say and try to brush her off.

"No—" she interrupts, but I stop her.

"I can't, Audrey. I can't be where my brother has been. That's a line I'm not willing to cross."

I can tell the moment she fully grasps what I'm saying and then she steps away from me, spinning on her heel slowly and closing herself inside the guest bathroom.

- THREE -

***AUDREY* - Four years later . . .**

Audrey, if you pick up one more damn box, I swear I'll lock your ass in my closet until I'm done unpacking this truck!" Lane yells at me, as he's backing the moving dolly stacked with three large boxes through our front door.

"Lane, I'm perfectly capable of carrying my own boxes," I say, laughing, while darting around him. Chuck weaves in and out between the two of us, excited about his new surroundings.

"You weigh basically nothing. I'm afraid you'll snap in half or something carrying these," Lane says. Once I set the box down, I reach out and pinch the tiny bit of extra skin on his lower back. I'm surprised I can even grasp anything with how tight and toned he's become. He swats my hand away and says, "Just start unpacking; I'll unload."

"I can help—" I insist, while trying to mess up his sandy brown hair.

He cuts me off with a ridiculous pouty lip. "Please, it'll make me feel better." No guy his size should have such a look. He knows that he's won because I can't resist his begging.

I was more than hesitant about this move, and I wouldn't have done it for anyone other than Lane. The fact that we were both accepted into the same master's program in accounting doesn't hurt either. Last year, I was shocked when *both* of our acceptance letters arrived in the mail, considering I had never even applied. Apparently, Lane took the liberty to apply for me. He told me that he didn't plan on leaving without me, but he needed a reason for me to come along. And besides my cousin Kennedy, Lane is my only friend. So, to be honest, I would follow him anywhere.

The only thing that made me hesitant about moving up here was that I knew I'd now be on the same campus as Jace. It was hard enough living in San Diego, which isn't too far from LA, for the past three years, but now I run the risk of actually bumping into him on a daily basis. If I see him, I know I'll act ridiculous again, and I can't chance that. I've embarrassed myself enough around the Riley boys.

One year ago . . .

After more than two years of gabbing about Jace, Lane has finally convinced me to go and do something about it. I'm sweating bullets as he drives me two hours north to where Jace and Jaxon are attending school. I hate that he has to leave and get back to class because this could backfire in my face and I won't have a place to stay. I realize how bold this is of me to just show up, but this is not something that can be done over the phone, and if I prepare him at all for my arrival, he'll just shoot me down.

I see their truck parked in a garage outside the apartment building, which tells me I'm at the right place. Lane wishes me luck and drives away with all of my courage sitting safely in his front seat.

As I make my way up the stairs, Jaxon sees me and hauls me inside his apartment, past the living room, and into his bedroom without saying a word. *Well, this is going fantastic.*

I can see by the daggers he's glaring at me that I'm not welcome here already. He's still mad at me for things that he never cared to find out the truth about, and I don't see the need to fill him in just to make him feel better. Plus, it wouldn't make him feel better. He just wouldn't hate me as much.

"What are you doing here, Audrey? I don't need this shit right now. Why the hell would you fly all the way out to California? Isn't this something you could have picked up a damn phone and called me about?"

I begin to tune him out at this point because he's on a roll and he apparently needs to get this out of his system. He has no idea that I live only two hours away and that I sure as hell didn't come up here to see *him*. The only good part about this little tantrum is that I can sit here and take him in.

He's all grown up now and I can only imagine that Jace is the same. Typically, a voice like his wouldn't bother me, but I've associated *this* voice with my big mistake. It was my first hint that something was wrong, the first clue that I should have grabbed on to and shook until I discovered he wasn't Jace. As I sit here, taking in his large shoulders and long, lean legs, I tune back in to hear him still reprimanding me. If he knew me at all, he would know that I'm an expert at blocking out harsh words. After dealing with it for the first eighteen and a half years of my life, the words just roll off my back now.

"Where's Jace?" I ask, not caring if I'm interrupting him or not.

He freezes for a second and frowns at me, and I wonder if he's trying to figure out why I'm asking him about his brother. "Audrey, are you listening to anything I'm saying? This is not a good time. I need to find Emerson, and you can't be here when I bring her back."

I don't know who Emerson is, but damn . . . poor girl. Jax and I "dated" for three months, and I'm still surprised I stuck around that long. Jax is wild and just too much to handle. He has a nice side, but even that had gotten on my nerves. He could never make a decision to save his life. Every time we'd sat in his Camaro trying to choose where we should eat, he and I would go back and forth, telling the other to just pick something. Meanwhile, all I could think at the time was, *I bet Jace would've just taken charge and we'd already be eating by now.*

"I don't need to be here when Emerson comes, Jaxon. Just point me toward Jace."

"Jace is fucking busy!" he yells. "He's out there making something out of himself. Shouldn't you be in Texas taking care of your child and screwing physics teachers?" I know he's upset, and maybe in his mind, he has a right to be. But something else has to be going on in his life, because Jax was never mean. Even when everything went sour between us, he had never been intentionally cruel the way he's being now.

"You don't know a damn thing about my life," I state in a hard tone and stand to make my way toward his door. I may be able to let cruel words roll off my back, but in the last few years, I've also acknowledged that I don't have to listen to them. And Jaxon brought up the one thing I wasn't going to talk about. Lane is the only person on this planet who knows what really happened. Lane is the only person who ever cared to ask. No one asked. Not my mother, not my father, not Jaxon—no one cared enough to even ask.

As I make my way out of Jax's bedroom, I find myself face-to-face with the one person that haunts my dreams. I want to hug him and I want to hit him. I hate that I still think about him. I mean, we'd met, gone to a coffeehouse once, and kissed twice. Why after three years do I still feel a connection with him? Have I just built him up in my head? Maybe it's because he'd been the first person, outside of Mrs. Thomas and Nico, to show me real kindness. Or maybe it's the fact that every time I saw him after that fateful day, he looked at me with such longing I swear I could feel it in my bones.

"Audrey . . ." he whispers in shock. He gives me *that* look, and I can immediately tell he still feels it. Maybe it's purely just an attraction, but the electricity buzzing within me proves there is still something between us.

Behind me, I hear Jaxon curse under his breath. "Ignore her, Jace. Get back in here, Audrey," he says, pulling me back into his room. I almost cry at being so close to Jace, and once again not being able to do anything about it.

This is icy territory that I'm still not sure how to approach. I could just blurt out the truth to Jaxon. I want to—God, do I want to. I want to tell him everything. I want to tell him how I've only wanted Jace since the moment I met him. In a way, I know Jaxon won't care that I had only been with him to waste time. He already knew that.

The morning he'd brought me back home for breakfast after Cole's party, he had asked me to be his girlfriend. Right away, I'd refused. But then he had explained that he thought I was a cool chick and we could have some fun together. He'd also wanted to get his mom and brother off his back, since apparently he'd been acting wild lately. He had claimed that if he had a steady girlfriend, maybe they would lay off him and not worry so much. Stupidly, I actually considered his crazy idea.

When I later realized that Jace was a lost cause, I explained to Jax that I cared about someone I couldn't have, and that the only way I would "date" him was if he knew that it wouldn't be going anywhere. I also wanted to get away from my house more often. He completely agreed, saying he really only needed a buffer to keep his mom at bay. I didn't have normal parents, so I had no idea what he was talking about.

We crafted this strange sort of relationship and friendship between us. I won't lie: we'd had a good time together. But there always had been something missing for both of us. If I could go back in time, I wouldn't have agreed to it, but I was young and stupid and just trying to find an escape from my home life.

For the next three years, I compared every guy I came across to Jace, and they always came up short. That's when Lane decided I needed to try and do something about it. I hadn't seen Jaxon in years and I hoped the fact that we had never been in love would help to sway Jace's opinion on the matter. Maybe Jace just needed to see that I never really meant anything to his brother and that it had always been him for me.

Nevertheless, when Jaxon pulls me away from Jace and back into his room, I realize it's not my story to tell. This is his twin brother we're talking about here. If Jace doesn't want him to know, I can't hurt him even more by telling Jaxon. I spend the entire week trying to get Jace alone, but he slips in and out of the apartment like a ghost and I can't get him to listen for even a second. Halfway through the week, he stops coming back to the apartment altogether.

When I finally meet Emerson, I instantly despise her. Not because she's beautiful, and not because I had sat around all week listening to Cole and Jax talk about her like she walked on water. None of that bothers me. What makes me seethe is that the first time I met her, Jace had his arm around her shoulders. Who the hell is this girl, and how does she have all of these guys wrapped around her little finger?

Cole's new girlfriend lives next door, and from what I'm able to gather, she's Em's best friend. I figure out that Jace has been hiding out over there, so every day I try to stay close to the door in hopes of catching him. One day I hear him outside the apartment calling out to Quinn, and I jump up to open the door. He's already running down the hallway and heading out toward the parking lot. I'm still in my pajamas and my hair is in a messy bun on the top of my head, but I don't care. My time is running out. Lane called that morning to ask about my progress, and when I told him I was still at square one, he told me that I need to kick it into high gear. I have classes to get back to.

Jace comes back down the hallway with one arm wrapped around a beautiful, blonde-haired girl who can only be the famous Emerson. His opposite hand is holding a large duffel bag. I wince, knowing that I'm going to have to do this in front of her. But before I can even get introductions in, I've already pissed off Jace.

I'm not trying to be snarky when I say, "You must be the golden girl, Em, all of my boys are talking about." I'm trying to lighten the mood and get her to hang around for a while. I know if she leaves, Jace will follow.

She doesn't even get the opportunity to reply. Jace icily tells me to go away, and then he slips into Quinn's apartment behind Em. Behind the closed door, I hear their muffled voices and thank the heavens I can't make out what they have to say about me. Right then, I realize that maybe I'm once again making a fool out of myself. I slide down the wall to the ground and cry quietly into my hands.

~

Since it's my last day here, I take a walk to try and actually enjoy this beautiful city. Last night, I finally came to the conclusion that this trip has been a failure. There's a thin line between determined and pathetic, and I had crossed over into pathetic territory. I need to go home and just get Jace out of my head. Yes, I wish he would have listened to what I had to say, but I can't keep thinking about someone who won't even talk to me.

After watching the early morning surfers, I decide to attempt a different direction back to the apartment and happen upon the giant campus where Jace and Jax attend. The grounds really are quite beautiful with their red brick buildings, spectacular fountains, and towering palm trees scattered throughout. The library alone is a sight to behold. There's a giant water fountain out front and a long garden filled with red and gold flowers. If I attended this school, I would love to sit out here between classes and listen to the relaxing sounds of the fountain.

Eventually, I come across Jaxon sitting under a tree in the middle of a beautiful courtyard. I hesitate for a moment, trying to figure out if it's really such a great idea talking to him again. I finally come to the conclusion that I need to at least apologize for taking over his living room this week, and let him know that I won't be bothering him again.

As I start to walk toward him, I notice Emerson approach him first. He lifts his head to look at her with a smirk on his face and a look of adoration in his eyes. I haven't spoken to Jaxon much while I've been here, since he's spent all of his time either sulking in his room or talking to Cole about Emerson. But if this week hadn't already proved it, that look alone would have told me how crazy he is about her. It's obvious she's really done a number on this guy, because I never thought Jaxon Riley would be this whipped by just one girl.

As I approach, I think about what I should say. Maybe if I joke around with them, they'll be more inclined to talk to me. Maybe if I get on Emerson's good side, she'll show me some female solidarity and help me find Jace.

I call out before I reach them so I won't overhear a private conversation. "There you are!" I smile toward them.

Jaxon slams his textbook shut and stands up, glaring at me. I decide to turn my smile toward Emerson, but she's only watching him.

"I've been looking all over for you, Jaxy," I say, while inwardly cringing at my awkward attempt at sounding lighthearted. I guess not having many friends throughout life has made me socially incompetent. I have never called Jaxon by that nickname in the past and I can't believe I just called him that now.

"What are you doing here, Audrey? I said I would come back to meet you at the apartment after my classes," Jaxon growls at me.

Think of something, Audrey. "What, I can't come hang out with my hubby? Besides, it doesn't look like you're in class anyway," I joke. Sometimes I still can't believe that we were so immature as to run off and get married. But then again, I had already made the biggest mistake of my life four weeks before that . . .

"Hubby?" Emerson gasps. *Uh-oh . . .*

"Audrey, shut the hell up!" Jaxon yells, while reaching for Emerson.

As he calls out to her retreating form, I realize that I just made Mess Number 7,594. She obviously didn't know about our sham of a marriage that was immediately annulled, and my big mouth just tried to joke about it.

"She didn't know? Jaxon . . . I'm so sorry . . . I figured since you two are together . . . she had to know . . . Shit! I'm so sorry. I was trying to make a joke."

He points at me and says, "Go home. Not my home. Yours."

I know Lane has a night class and I don't want him to have to skip, so he'll have to come back up to get me tomorrow morning. "I leave first thing in the morning," I assure him.

"You bought a ticket?" he asks tersely.

"Sure," I reply and begin my walk back to the apartment. Once Jace finds out I've pissed off Em, he definitely won't want to talk to me either.

Basically, the whole week has been one big, fat flashing neon sign telling me to forget about this whole pipe dream I've had and move on. The one thing I can say is that I'll never have to look back on this time and regret not trying. I've made the effort and gone the distance. Once again, no one has put in any energy toward me. I need someone who wants to meet me halfway, and I deserve it. Besides, I need to stop lusting after a guy I met three years ago, and who has barely said a handful of words to me since.

Jace doesn't want me—I finally understand that—and Jaxon never even tried to speak to me amicably. Anytime I approached him, he practically snarled at me. If this had been four years ago, I would have been able to think of a million different reasons why people should hate me. Not now, though. Now I think Jaxon is an asshole and Jace just doesn't care.

~

Present day . . .

I slowly return from my painful memories to hear whispering coming from outside of the kitchen. I'm supposed to be unpacking, but the furthest I've gotten is taking three glass mugs out of one cardboard box.

"Watch this, boy." I look into the dining room and see Lane sitting at our table with Chuck between his legs. "And . . . she's back," he says, patting Chuck's copper-colored fur. "Wow, doll, that must have been a good one."

I have always had a habit of zoning out for long periods of time, which is probably a side effect of my past. If you imagine yourself anywhere else, you just might forget about what's happening in the present. While I don't get beaten up anymore, I still find myself getting lost in thought all of the time. It's easy for my mind to slip in and out. Lane likes to make light of the subject, but I can tell it worries him.

"How long was I out?" I ask, as I begin putting the remaining mugs into the cabinet.

"I'm not sure, but it was a while. I finished unpacking the truck, and then Chuck and I sat here waiting for your return."

Moving here has been throwing me off lately. "Damn, I really need to snap out of it. How am I supposed to pay attention in class again soon?"

"I hate to say 'I told you so,' but you shouldn't have gotten a taste. Ever since winter break, it's only gotten worse. You should have already learned your lesson from your disaster visit up to see him. You need to go out there and just bang someone new. It'll help, I swear," he chuckles, while giving me his devilish grin. I know he's full of shit because he rarely lets any guy near me.

"I told *you* we shouldn't have gone to Texas, just so you could see what a loser I actually was!"

"Hey, I wanted to see where my girl grew up," he says, shrugging his shoulders.

I still can't believe he convinced me to go all the way back to Texas with him for winter break this past year. He'd been asking to go since we moved in together my freshman year because he wanted to see where I came from. I never had any desire to go back and I still don't understand what he wanted to see.

It's not like I have any good memories from there. Just one pissed-off guy I left behind and that's only because I took Chuck, not because he misses me. I like to think of taking Chuck as my way of sticking it to my dad without actually having to see him. Besides, Chuck's happier here anyway, since he never has to scrounge for food with me.

JACE - Winter break, eight months ago . . .

Jax and I have only been living in California for about five months now, and I already miss Texas like crazy. As we drive through our little town, I think about how this place is home to me. California is fun, but I'm ready to be done with school so I can get back here.

I've been looking forward to our trip home for a while, but more so in the past couple of weeks. Cole's always locked away with Quinn, and Jaxon is so far up Em's ass I don't even recognize him. I love Em to death, and she is by far the best thing that's happened to Jax, but damn, I'm jealous.

I want a girl riding next to me in my truck or on the back of my motorcycle. I want a girl to just lie around in bed with me for hours on a Saturday. When I see the way my brother looks at Em when she's not paying attention, I want that. Yeah, I'm in college and I should be out there living it up with a different notch on my belt every weekend, but that's just not me.

"Don't think I've forgotten we're getting you laid on this trip, man," Jax interrupts my thoughts.

"I think I can take care of myself," I reply, while watching the shops pass by out the window.

"Nah, you're a cranky bastard. It's happening," Cole says from the backseat. "We should hit up that party tonight at Hunter's lake house."

"Or we could just find you a chick right now," Jax challenges, pointing to the back of a brunette walking down the street.

"You mean the girl with another dude's arm wrapped around her?" I ask.

I can't help staring at her ass, though, and there is something about a set of long legs on a girl. I'm tall, so I like my girls tall as well. All that bending-over shit that Jax and Cole do with their girlfriends is not for me. I'd still like to be able to stand up straight when I'm seventy.

"She is pretty hot, though, I'll give you that."

As we drive past them, my eyes are glued to her. "Fuck, isn't that Audrey?" Cole asks. *Yes, it sure is.*

"Who the hell is she with?" I growl. "Have you ever seen him before?" My head is still turned and my eyes can't seem to stop looking at her.

"I don't give a damn who she's with," Jaxon states in an annoyed tone and continues driving forward. Meanwhile, all I want him to do is turn the fuck around.

"She looks . . . good . . ." I try to say only to myself. When she's too far away to see, I turn back around in my seat. I notice that Cole's too quiet, and when I glance back at him, I see that he's studying me. Inquisitive bastard.

~

Two hours into the party, Jaxon's being a pussy and leaving because he needs to call Em. Cole is already passed-out drunk on one of the couches, which just seems like bad news for him. I should probably call Quinn later and tell her that he's okay. We ended up taking two cars because I figured at least one of them would need to report in to his ball and chain.

Now that I'm alone, all I can think about is the dude with his arm around Audrey earlier today. Jax and I are not small, by any means. Thankfully, we got our build from our dad's side of the family. When my dad died, he was thirty-five years old, but he was six foot three and could still bench press double his weight.

That guy with Audrey today looked threatening. Not saying I couldn't take him; I've had plenty of experience my whole life fighting with Jax. He's probably tried every move in the book on me, and I've always been able to counter them. And why the hell am I thinking about taking out Audrey's boyfriend anyway?

For the first time in years, I consider getting wasted. I went drinking with Jax and Cole a few times when I was seventeen but hated the stuff, so I haven't touched any alcohol since. However, it seems to help others when they want to forget hostile thoughts, and Audrey's boyfriend is definitely making me feel aggressive tonight.

She seems to be a recurring weak point for me. When she came out to California to see Jax a couple of months ago, it took everything inside of me to stay away from her. I knew that if I let myself even stop to talk, I would end up grabbing her and holding her hostage in my room. Then I would definitely have some uncomfortable explaining to do.

A bubbly, short blonde stumbles up next to me with two plastic cups in her hands. She tries to mesh her body up close to mine, but her head only reaches my chest.

"Here, handsome, I got you a drink," she says, with her face tilted all the way back so she can look me in the eyes. She smiles and I can see that she's already wasted. I grab the drink, and without looking to see what it is, I put the cup to my lips and swallow the contents inside. Shit, this is terrible. It's a mixture of liquor that someone tried to disguise with Coke, but it's still fucking awful. With my mouth closed, I cough down the burn. This crap is poison, but the spacey, warm feeling that follows entices me to grab another. And another.

Soon after, I grab the blonde's hand and drag her out to the bonfire near the lake. Hunter has his truck parked down by the dock with all of his doors open and the music blasting. She leads me into the middle of the crowd of dancing couples and I spin her around so her back is against my chest.

I'm impressed by how fast the alcohol reaches my system, and I guess this would be the one time in my life when I'm considered a lightweight. Mentally, I'm scanning through my textbooks, trying to determine my blood alcohol concentration level, but it's all a jumble. All I know is that I want to go one way, but my body starts shifting another. This blonde chick is grinding against me and it feels fucking great. Right before I grab her to spin her around, I send out a silent "thank you" for the fact that Jax left and Cole is out for the night.

She turns on her boot heel and looks up into my eyes. I cup her face haphazardly and can practically taste her arousal on my tongue already. She wants me. She continues dancing in front of my hips with her hands on my chest, while I scan the area for a place we can hide together. This is going to be quick.

Looking over Blondie's shoulder, I suddenly catch the stare of big, brown eyes. I try to make myself focus on anything but those long, tan legs under her short, red sundress. It's too late, though. She notices that I've spotted her, and she reaches out to snatch a beer from some guy's hand. Without removing eye contact, she places the glass bottle against the sides of her face, as if she's trying to cool off from being overheated. She can't turn away and neither can I. We both want each other. We always have, and I just might be drunk enough to finally let myself indulge.

I finally notice that the guy next to her is the ripped-up dude she was walking through town with earlier today. When he clutches her chin in one hand, turns her to face him, and shakes his head while mouthing the word *no* at her, I start shoving my way through the dancing bodies. If she wants me, even if it's only for tonight, then he's going to fucking step aside.

I continue walking until I'm standing with my toes touching hers. I hope she doesn't have any personal boundaries because I don't plan on recognizing them tonight. I can see the cold condensation on the beer bottle that she now has smashed against her chest. She rolls it across, leaving a wet trail in its wake. I can't stop myself from reaching out and touching the chilled skin. When my fingertips graze across the area underneath her collarbone, her lungs swiftly fill with air.

Her boyfriend smoothly pushes me aside to stand directly in front of her. My body is intoxicated enough to stumble away, otherwise that wouldn't have been so easy for him. He's a shitty-ass boyfriend, if you ask me. I damn sure wouldn't allow some guy to put his hands on her if she were mine.

"Doll, this is not a good idea," he says to her in a warning tone.

"Lane, I'm a big girl," she replies back to him kindly.

I'm already done with this little get-together of theirs. Thankfully, Lane shrugs and steps away. I'm finally looking down at her beautiful face again. She's just as stunning as she was when we were eighteen-year-olds on the sidewalk outside of the bookstore. Her hair is a little longer and I've never seen her dressed up all sexy, but she's still my same girl from that day. Except she never was my girl . . . *Don't forget that, Jace.*

She cocks her head and studies me with curiosity. She's thinking hard about something and looks so damn cute doing it.

"Why are you drinking?" she questions. I start to wonder how drunk I actually am if she can tell even though I'm no longer holding a cup.

I smirk at her query and reply, "I thought I'd try something new tonight." She catches my double entendre, and I love watching her surprised mouth open and shut. I know another way I would love to see those lips move like that. She starts to grimace, but before I can ask what's bothering her, I feel warm hands come up from behind and glide across my abs. Shit, the blonde.

"Come on, sweetheart. Trust me, you don't want in the middle of *that* crazy," Lane says, while grabbing Blondie's hand. When she gets a good look at him, her eyes light up and she follows after him like a damn cat in heat. Fuck, I don't know whether to fist-bump him for being the best damn wingman ever, or slug him for being the shittiest boyfriend known to mankind.

I stalk forward, causing Audrey to reverse slowly. After fifteen steps or so, she backs into a large tree trunk. My hands hit the tree on either side of her face.

"It's not fair that every time I see you, you look even more delicious than the last," I whisper into her neck.

"I don't think you realize what you're doing right now." She shivers under my lips.

"Why did things have to get so screwed up?" I ask, dragging my lips across hers. "Do you think we would be together if you hadn't run into Jax?" I know I'll regret this tomorrow, but I really don't care right now.

"I can't let myself think about things like that, Jace." Her words are said like a prayer.

"Do you still think about me?" I whisper, while running a finger up the inside of her bare leg.

I feel her tremble before she admits, "Every single day."

"Well, at least I'm not alone."

My lips graze across her soft, plump ones. Her eyelashes flutter and she relaxes into me with closed eyes. I run my tongue across her bottom lip lazily before giving the same treatment to the top one. Her breath hitches when I lean back a fraction, and then, ever so slowly, I move in. I want to drag this out. I never got my moment with her, so tonight I want to take my time.

Our lips finally touch and she moans with pleasure. My fingers drag upward from the back of her neck into her loose curls and I pull her in tighter. Her hands brace themselves on my chest. Gradually, the slow, lazy kiss becomes heated and needy.

When her hands glide down and skim across my waist, I pull back instantly. Grabbing her hand, I quickly start dragging her off toward the driveway. We both need to get out of here before any other thoughts enter my head. When we finally reach Jax's black '67 Camaro, I realize she's tugging on my hand.

"Jace, where are we going?"

"I need you without an audience." I try to unlock the passenger door for her, but I can't seem to get this tiny-ass key into an even smaller lock. "Fuck! I can't work this thing."

She reaches out and wraps her little hand around mine, taking the key from me. "You're drunk."

With what I hope is a smug grin, I reply, "Yup, and *you* are beautiful." I emphasize this statement with a tap on the tip of her fucking adorable nose, while catching a whiff of something that smells like coconut.

"I don't like it."

"You don't like that you're beautiful? Well guess what, babe? I don't like it either."

"No, I don't like you when you're drunk."

"I'll never do it again." I lean down to kiss her perfect lips. Emotions that I can't comprehend are buzzing through me, so I reach out and squeeze her upper arm three short times.

She pulls back, but I stay there with my lips puckered out, hoping she'll return. "Promise?"

"I cross my heart, baby. I just wanted to forget about seeing you with your boyfriend. Shit . . . I didn't mean to say that part out loud." I try to lean back down to kiss her again, but she swiftly unlocks the door and pushes me inside. When she comes around to the driver's seat and hops in, I realize she's about to fucking try and drive this car. "Whoa . . . whoa . . . Audrey, only three people have ever driven this before. My dad, me, and Jax."

"Guess there's about to be four." She smiles confidently and lifts her hand to show me four fingers, although I'm seeing about twelve at the moment. I hear her push in the clutch to start the engine.

Damn, every time I hear this baby start up, I'm turned on. Add Audrey and I'm seconds away from coming in my pants. I have to have her and it needs to be soon.

She backs out of the drive, and when she shifts into first gear, I can tell that she feels the power under the hood. She may not understand what it means, but that little smirk tells me she likes controlling it.

At this point, I'm completely turned toward her, staring as she shifts into second. "Stop making that face," I say to her, while groaning and readjusting myself.

Her adorable nose scrunches up in confusion. "What face?"

Third gear and I'm having a hard time staying in my seat. I can't distract her from driving, but I'm dying to touch her. In the moonlight and soft glow of the dashboard lights, her skin looks like porcelain.

"The face with that little smile that says you're enjoying my car way too fucking much." Technically it's not my car, but I've put enough sweat and blood into this beast to call her mine. Just then, she turns down a familiar drive. "You're taking me home?"

"Yeah, you're drunk, remember? You need to go sleep it off." There's no way in hell I'm going to sleep right now. I direct her to pull over behind some trees. "No, Jace, I remember there being huge bushes over there." She does it anyway, and just then I hear a loud, scratching sound. She instantly stops, pushes in the emergency brake, and turns off the ignition. "Damn it, Jace! See!?"

I should be angry but I'm not. Hearing that little dirty word come out of her pretty little mouth makes me want to pull her into the backseat. So after I unclick her seatbelt, that's exactly what I do.

"You'll be pissed about that in the morning," she says. I position her underneath me on the black leather seat, and the way she's lying over the hump caused by the driveshaft makes her arch up into me. She's gorgeous, so damn gorgeous.

"I'll be more pissed if I didn't take advantage of this situation."

"What exactly *is* this situation?" she asks breathlessly.

"Your lips needing mine," I respond and press my mouth to hers before she can question my words.

I start slow, wanting to test the waters and needing to know if I still feel that spark that I've been craving for the past three years. The second her fingers thread through my hair, I feel it—that undeniable charge that only Audrey has been able to cause.

It's like a trigger has gone off and I can't slow down. I pull her shirt up over her head and she's already got her hands on the hem of mine. I try to help her out by pulling it over the back of my head, but I'm so wasted that it gets stuck. Her patience wears out, so she jerks it all the way off and tosses it aside.

My hands are everywhere and I still can't touch enough of her skin. Her hands are like a fire that I can feel through my jeans as she's unbuttoning them. This is happening. This is finally fucking happening, and I can't get all this damn fabric between us away any faster.

"Jace . . ." she moans, and my mouth is instantly back on hers. I plunge my tongue inside and can't hold in my own groan. I hate that she had to do most of the work because of my fumbling fingers, but I love that there is finally nothing between us. I dip my fingers inside of her and am even more turned on to find that she's so ready. I can't wait to feel all of her. As I stroke in and out, I remember to grab a condom from inside of my wallet. Before I can botch it up, she grabs it from me impatiently and . . . hot damn, her little hands are rolling it on me. This could get embarrassing if I don't take back control.

"Put your hands above your head, babe," I say in a raspy voice. She immediately complies without question. "Grab the seatbelt."

With her big, brown eyes looking up at me, I reach out and loosely wrap the nylon strap twice around each of her petite wrists. "You okay?" I ask, hoping beyond hope that she's fine with this. Her body language says that she loves it, but I need her confirmation. "You realize that I would never hurt you, right?"

I suddenly recall that I uttered a similar phrase to her the day we first met, and I groan when I see the gleam in her eye, telling me that she remembers too. "Jace, I trust you."

Without missing a beat, I slide into her and pause, needing this moment to grasp ahold of my sanity. Having her body underneath mine is so overwhelming that I can't seem to remember to breathe. She whimpers below me and tries to move against me. Ah . . . my girl needs a release already. I pull her legs up over my shoulders, while trying to keep my knee from slipping off the edge. With one leg bent up on the leather seat and the other foot braced on the floorboard, I finally gain the correct leverage.

Looking down, I'm captivated by the space where we're connected. *Holy shit.* I can't believe how good she feels and how good we look together.

"Gorgeous . . . you're fucking gorgeous, Audrey," I whispered.

"Jace, please . . ." she begs. Before I start moving, I lean down to kiss her again. I can't stop kissing her.

"How are your hands, babe?"

"Jace, please . . . just please . . ." she says, almost incoherently. I can't wait any longer either so I begin to quickly thrust in and out. The backseat of the Camaro provides very little room for my six-foot frame to navigate her body, but I learn to work with what I've got. Because what I've got under me right now is incredible.

I spent four months of my senior year lusting after this body. I watched the way she walked, the way her hips swayed, even the way she lounged on the dock out by our pond with Jax. After she disappeared, I spent the last six months of my senior year recalling this figure in my dreams. The curve of her waist, the length of her silky, white legs, and the way her long, brown hair curled up in the humidity.

My chest squeezes at the idea of getting to know every inch of her body and finding out exactly what she wants. I love that her hands are restrained, allowing me to give her all the pleasure. They're also not in the way of my mouth as I nip and suck my way across her chest. The farther I push her legs forward, the louder she gets. And the harder I push into her, the tighter she feels.

"Jace . . . Jace . . . Jace . . . yes, like that . . ." she chants without shame.

I need her to let go because I can't hold off much longer. Drinking tonight was not my best decision, and if I had known Audrey was going to be grinding underneath me, I wouldn't have touched the damn stuff.

I reach up and pull the seatbelt to constrict tighter against her wrists. In the next second, her whole body locks up and I feel her contracting around me as she's screaming my name. Pleasure shoots through me and I ride out the spasms by kissing her face from ear to ear and down to her neck.

"Damn, I needed that," I say, blowing out a hard, ragged breath. "Thanks, babe."

I collapse on top of her and then maneuver her body around so she's cradled in front of me. I reach up and untangle the belt from her wrists, and she slowly flexes them in a circular motion.

I pull her in close and bury my face in her hair, memorizing her delicious scent. My lips kiss the back of her neck for as long as I can stay awake. Squeezing her tighter against me, I hold on for dear life so she can't go anywhere. It doesn't work, though. I wake up the next morning in the backseat of my brother's car . . . alone, with only the scent of coconut that lingered on her skin.

- FOUR -

AUDREY **- Present day . . .**

So how did your first day of graduate school feel?" Lane asks, while wrapping his arm around my shoulders and swinging his backpack up onto his own.

"Pretty much the same as undergrad, honestly." Though my reaction might not indicate it, I really am excited to continue my education. I just wish Lane had tried harder to attend a school in San Diego, where we were already living and where Jace *doesn't* live. Being in the same city and on the same campus as him feels weird, especially with the way things were left between us. However, I know I shouldn't be picky about where I get accepted into highly prestigious programs. It's still overwhelming sometimes to think about all I've accomplished in the last couple of years.

"That's what you get for being so damn smart. Some people just can't be challenged," he teases, interrupting my thoughts.

"Look who's talking, smarty-pants," I say, laughing, and bump him with my hip. Lane graduated last year with the fourth-highest GPA in our class and was only a fraction of a point away from being the second salutatorian. He believes that, just because I graduated within three years instead of the typical four, I'm some kind of genius. Lane was the only reason I was able to accomplish that, though. He stayed up to study with me for endless hours on countless nights, and he even helped throughout his winter and summer breaks when I continued taking credits.

"I still think you should have let me sleep with the dean. I could have been valedictorian," he complains.

"Ew, Lane . . . I still don't believe you would have done that. She was like ninety!" I say with a gasp, while he directs me out to his car.

"She wanted me." He shrugs his shoulders, as if this is just a simple fact.

"Most girls do." And to prove my point, a short little blonde walks by with boobs that I know aren't real, giving Lane her finest bedroom eyes.

"Except you, doll, except you," he teases, while looking over his shoulder at the passerby. "Hang tight, I'll be right back . . ." He heads off to catch up with her. Rolling my eyes, I walk toward his black SUV and open the passenger door. I flip through my new textbooks while I wait for the playboy. A few minutes later, Lane's giant frame rattles the car as he climbs into the driver's seat.

"Shit, it's hot in here. Sorry about that," he apologizes. I shrug my shoulders because I honestly hadn't noticed. "Okay, so where were we?" he asks and turns the key in the ignition.

"Hmm . . . we were either trying to get our dick wet or talking about how I'm not most girls," I inform him with a smile.

"Jealous, doll? Do you want to join Harmony and me later? Can't say I wouldn't like having you there, but it might get a bit weird on the friendship, don'tcha think?" Then the sarcastic ass has the nerve to flash me his dimples.

"No . . ." I gasp. "Tell me her name is *not* really Harmony." I roll down my window to let some of the cool ocean air in. One thing I'll never get tired of is the breeze off the coast.

"It sure the hell is, and later we're gonna . . . harmonize." He winks, and I can't hold it in any longer so I burst out laughing. Thank God, Lane doesn't bring girls back to our apartment. I'm relieved I won't have to overhear that "music" session. "But that's cool if you don't want to join us."

"Hey, don't act like you're insulted that I'm not one of your groupies," I add.

"Well, when we met and the second sentence out of your mouth to me was 'I'm not sleeping with you,' I'll admit I was wounded," he says, clutching his heart dramatically. "But now I love ya too much, so it's a good thing I never actually *tried* to charm you."

"Something tells me even that wouldn't have worked." I chuckle.

Just then, I spot Jaxon walking across the parking lot with his arm wrapped around Emerson. I slouch down in my seat, even though they're too far off in their own world to see me. I'm honestly impressed that those two are still together. I wouldn't have guessed that Jax had a long-term-relationship bone in his body.

"Ahh . . . and so it begins. Is that him?" Lane has only ever seen Jace once before, so he doesn't know how to tell them apart.

"Nope. It's Jaxon." My teeth grind together, because I still have some hostility toward him. "I'm hoping to hide out for the remainder of the year, and then we can hightail it out of California unscathed."

"Good luck with that," he teases and begins to back his car out of the parking spot. My whole body tenses up when I see *him* jog down the sidewalk to catch up with his brother. My eyes are glued to Jace as he runs past them, smacking Emerson's ass in the process. She just laughs, but Jaxon takes off after him and wraps his brother in a headlock. I'd forgotten how amusing the twins were together.

"Stop, Audrey," Lane says, breaking my trance as he drives off the lot. "Did you ever go check out those bars I told you about?"

I grin at his not-so-sly subject change. "Yeah, I applied to all of them. I actually got a callback for an interview tonight at the one that's closest to your gym."

"Good. I prefer that one so I can keep an eye on you."

"Lane . . ." I warn, "I don't need you scaring off every guy I meet."

"Pick better guys," he says simply.

"You scare them all off."

The downside of having Lane as your best friend is how intimidating he looks and acts. He may be a whiz with numbers and calculations, but he's far from being just a number cruncher. He religiously works out at a boxing gym and tries to get in the ring with everyone at least once. We couldn't even move up here until he found a gym he liked because God forbid there was a small gap in training days.

A couple minutes later, we pull up in front of our new apartment. The white stucco walls and red tile roof still make me smile; this complex is beautiful and I commend Lane on a great choice. We live on the first floor, which is nice because I can let Chuck out easily and our neighbors don't have to worry about a seventy-pound dog stomping around above them.

I walk beside Lane up to our door, but before he can push it open, a red blur comes dashing out and begins circling our legs. I scratch behind Chuck's ears and ask him about his day.

Quickly, I run off to the bathroom to shower and get ready for my interview tonight. When I finish, I exit the steam-filled room and walk toward the kitchen in my bra and panties. I had forgotten my clothes were still in the dryer.

I hear Lane in the kitchen, pulling an assortment of vegetables out of the refrigerator. I swear he eats every thirty minutes. He's also the health food police. Once, I brought home a package of Oreos and let's just say . . . my delicious chocolate cookies went straight into the Dumpster. Typically, I don't mind, though. It's nice to eat healthy meals for a change. When I told him I basically survived off ramen noodles and peanut butter sandwiches before moving to California, I think he about had a small heart attack.

He glances at me when I walk into the kitchen and does a double take. I pass right by him and walk into the laundry room to grab my clothes for tonight. With the pile in my arms, I make my way back through the kitchen.

"Doll, you know I'm not your *gay* best friend, right?"

"Lane, I've seen you with too many women to ever think that."

"Just checking," he smirks, while blatantly checking me out.

"It's nothing you haven't seen before," I say and roll my eyes.

"Doesn't mean I won't appreciate the view," he replies brazenly.

I stand in the middle of the kitchen and pull on my jeans and a white T-shirt. When I'm fully clothed again, I grin at him and turn to hunt down my own food.

"You really don't need to work," he says, and I know exactly where this is going. "I hate when you work the bar late at night, especially when it's not necessary. You know I can take care of everything."

"Not this discussion again, please. I like working and I like the atmosphere in bars. Usually it's lively and upbeat, and I need to be around *happy*. Besides, it's kind of empowering to cut off the drunks."

"Fine, fine . . . let's not fight." He raises his hands in surrender. I walk around the counter and hug him around the waist.

"You know, for someone who fights as much as you do, you sure are sensitive about arguing," I say and then add, "which we weren't, by the way." We actually *never* argue. He's a beast in the ring, but outside of it, he's probably the calmest person I know. I have no doubt I was meant to have him in my life, especially after the years of violence I endured while growing up. "I'm going to go finish getting ready."

He kisses me on the top of my head and says, "I'll drop you off on my way to the gym."

~

"So I'll just let you get comfortable with the bar. Feel free to look around and start learning where everything is. Our other bartender should be here soon, and she can start training you. Meanwhile, let's head to the back and see if we can find a shirt that will fit you."

I haven't been to many interviews, but I'm pretty sure that was probably the easiest one a person can go to. Ed, the owner and manager, didn't even ask me for my bartending license or past experience. I don't know if I should be happy to have such a laid-back boss, or wary that he may be too lackadaisical and thus careless.

Ed walks me back to what looks like a storage room and tosses me a black shirt. "Bathroom's down the hall. Change over and come out front," he says in his retreat.

Walking back out to the bar, I tug on the uncomfortable shirt Ed gave me. If I pull it down to cover more of my waist, the V-neck shows too much of my chest, but if I pull it up, it shows my stomach. Screw it—I'd rather show a little stomach than my nonexistent breasts. Feeling as uncomfortable as I probably look, I push open the doors.

"Here she is, Em. Train her up." Ed scoots past me as he departs for his office.

"Ed, you numbskull . . . her name isn't Aubrey, it's Audrey," Emerson states, enunciating the *d* sound.

Well, damn it.

"Oh good, you two know each other," he says over his shoulder.

"No, we actually don't know each other at all," I reply, knowing he didn't hear me.

I slowly walk behind the bar and then decide to backtrack a few steps. Still tugging down on my shirt and then pulling it back up, I say, "I should . . . go . . ."

Before I can push the doors open to go and grab my stuff, she calls out, "Audrey, wait." I spin on my heel to look at her. "We can make this work. You obviously need a job and I need someone to pick up more shifts for me."

"It'll be weird. Really, really weird . . . and uncomfortable."

"Yes, it probably will," she acknowledges with a sigh. "Why *are* you here, by the way? Don't you live in Texas?"

"I haven't lived there since I graduated from high school."

"I thought Jaxon said . . ." she starts to say.

I quickly interrupt. "Jaxon doesn't know anything about me. And to answer your other question, I was just accepted into graduate school here." I don't elaborate further and she doesn't push for more.

We work through the next hour and it's anything but enjoyable. Emerson points out all the buttons on the register and shows me their protocol for starting a tab for customers. She demonstrates how to open a table and where to put everything when I'm done with it. She points out the black recipe book, but I doubt I'll need that.

After talking for an hour straight, she finally takes a deep breath in and out. She must be the type to ramble when she's uncomfortable. The more I think about this situation, the less I feel like this is a good idea. There are plenty of other options for me out there, so there's no need for me to torture myself here. I wanted to be around happy, and I can tell that would be the last word used to describe how she feels working with me.

"I really do appreciate you showing me all of this, Emerson . . ."

"Call me Em."

"Em, I appreciate it, I really do. But I just don't think this will work out."

"Why not?" she asks, and I have to stop myself from laughing at the asinine question.

"Frankly, there's just no reason for me to work somewhere every day where I know I'll be despised. I've had enough of that in the past to last a lifetime." Thankfully, we don't have any customers yet, because this conversation is not work-appropriate.

"Audrey, I don't hate you. I don't even know you," she says in a softer voice. I raise an eyebrow at her, silently telling her to be honest with herself and me. "Okay . . . okay. I'll admit, I'm not your biggest fan, but I don't *hate* you."

Feeling as though I need to busy my hands, I grab a lime and begin slicing wedges. I don't know what kind of crowd this place draws, but limes are always necessary in a bar. I slice three before I begin talking to her again.

"Okay, so you don't hate me. But you have to admit you wouldn't choose to work with someone who holds distorted notions about you," I mumble, while continuing to look down at the knife and fruit in my hands.

I hear glasses clinking behind me and then see her move on to scrub down the bar top. I don't budge from my spot. I've never enjoyed confrontation, and I'm still hoping to slip out of here gracefully without causing a scene. A full five minutes pass before she decides to speak again.

"When you say distorted . . . are you implying that Jaxon lied?" she questions, leaning against the counter next to me.

"I don't know if I would call it lying, because I don't know what he's said, exactly. But I do think he's an asshole that couldn't even give me two seconds to speak," I grind out between clenched teeth. I take a deep breath and let it out long and slow the way Lane taught me to do when I work myself up. I finally turn to face her. "I'm sorry. I shouldn't have said that, especially to his girlfriend. Sometimes I get carried away and say exactly what's on my mind without a filter."

"Do you still love him?" she asks candidly.

"Jaxon?"

Her eyebrows scrunch in confusion when she says, "Yes, of course."

"I've never loved him." I turn and walk to the opposite bar top, but she follows right behind me.

"Okay, now you have to tell me everything." I'm confused by the one-eighty in the tone of her voice. It doesn't sound demanding or mean, more like a best friend asking for the latest juicy gossip. I turn to look at her expression and see that she has a tiny smirk at the edge of her lips.

It takes me a moment to respond, and in the meantime I stand there and observe her. We couldn't be more opposite: I'm a brunette and she's a blonde. I consider myself tall and lanky, whereas Em is on the shorter side with curves in all the right places. Lucky bitch. In this moment, I wonder if Jace has ever been attracted to her and then I try to recant that thought. Looking at her, it's hard to imagine who wouldn't be.

"We look nothing alike." The words spill out of my mouth involuntarily.

She smiles and says, "Yeah, I don't think he has a certain type."

"Who, Jaxon?" I really need to snap out of it, because while she must think I have Jaxon on the brain, it's actually Jace that haunts my thoughts. "No, I wasn't even thinking about him." I should leave it at that.

She eyes me and says, "I don't know what it is, but I think I like you. Even though I feel like I shouldn't. It also makes it easier knowing you aren't in love with my boyfriend."

"Um . . . thanks?" What am I supposed to say to that? She shrugs her shoulders unapologetically and I decide to give her a little bit. "I met Jax by accident. After a big mistake, he and I ended up . . ." How do I say this to someone's girlfriend?

"Having sex," she suggests, nodding her head. "Go on . . ." She laughs as if it's no big deal to talk about her boyfriend's past sex life. Em is easy to talk to, and though I don't want to like her, I do. Kennedy is the only female friend I've ever had, but she lives all the way on the East Coast.

"Yeah, that. Soon after, Jax asked me to date him, purely as a buffer for his mom and brother. I guess he was going through a rebellious stage and they were always on his case. When he first asked, I said no. But after realizing I never had a chance with the guy I actually wanted, I latched on to him as an escape from my . . . um, less-than-ideal home life."

Before Emerson can ask any more questions, the music cranks up and customers begin to pack the bar and pool tables. We work smoothly around each other. She cashes out the pool tables and I fill drinks. She doesn't have to give me much direction because I already know my way around a bar. Occasionally, we get slammed and work as a team. Rum and Coke? She pours the rum and I dispense the Coke. Seven and Seven? She pours the whiskey and I top it off with 7-Up. When a table of eight orders a round of beer, I grab the bottles out of the fridge and line them up. Em comes up from behind and pops all the tops. Somewhere along the way, we became a fully functioning team without even talking.

At one point, things cool down for a moment and a cute little old man perches up on a barstool. "Hey, Em, who's this lovely lady you've got back here?" he asks.

"Hi, Joe." She smiles at him while pulling clean glasses from the dishwasher. "This is Audrey. She works here now." I can feel her eyes on me, probably wondering if I'll refute her statement. "Make sure you tell your wild crew over there to be nice to her." When she shakes her finger back and forth at him, I can't contain the giggle.

Em hands him a Sprite and he winks at me on his way back to his table. "Nice to meet you, Miss Audrey."

"Joe's here all the time," she tells me. "He's great. If you have family issues, he's the man to talk to. He lays it out straight, no bullshitting around. I've gone to him more times than I can count."

"I might actually take advantage of that . . ." I say as I stare after the kind, old man.

I've never had grandparents. When I was younger, I use to daydream up these wonderful, make-believe families. A dad who came home from work with open arms, wanting hugs from his whole family. A mom who would help me get dressed for school dances and, one day, my wedding. A grandpa who would let me sit in his lap while we drank sweet tea on the porch. I even had a grandma who pinched my cheeks and made the best peach cobbler. I've had these fantasies for so many years now, they almost feel real.

The night begins to wind down and our bouncer, Mark, begins to escort out the stragglers as the bar closes. Em and I walk by all the tables and pick up any glasses we missed during our earlier cleanup.

"Can I ask about your home life? Or is that rude?" Em asks while I'm scrubbing glasses.

"Are you asking for yourself, or do you plan on sharing this with a certain boyfriend?"

"He doesn't know?" she asks, sounding shocked.

"You guys don't talk about past relationships, do you?"

She laughs. "Well, this is my first relationship, so there wasn't much for me to talk about. Jax skimmed over his past and I never really felt the need to know details." We finish our closing duties and decide to sit down on the bar stools and continue our conversation.

"Jax never mentioned me before I came up here last year, did he?"

"No . . ." she says with a worried face.

I hurry to reassure her. "That's because Jax and I didn't mean much to each other. We came to an agreement and we had fun. Things got all screwed up, but that's it. There never was anything significant going on there."

"I guess I can understand that. I think I just assumed since you guys were married, that if you broke up, it would be heartbreaking. I've only ever had one relationship and I know I'd be devastated to lose him."

"But it wasn't ever like that with us. Plus, we were in high school. We were both young and stupid." I sigh at the memories and then change the subject. "Can I ask you to not tell anyone that I'm working here with you? Not Jax or Jace . . . I know they'll eventually find out, but I'm just not ready. The first thing they'll think is that I did this on purpose."

"I can't lie to Jaxon, but unless he specifically asks, I won't tell." She makes a crisscross motion over her chest and I feel a bond forming with her.

"My parents hated me. Well, I'm sure they still hate me," I say in a quiet voice, answering her earlier question. "They never wanted a kid, but it ended up benefiting them money-wise to keep me around. My mom was rarely home before she eventually ran off for good, but my dad . . . he was . . . violent."

Em sucks in a quick breath and then apologizes for her reaction, "I'm sorry. Go on."

"Well, there's not much more to it. For as long as I can remember, I was hiding bruises and cuts. Dating Jaxon was nice, only because I had a place to hide out from my house. I worked a lot too, so I spent most of my time either at the restaurant or with him. Honestly, though, I would have chosen anything over being at home. I never had any friends because I didn't want them asking questions. Jax was pretty self-involved back then, so he never noticed anything."

"He never asked about your bruises?" she huffs out in frustration. When I shake my head back and forth, she says, "Jerk."

That makes me laugh. "He was in high school, a teenager going through his own losses." I start to wonder why I'm defending him. "Clearly he's changed, though."

"That doesn't excuse his behavior," she replies. Is she sticking up for me? In another beat, she smiles and says, "Hey, next Saturday there's a bonfire on the beach and lots of new people for you to meet. You should go with me."

My mouth drops open in shock that she's asking me to hang out with her. When I recover, I say, "I don't know. Last time I was around your group, it was clear that I wasn't welcome."

"Well, since I'm the one inviting you, then you're welcome in my book. And that reminds me, you still need to tell me about that trip last year. Jaxon and I were dealing with our own drama, so I didn't really know what was going on."

"Hey, girls," Mark interrupts us from the front doors, extending his arm to keep his cigarette on the outside. "Let me walk you out. There's a big dude out here just standing by his car, and I don't like it."

"Black SUV? Sandy brown hair and way over six feet tall?" I call back.

"Yup. He's not stalking you or anything, is he?" I can tell Mark's hackles are up and I'm surprised by his protectiveness, especially considering we just met.

I hop down from the bar stool and Em follows behind. When I reach the door, I stick my head out and holler, "Get over here, Lane! You're making the bouncer edgy." I turn back to Mark. "Thanks, but that's my roommate. You don't have to worry about him."

As Lane strides across the parking lot, everyone watches. It's hard to not stare at Lane, I'll admit.

"Shut. Up. He's yours?" Em whispers in awe.

"Well, he's mine in the way a sister claims a brother, even though we aren't blood-related."

"No way, girl. If you're single, you cannot let *that* go to waste."

I nudge her with my elbow. "Em, you're taken, remember?"

"I'm still allowed to appreciate God's work," she giggles. "And damn, God was in a good mood the day he made that man."

"You're ridiculous," I say, laughing, as Lane approaches. I introduce him to my new coworkers. Em and I walk back to get our purses and then return to the front.

"If we're ever working together, I can give you a ride home," she offers.

"Why are you being so nice to me?" I cringe at the drama of it all.

She halts in her steps. "Because I'm starting to think that there was some kind of huge misunderstanding, and I want to know the truth. You and I seem to click well and we're going to be working together." She shrugs as if it's a no-brainer. "So about that party next weekend?"

"I'll think about it."

"That's all I'm asking. We work together a bunch this week. I'll convince you by then," she says confidently.

I laugh at her boldness. "All right. Well, thanks, Em. I'll see you later."

Lane eyes me curiously as we walk arm-in-arm to his car, and I know he's about to bombard me with questions.

- FIVE -

JACE -

With my shirt draped over my shoulder, I walk into the kitchen to grab water from the fridge. "You guys going to that bonfire thing Saturday night?" I ask Jaxon and Em, who are lounging on the couch.

"Yeah, Cole and I are going right after we get out of practice. You gonna take the girls?" Jax asks with his arm tucked under Em.

"If they need me to, I will. Otherwise I'll see you guys there." I chug my water and pull my shirt off my shoulder.

"Where you goin' tonight?" Jax questions. "It's Thursday."

"I'm hitting up that country bar with some friends from class. You know, it's okay to go out on a school night . . . we're not twelve anymore," I chide.

"I bet those premed guys can really let loose," he laughs.

"Yeah . . . something like that," I retort.

Em sits straight up. "Jace, when did you get a bunch of new tattoos?" she asks, sounding surprised.

"He's been filling up on those all summer, babe," Jax answers her. I shrug my shoulder while pulling the black T-shirt over my head.

Her bottom lip pouts out and I ask, "What's wrong?"

"You're not identical anymore."

"It's about damn time," I exclaim. That was probably a dick thing to say, but I'm so tired of getting confused for my brother. This summer I went a little crazy with the ink. It was a blast. Everything about Jax and me is identical. We have the same build, same height, same hair, and the same eye color. We even have the same damn teeth. Our voices differ, but not many notice. Lately, I've been having some kind of identity crisis and have been craving to mark myself apart from him.

The jarring tone of OneRepublic's "Apologize" blares from a cell phone and startles all three of us. Em snatches it up from the coffee table and heads for the door.

"I have to take this. I'll just be next door." She points toward her apartment and walks out.

I give Jax a puzzled look and he asks, "So it's not just me that thinks that was bizarre?"

"It *was* bizarre, but Em is weird like that sometimes." I try to shrug it off because, knowing my brother, he's brooding over who's on the other end of that call.

"No, she's been doing that shit all week. Who the hell do you think she's talking to? You haven't seen her with any guys, have you?" he begins to ramble.

"No. Calm down, crazy," I sigh. "If you don't trust her, you should probably talk to her."

"You're right: I'm going fucking crazy. I do trust her, but . . . what if she's just done with this whole relationship thing?" As he starts to overthink his words, his face changes to a sickly pale color. As per usual, I get a sinking feeling deep in my gut when Jax feels sick. My mom always calls it our twin bond; it's freaky shit, is what it is.

Before I can tell him that people don't usually up and decide to be done with the person they love, Em walks back in the door.

She no longer has her phone, so she must have left it at her place. I see Jaxon staring at her empty hand, and I know this is not lost on him.

With a big grin, she jumps on top of him. Em sure as hell doesn't look like a chick that's done to me. When she lands in his lap, her hands automatically graze up his chest. Then she pulls back when she sees his face.

"Are you sick, babe?" she asks, concerned. "I'm *really* hoping you're not, because I thought we had plans tonight." She leans in close to his ear. Now I feel like I'm interrupting.

He stands up with her legs wrapped around his waist and holds on to each side of her face. "You're mine, right?"

"Considering I got this, I damn well better be." I watch as she points to the inside of her right palm.

Shortly after returning from her internship in Africa, Emerson had the word "Mine" in Jax's handwriting tattooed on her palm. He had the same thing tattooed on his chest, except the mirror image. I don't fully understand it, and it seems really fucking corny, but I can't say I'm not envious of what they have together.

I leave the room before their show becomes unsuitable for all audiences. They often forget where they are and who else is around. I've lost track of the number of times I've had to ask Em to try and not take off my brother's pants while I'm still in the damn room. Quinn and Cole aren't any better. Being the fifth wheel really fucking blows.

I was hoping to use this time to talk to Jaxon about certain issues that have been weighing heavily on me, but I guess that's not happening again tonight. I make my way to Cole's room, so I can try and unload some of this shit before heading out.

I know they don't mean to, but it's really taken a beating on me to have to squeeze in time to talk to my own friends lately. I shouldn't have to fucking schedule appointments with them.

Whatever happened to "bros before hoes"? Not that Quinn and Em are "hoes." Well, Quinn never was, and Em's not anymore.

I knock twice and hear Cole's deep voice call out, "What's up?"

"Everyone decent?" I ask, covering my eyes and pushing the door open.

"Get in here, douchebag," he replies.

Cole and Quinn are lounging on his bed. She's reading a book and he's typing away on his laptop. It's so . . . simple. I never thought I'd see the day that Cole West would be in for the night before two a.m., let alone nine p.m.

"Is the doctor available?" I ask, in reference to an old joke.

"Uh-oh, what's up, man?" Cole responds and immediately and sets his laptop aside.

"The doctor?" Quinn asks, confusion written all over her face.

"Cole used to be our therapist, I guess. We called him 'Doc' because he was the guy to go to with problems."

"Yeah, he is great like that." She stares up at him dreamily. Freaking nauseating. "When can I be a patient?" she whispers while rolling closer to him. That's my cue to leave. Yet again. I turn on my heel and grab for the doorknob.

"Stop, man," Cole says with a laugh. "We're just messing around."

"Nah, I'm so sick of this shit. I can't ever say two words to you or Jax anymore without interrupting some kind of lovefest." I'm ranting like a pussy now.

"Aw, I'm sorry, Jace." Quinn pats the bed next to her and I park my pathetic sorry-ass down. "I can leave if you guys want to talk."

"No, I don't care if you're here. I just need one conversation where someone isn't down someone else's throat."

"Deal," she says. "Give them a break, though," she says, pointing to the door. "She just got back, so they're in the honeymoon phase again."

"I know, I know." I hold my hands up in surrender. "That's why I haven't blown a fuse in front of them yet."

"What's up, son?" Cole smarts off again. I stare at him, not saying a word. "Okay, okay, I'm sorry. I'm done fucking with you, for real this time."

"I dropped premed." With Cole, it's best to get straight to the point. He doesn't have the attention span for beating around the bush.

Quinn's mouth drops open and Cole looks equally stunned. "Uh . . . what? You dropped out of school? It's your senior fucking year, man. You couldn't go one more year?" he scolds.

"I didn't say I dropped out of school. I said I dropped premed."

"What the hell else are you going to do now? Changing your major this late in the game is not going to be easy."

"I've been double-majoring."

Another set of stunned faces.

"I never wanted to be a doctor. Okay . . . well, I did once when I was sixteen and my dad and Jax stuck to the idea like glue. When Pops died, I just felt it was . . . right, you know?"

"What's your alternate major?" Quinn encourages me to continue.

"Finance and business economics. Business, basically," I reply with a shrug. "Okay, guys, seriously. The stunned faces don't fucking help."

"Go on . . . tell me the reasoning behind all of this," Cole requests.

"Look, I always saw myself taking over my dad's business one day. I used to talk about it all the time with him. Then I spoke of being a doctor for like a week, and he acted like I walked on water for something I hadn't even accomplished. Jax later took over that notion for him. I hear the way he talks about me to people, like I'm going to cure cancer."

"Is premed too hard?" Cole asks calmly.

"Fuck, no. I was actually pretty good at it. I just don't *want* to do it. I gave it a shot; I tried to love it. What I want to do is take over Pop's company when my uncle retires."

"I've never even heard you say what your father did," Quinn reflects.

"Security," Cole's gruff voice responds.

"The Riley Group." I smile with pride at all my dad and uncle achieved together.

The Riley Group began as a small business meant for personal and corporate security in the Dallas/Fort Worth metroplex. Together they built a humble empire due to their high success rate and numerous government contracts. I love that it still has that small business feel, though, and I hope to maintain that.

Uncle Logan, who coincidentally is my dad's twin, has been responsible for all of the executive work since my dad's death. The past couple of years he's been keeping me up to speed on the company and trying to recruit me to take over when he retires. Seeing as the company is called the Riley Group, he wants it to stay in the family.

It has always interested me, but I thought I needed to follow through with medical school. I finally recognized how absurd it was, trying to be something I had no desire to be. The day I walked into the registrar's office and dropped premed, it felt like a thousand-ton weight had been lifted from my shoulders. Logan was thrilled, and has been in constant communication, trying to teach me the ropes.

"You're having a hard time telling Jax," Cole states.

Even though it wasn't a question, I answer, "Yeah. I don't want to disappoint him and I'm hoping he'll join me. I haven't heard him talk about the company once since Dad . . ." I trail off. "So I don't think he has any interest." Here's the kicker . . . "I want you to join as well."

Quinn's smile lights up the room, and if Cole was hesitant before, her smile just shifts his focus away from anything negative.

"Dude, I'd take any opportunity to work with you," Cole says with a smile. "I never imagined we'd have the chance to."

"I know you and Jax are majoring in business journalism, so this is stretching the usefulness of that degree. But it just wouldn't be the same to do this without you guys."

"Stop worrying about what Jax will think, Jace. He just wants to you to be happy. Whether he shows it lately or not," Cole adds. "You also don't need to try and hire us to keep us close. Although I'll definitely take you up on the offer."

"Aww, you guys really are like brothers. Like triplets, except Cole is the hot one." And Quinn ruins it all.

Cole's bedroom eyes immediately lock down on her. I swiftly get up, kiss Quinn on the cheek, and tap knuckles with Cole. "We'll talk more later. Thanks, Doc," I say, as I head for the door. "Love ya, Quinny."

"Anytime," he says through a mouthful of Quinn. At least they let me get halfway to the door this time.

The guys from class have been trying to coax me into going out with them since last year. However, most of my days have been spent studying for two majors and squeezing in time with my brother and Cole. There have never been enough hours in the day. Another reason I'm excited to drop premed: more time to have fun and be an actual fucking college kid.

I still need to call Mom and talk to her about all of this, which stresses me the hell out. Although right now I need to stop thinking about that. I promised Max I would go check out this "country" bar close to the tattoo shop I've been frequenting. Max has done the majority of my tats. I won't lie—he does some pretty badass work. I'm not sure about his taste in venues, though. I mean, a country bar in southern California?

"Fucking Riley! You actually showed." Max slaps me on the shoulder as I squeeze past the crowd.

"Said I would," I holler over the noise.

"Hey, Texas! You feel like you're at home now?" Danny asks, while passing me a beer. I shake my head and scoot it back. When I promised Audrey I wouldn't drink again, I meant it. Even if I hadn't promised, the hangover the next morning would have been enough to convince me it was a terrible idea.

"You do understand that we don't all wear cowboy hats, ride horses to work, and line dance, right?" I say, laughing.

"You don't? Huh . . ." Danny says, sounding disappointed.

"I'm gonna grab a drink." I point to the bar. The thing I've learned from the few times I've been able to hang out with these guys is to always have a drink in your hand. If you're not drinking, they'll pester the living shit out of you until you get one. I shoulder my way through the people up to the bar.

I catch the cute bartender's attention and call out, "Coke in a short glass."

"Got it, sweetie," she winks.

I lean up against the bar with my elbows bent and take in the crowded room. This place isn't bad. I notice a set of pool tables upstairs, a dance floor on the first floor, and tall tables surrounding it for people to hang out and drink. The music is obviously country, which I prefer. And the girls are all wearing short dresses and cowboy boots, which I love.

"Y'all are sweet, but I don't drink," I hear a sultry female voice say over the music. An honest-to-God southern accent pulls me from my people watching. At that moment, the bartender comes back with my drink in a tumbler. Perfect—this could easily pass for a Jack and Coke. I hand her a ten and tell her to keep the change. She tries to chat me up but now that I've heard it, I'm on the hunt for that voice.

"Since you won't let me buy you a drink, let me at least have a dance."

"Okay, just one, though," I hear her say flirtatiously.

I watch a guy in a button-up Affliction shirt guide her toward the dance floor, and I know exactly who's under his arm. I should have known from the first "y'all" she spoke. The douchebag twirls her once they reach the wooden floor and I see her laugh. I instinctively follow after them so I can get an up-close view, and I lean up on the railing that surrounds the floor. Why is she here again? And why does she still look so damn beautiful?

There's something about knowing how it feels to be with a certain girl, yearning for it, and knowing you can't have her. I've had Audrey; she should be a distant memory at this point. But I still crave every dip and curve of her skin. My body knows where she fits perfectly against me and it won't be satisfied until it has her again.

"Staring pretty hard at my girl," a deep voice booms from behind me. I already know who it is. Lane. I wouldn't forget that guy.

Without turning around, I say, "I guess you get off on seeing other guys with *your* girl. You sure as hell suck at keeping her *yours*, though."

He chuckles and positions himself right next to me, beer in hand. He leans his elbows up on the railing and looks out after Audrey. Just like I'm doing. "I don't know . . . I think I do a pretty damn good job, seeing as she's been living with me for over three years now."

I flinch at the idea of her living with any guy. Unwarranted jealousy flares through my veins and I can't stop the bombardment of images in my head. What would it be like to have Audrey all to myself, to be able to touch her whenever I wanted, and to see her sleepy face every morning? I rub out an ache in my chest and continue to watch the loser with his hands on her hips, trying to pull her in closer.

"How can you stand it, man? I mean, how the hell can you watch other guys put their hands all over her?" He has to have known what I was up to over winter break when I dragged her off alone. It's probably best to leave that be. No reason to bring up the best damn sex of my life, which just so happened to be with his girlfriend.

When her dance partner dips her backward and I catch him trying to look down her shirt, I begin rubbing my chest again. And despite what's happening on the dance floor, Lane's watching every move *I* make.

"You act like a lovesick puppy, and yet you've never given her the time of day."

So she's talked about me to him? That shouldn't feel as good as it does. "You two have a weird relationship," I state with feeling.

"I guess it would be weird if I were sleeping with her. But I'm not." My fists clench, because I'm not sure what to think of his words. "She's like my little sister and I love that girl to death, meaning I would destroy any asshole that breaks her heart."

The threat isn't lost on me. "Can't break what was never yours."

"That's where you're wrong," he replies.

Just then, Audrey dances past us and our eyes connect as her idiot partner spins her around. Her head whips back to look again and I can see the confusion on her face, probably wondering why Lane and I are talking. Lane wiggles his fingers at her and she gives him a tense smile.

"She's worried I'll hurt you," he says, still maintaining forward focus.

"I'm sure you could," I state, "but she should also be worried that you would get hurt while trying." He throws his head back laughing, and it pulls Audrey's confused glance back to us. I almost want to laugh with him, because her partner is starting to get annoyed at her lack of attention.

"There's too much shit between us," I declare.

"Maybe if you took your head out of your ass long enough to hear what she has to say, you'd change your mind." When I give him a questioning look, he continues, "Have you *ever* let her talk?"

I shake my head back and forth because it's true. If I let her talk, she could convince me to do just about anything. Even betray my own brother by dating his ex-wife, who cheated on him and got pregnant by another man. Shit . . . that's a hard pill to swallow.

"Fuck . . ." I continue rubbing because I have a feeling Lane's about to make me feel like the biggest asshole known to man.

"She came up here last year to talk to *you*, not your dickhead brother. But you guys wouldn't know that, because you never let her say more than two words before cutting her off or ignoring her completely."

Huge asshole–check!

"Oh, and before your ego grows any bigger . . . she's been living in California since the day after she graduated from high school. She didn't make this huge trek out to talk to you last year. I sure as hell didn't want her to waste her time driving even two minutes to see you."

"You both live here?" I ask, shocked.

"You either quit staring at her like she's holding your next breath or you go talk to her," he says, ignoring my question and pushing off the railing.

"You're kind of an asshole, you know that?"

"Nah, just protective of my girl." I don't need to turn around to see that he's walking away. I guess this conversation is over. I wish he would fucking stop calling her his girl, though. It's unnerving how one guy can make you grateful that he's around and enraged at the same time. If it weren't Audrey that stood in between us, I think Lane and I could be friends. I can appreciate his no-bullshit policy.

The song is finally ending and I can already see Audrey's partner trying to persuade her to go another round. Not gonna happen, buddy.

- SIX -

AUDREY -

Pete, or Paul, or was it Parker? Whoever this guy is, he reeks of cologne. My nose is stinging badly, my eyes are about to start watering, and my head's beginning to pound. The entire dance I've been begging for the song to just end already, and now I need to tell him to take a hike. He got his one dance. I also need to find Lane ASAP to figure out why he was talking to Jace.

The guy with a name that starts with P is still holding on to my hands as I'm trying to gently pull back. The upbeat country song we were just dancing to starts to blend into a slow song. Hell. No. I can't have my face that close to his body or I'll pass out from the toxic fumes. Why do guys insist on spraying themselves down with this stuff? It's not a magical pheromone that's going to have the ladies chasing you.

"Mind if I cut in?" Jace's voice growls from beside us.

I don't even have to think twice about his question. Immediately, I extract myself from Mr. Smellgood and grab Jace's hands. I can hear the guy's protests, but Jace moves us toward the opposite side of the dance floor. His movements are fluid and easy to follow.

"Whatever reason you have for dancing with me, I don't even care right now. Thank you for getting me away from him," I say, smiling up at him.

He places his hand on my waist and pulls me in closer. His nose scrunches up in disgust. "Damn, he should have just pissed all over you instead."

"Oh no," I groan into his shoulder, "is it on me?"

With my eyes closed, I feel the tip of his nose run from my temple slowly down to my neck. He's sniffing me and it feels primal, possessive, and way too sexy. It's everything I'm attracted to in Jace: his commanding touch mixed with his sweet softness. My nerve endings are on fire at the memory of what his touch can do to my body.

"Don't, Jace," I breathe out in a whisper.

"Hmm?" he mumbles, his nose still burrowed in my neck.

It's difficult to think straight because, unlike my previous partner, Jace smells clean and delectable. Not an ounce of cologne, just soap and aftershave. "Stop, Jace, I'm trying . . . I just want to get over you," I stumble out candidly.

The warmth of his breath tickles behind my ear. "I like it better when you're under me." I force myself to pull out of his grasp and walk toward the exit. I can't do this right now. Jace is much too tempting and not healthy for my mental well-being. He grabs my hand and spins me back into his chest. "I'm sorry; I'll behave." I place my left hand back on his bicep and my right hand in his larger hand. We continue dancing in a comfortable silence.

"Who would have thought two kids from Texas would meet back up at a country bar in California?" I ask, trying to lighten the mood.

He smiles and declares, "I have to admit I was skeptical about this place."

"Me too."

As if on cue, the slow song fades. The lights begin to darken and a fast beat begins pumping through the speakers. It's definitely not country music anymore. It must change over after a certain time. The crowd descends onto the dance floor as if they were waiting for this music all night. A secret they were all clued in on, unlike me. The temperature rapidly escalates with the drastic increase of body heat.

"And . . . that's exactly what I was expecting," he chuckles into my ear. I reach back and grasp my hair into a handheld ponytail so I can cool down. Jace grabs on to my hips and begins dancing in front of me. I look up into his eyes and he shrugs as if saying, "Might as well." He spins me around so that my back is facing him and then blows cool air across my neck. It feels wonderful and much too intimate at the same time.

Looking around, I watch how others are moving. I've danced like this before, alone in my bedroom with the music blasting, but never in public. And never with Jace behind me. I don't know how to do this with a guy, or how to keep a rhythm. I'm sure I look like a complete idiot just standing here. Jace continues to blow on my neck and I'm so overheated, it feels fantastic. Problem is, it's creating an unwanted need between my thighs.

"Relax," his deep, melodic voice whispers from behind my ear. When I shiver, he squeezes my hips and pulls them closer to him. Slowly, he begins to slide against me and I mimic his movements in front of him. After watching the girls around me, I soon feel confident enough to turn in his arms and roll my hips while looking up into his eyes. Gradually, I loosen up and begin to have fun.

"Every guy here is so damn jealous of me right now," he says into my ear. I look up and roll my eyes at him, but he's able to eventually elicit a smile from me in the process. An hour passes in the blink of an eye and we're both laughing and having a good time, but it's sweltering in here and I need a break.

"I'm gonna grab a water. I'll be right back," I holler close to his ear and gesture toward the bar.

"I'll come with you," he mouths back.

Shaking my head, I yell, "Just stay. I'll come back and find you." Without waiting for his response, I head off the dance floor, welcoming the immediate rush of cool air I feel once I leave the mass of writhing bodies. My skin is damp with sweat and I'm sure my hair is looking less than perfect. I can feel my limp brown curls sticking to the skin of my neck. I push my way to the bar and ask for a glass of water. When the bartender returns with it, I gulp down the refreshing liquid quickly.

"Doll, you're club dancing?" Lane calls out from beside me. His animated smile tells me he's either excited for me or he's drunk. Maybe both. I nod my head because my voice is already getting sore from shouting over the crowd. "With Jace?" he asks and I nod again. "Another checkmark in the box of things you haven't done yet!" His excitement is contagious.

I pull him in for a hug and laugh. "You look like you've been having a good time."

"Yeah, I have, actually. Would you hate me if I headed out with Christine?" He points his thumb behind him to a waiting blonde that I've never seen before. "Here are the keys to the car. Will you be all right driving home alone?" I nod my head in shock because this is so unlike Lane. He never just leaves me. "Promise you'll stay near Jace and that he'll walk you out to the car?"

"Why do you trust Jace, but not anyone else?"

"I don't know. I just got this vibe about him, that he wouldn't let anything happen to you. Should I go talk to him about this?"

"No, Dad, I don't need a babysitter." I shove him in the chest playfully.

"Promise me or I'm staying."

I stick out my pinky and say, "Promise." He wraps his smallest finger around mine and kisses my forehead.

"How late do you think you'll stay?" he asks, while Blondie starts grabbing for his hand.

"No, no, Papa Bear. You've done your duty; time to go." I shove him and make my way back to the crush, pushing his keys into the front pocket of my jeans.

When I left Jace on the dance floor, I had a one-track mind: get water and clear my head from the lust-induced Jace-fog. I never thought about what he would be doing while I was gone. Of course he would continue dancing. Did I expect him to just stand there and wait after I'd asked him to stay? Regardless, seeing him dancing with two other girls, one in front and one behind, still has my heart pounding erratically.

I stop my forward motion and watch from a distance. There's a split in the crowd that allows a direct view of the show. Jealousy flashes through me at the sight of the girls' faces that are thick with desire and their hands that are all over him. His hands are out away from them, but their bodies still connect with each beat of the song.

When another set of hands grabs on to my waist from behind, I flinch and look over my shoulder. A tall, dark-haired man smiles down at me.

"Mason," he introduces himself.

"Audrey," I call back in a hoarse voice.

This guy is handsome. His jaw is defined and yet he has a hint of a baby face, which is endearing. His messy brown hair is tossed about and damp. I smile and decide to relax. This is what people do in dance clubs. All small talk is thrown out the window. The conversation is spoken with the movement of our bodies. Besides, I don't feel like trying to break up the threesome in front of me.

When I turn back around, I see that Jace is frozen, staring directly at me with his bright blue eyes. His groupies are practically begging for his attention and becoming needy with their hands. Neither of us makes a move toward the other. We're locked in a stare-down.

Mason's hands move from my hips to my waist and back down again. I begin to move against him. Jace drives his hips forward at the same time. When one of the girls aligns her body with his and grinds up against him, I roll my hips and do the same to Mason. I'm instantly turned on when I see Jace's mouth form a small *o* shape. His eyes never leave mine as he spreads one hand out on the girl's stomach and I move Mason's over mine. Fire ignites in Jace's eyes and I'm spurred on.

Before I realize what's happening, Jace and I are dancing together, only we're ten feet apart with different partners. When he rolls forward, I grind back. Every movement Mason makes feels like Jace in my head. I wonder if Jace is thinking the same, since his eyes haven't budged from my face or my body, not even for a second.

We continue this hypnotizing dance for what feels like an eternity, mirroring our movements with each other's. The way his body flows with the music is almost like living art. He's a masterpiece in the middle of this packed wooden dance floor, a God among men. His tall frame should appear out of place, but it draws in all the eyes around him. The black T-shirt he's wearing is putting up a tough battle against his flexing muscles, and I wish it would surrender already. My fingers ache to pull it off over his head to reveal the lines and curves of his chest and stomach that I've stroked once before.

He hasn't put his hands back on the girl in front of him, but that doesn't stop her from rubbing her body all over his. I've never been captivated like this before . . . it's almost erotic, and yet I'm envious at the same time. I hate that she's feeling every ounce of muscle on his solid chest that I should be feeling. However, I don't move forward and neither does he.

I can't help thinking about the way this whole scene reflects the relationship that Jace and I have always had. So close, yet always so far away.

"You're a great dancer, gorgeous," Mason says into my ear. I close my eyes and try to block out his voice. I hold the image behind my eyelids of Jace, who's not even ten feet away from me, moving his body seductively. I'm lost in the withdrawal from Jace's intoxicatingly blue eyes, and I have no idea how to respond to Mason. *You're not so bad yourself, but I've actually been dancing this whole time with the smokin' hot heartthrob that's dancing ten feet away?* Might be a mood killer.

"Need something, Riley?" Mason's voice shakes me out of my reverie.

I freeze, knowing Jace must be close, but I can't open my eyes to look. A warm hand touches my hip and his tantalizing voice says, "You found my girl." I hear the smile in his tone and I tense at his words. "Look at me, gorgeous," he whispers, too close to my lips.

Because I can't seem to convince my traitorous body to defy him, my eyes snap open. Just as I imagined, he's bending down and looking directly at me. If I wanted to, I could move a fraction of an inch and have my mouth on his.

"Did you enjoy teasing me?" he inquires softly so that Mason can't overhear. I'm thankful, because it was rude of me to get lost in Jace while dancing with someone else. I don't want Mason to know about that.

And because I'm generally honest to a fault, I respond with a simple and breathless, "Yes." His eyes flare with excitement and his grip on my waist intensifies. He enjoys when I obey him, but he also likes to be teased. Huh . . . good to know. Not that this will ever happen again.

"Seriously?" Mason groans, interrupting our stare-down. "What's with you and Jaxon taking the good ones?" he asks Jace.

Then he looks at me, saying, "Thanks for the dance, Audrey," and turns to walk away.

"Thanks, Mason. Anytime you want to dance again, let me know. Jace and I aren't together," I hurriedly say before he can get out of earshot.

Mason abruptly halts his movement, but Jace quickly stops whatever he might be thinking. "Move it along," he growls and pulls my hips to his.

With a scowl, I turn and say, "It's time for me to go home. Walk me to my car?" I wish I didn't even have to ask him, but I've promised Lane.

He takes my hand as we leave the bar, and I decide that pulling it away is not a battle I feel like having with him at the moment. He's gripping me tightly and his eyes haven't left my face. I feel as if he thinks I'll run away, which is exactly what I feel like doing right now.

"Are you mad at me?" he questions.

"No."

"I can always tell when you lie, Audrey, so don't."

"How about *you* don't do that again? You've made it perfectly clear how you feel about me, so don't stop me from being with someone else." I continue walking toward Lane's SUV and click the unlock button on the key fob when I reach it.

He turns me around and backs me up against the door. "And tell me, how *do* I feel about you?"

"I think you're attracted to me sexually," I admit. He nods his head and I continue, "But you finally got that urge out of your system over winter break. In regard to everything that happened in high school, I don't care what you think."

His stare becomes hard and cold when he hears my words. "What the hell?" he practically yells.

I quickly shrink away from him, ducking my head and averting my eyes, but I can't move too far because he has me blocked in. My conditioned response is the only one I've ever known. In my experience, the actions that come after words like that are not pleasant. In fact, they are the furthest thing from pleasant . . . they are painful. As in black eyes, broken ribs, and bruised arms.

A minute passes and no blows are thrown. With my head down, I look back in front of me and see Jace's shoes. Jace. It's Jace. *What the hell am I thinking?* Jace is not my father and he would never hurt me, not physically anyway. I silently berate myself. *Knock it off, Audrey; you're not that girl anymore.* Looking up at him again, I cringe at the fear in his eyes.

JACE -

What the hell just happened? First, she pisses me off by saying that I got an urge out of my system when we were together, and then she recoils away from me as if I would strike her. All of a sudden, she's the girl I found on the sidewalk again. "Approach with Caution" is back on her chest. Did she really just think I would hurt her? The sight of her withdrawing that way makes me physically nauseated. Why would she react like that around *me*?

Slowly, I lift up my hands and show them to her, before gently placing them on her arms. Thankfully, she doesn't flinch, so I proceed. I need to calm my voice. I don't care how angry she made me with her words; this is not the time for a heated argument.

"Audrey?" I ask, and her big brown eyes widen as they look directly at me. "What just happened?"

"I don't know . . ." she trails off hesitantly. *Bullshit.*

"Did I scare you?" She nods her head at my question, and I have to step away from her. I hate not touching her, but if I frightened her, then I need to give her some space. Shaking my head back and forth while trying to think, I say, "I would never . . . I never . . . shit . . ." I'm stuttering with frustration. "Have I ever given you the impression that I would hurt you?" I never thought I would have to say those words to a girl. I would absolutely never lay hands on her, or any girl, for that matter.

She steps closer to me and says, "No, I know you would never hurt me like that. It wasn't your fault. That had nothing to do with you. It just . . . happens."

"If it had nothing to do with me, who does it have to do with?"

"I need to go home; it's late." She turns back toward the car and I lunge for her. I hold on to her hips from behind and lean down to whisper in her ear. If she can't look at me when she says it, that's fine, but she's going to say it. She'd better fucking believe I'm going to find out who did what to her. So help me, God, if it's Lane, we'll be attending his funeral by Monday.

"Who?" I ask in a low growl.

Her shoulders slowly slump in defeat. "My dad."

"Your dad? What are you talking about? When? How?" My questions begin spilling out.

"I don't want to discuss this with you. Not here. Not right now." She reaches out and opens the door to her vehicle.

"Where's Lane?" I ask, as she climbs into the driver's seat.

"He left with some girl he met."

"Shit, he just left you here?" I ask, trying to keep my tone calm. Placing my hands on her thighs, I try to regain my composure. Are we talking about the same guy who always has one eye on her at all times?

"He made me promise that I would ask you to walk me out here."

"I'll follow you home, then, so I know that you got there okay."

"Jace . . . don't."

"I'm following you home, Audrey. I'll be right behind you." I close the door, leaving no opportunity for any argument she may attempt.

When I pull up into her parking lot, I'm relieved to see that she's in a nice part of town and only a few blocks away from me. This is the area where most students live who are attending the university, and I wonder if she's going to school here now. She parks in her designated spot and I have to force myself to stay in the car. If I get out, I'll never get back in.

She glances at me on her way out of the car and then walks to unlock her door. A dog dashes out and excitedly greets her when she gets the door open. Damn, that dog just put a smile on her face that could make a grown man drop to his knees and pray for more. If she doesn't stop, that's exactly what I'll end up doing. Damn lucky dog.

With a final look in my direction, she closes the door. She was probably wondering if I would get out and say something. I slam my palm against the steering wheel. Why is she wrapping me around her little finger again? I'm supposed to be over her! But right now, all I can think about is smashing my fist into her dad's front teeth for whatever he did, locking her away in my bedroom, and keeping her all to myself. Just for good measure, I slam both palms into the steering wheel again.

A light comes on, and I can see her moving around in what must be her bedroom. I fantasize about her peeling off those tight-ass jeans and her button-up shirt with the top three buttons undone. Standing above her while dancing, I had the perfect view down that shirt. Fucking Mason probably saw down it as well. I have to stop before I beat the shit out of my poor leather steering wheel.

Her light switches off and I'll bet she's curling up in her bed. Slipping that delectable body under her sheets, turning on her side, and sleeping with her hands tucked up under her cheek. I can picture her beautiful, dark brown hair spread out across her pillow, just waiting for someone to run their fingers through the silky strands.

I step on the gas and pull into a visitor's parking spot. She has to know I'm still here. Even idling, my V8 can be heard from a block away. My neighbors fucking love me. Ever since Jax handed over the keys to his '67 Camaro, I've been fine-tuning the engine so it purrs, nice and loud.

My body pulls me toward her apartment, even though I should get back in the car and drive home. Out of curiosity, I make my way to her window first. It must be in my blood to check security because I test the lock and push on the metal frame. When it easily glides up, my jaw clenches in anger. Her window is fucking unlocked. Why the hell isn't Lane checking for these kinds of things? I push her vertical blinds aside and quietly crawl into the darkness, which is not an easy feat when you're six-three.

I hear a soft, muffled *thump, thump, thump* on the carpet near my feet. I let my eyes adjust to the darkness, taking in her room by the glow of the street lamps. I see that her marvelous guard dog is still lying on the ground with his tail wagging, despite my illicit approach into his owner's residence. I bend down and scratch his stomach. I guess I should just be thankful he didn't bite my head off.

She shuffles in her bed and I'm surprised she hasn't freaked out by now. Usually when someone starts climbing in your bedroom window, you should have your guard up. I walk over to her bed and see that she's completely passed out. She has one arm thrown over her head, and the covers are tucked all the way up under her chin. Damn, how did she do that? I literally watched her walk into her house not even ten minutes ago and she's already dead to the world.

Her body is practically screaming for mine to join her, or maybe it's just my body doing the screaming. Well . . . far be it for me to ignore this opportunity. I sit down on a chair and take my shoes off, and then decide to make myself at home by removing my jeans and shirt as well. I leave my boxers on, even though I hate sleeping in clothes, because I should at least be somewhat courteous at this point. I mean, I did just break into her room and now I plan on climbing in bed with her, all while she's fast asleep. She's going to be pissed when she wakes up, and I can't wait to see her cute little angry face.

With a smirk, I try to figure out the best possible way to climb into this tiny excuse for a bed without waking her. My knee hits the mattress and I groan. This isn't a tiny bed, it's a fucking futon. I hate futons. There's always a metal bar in your back that you can't escape. When the damn thing practically growls under the weight of my body, I wonder if it'll be able to hold both of us. Fuck it. If I break this thing, at least I can buy her a real bed.

I crawl up behind her and slip under the covers. I stifle a chuckle because unbelievably, she doesn't move a muscle as this thing creaks and cracks noisily in the quiet room. Tomorrow morning is going to be fantastic. Her reaction alone will be priceless.

I lie down beside her and shift to my side so we can both fit comfortably. She mumbles under her breath, and I freeze as she scoots her body closer into mine. Her hair is thrown up messily on top of her head and I'm aching to pull it all down. God, she smells delicious. The faint scent of coconut lingers, and I'm instantly thrown back to our first and only time in my car.

Her mumbling continues and then she murmurs, "Jace . . ."

Holy hell, she's dreaming about me. I inch closer, in hopes that if she speaks again I'll be able to hear every word that comes out of that pretty mouth of hers. My hand slides over a bare hip and I freeze. Slowly, I slide my fingers farther up and feel the tiniest string. If I could smack my forehead without waking her up, I would. She has a fucking thong on and if my instincts are correct, that's *all* she has on.

My hand splays out across her soft stomach and I pull her in closer to my chest, burying my nose in her hair. After everything she told me tonight, even though it wasn't nearly enough, I just need to hold her tight. I can fight those demons for her, and I need to make sure they never return.

The soft in-and-out of her breathing begins to lull me to sleep. This was a fucking dumb idea. I'm never going to want to sleep anywhere else again. Futon be damned.

On a long moan, my name escapes her lips again. I'm instantly hard and that fucker has no plans to surrender anytime soon. There's no doubt in my mind as to what kind of dream she's having . . . about me. This is going to be the longest and most excruciating night of my life. I'm two seconds away from flipping her around and waking her up, but she shifts onto her back and lets out a contented sigh. Well, at least it looks like Dream Jace did a damn fine job. *High-five, my man.*

- SEVEN -

AUDREY -

So maybe turning the air conditioner off last night during this September heat wave was not the best idea. But if Lane isn't here, I always turn it off. I'd rather deal with being uncomfortable than spend unnecessary money on utility bills. Whenever I fall asleep, my inner heater cranks up to its highest setting, so I typically sleep in as little clothes as possible. It doesn't seem to be helping right now, though, because my skin feels like it's on fire.

Slowly, I stretch out my legs and roll my ankles until they pop a few times. It's a nasty habit, but it feels too good to stop. My hands extend out and touch skin. Not my skin. And Chuck sure as hell doesn't feel like this either. Panic mode hits me fast, and I immediately start kicking to get myself out of the bed. In terror, I launch myself off whoever is in my bed and onto the floor, all while dragging the sheet with me.

A loud, painful-sounding grunt comes from the bed. I pull the sheet up over my chest and take in my late-night intruder. The muscles in his arms flex and move as his body collapses inward. His gorgeous chest is one that I am intimately familiar with.

"Jace?" I gasp loudly.

"Ahhhh . . . fuuuck . . . I think I'm gonna hurl!" His hands cover his crotch and his eyes are squeezed shut in pain.

"What the hell, Jace? How did you get in here? And why?" I screech, while trying to keep myself covered. He continues to roll back and forth, groaning in agony. My door instantly slams open with a wide-eyed Lane standing in the doorway. He still has that sleepy look, but his fists are clenched tightly and I can tell he's ready for battle.

"Audrey?" he huffs out, which further signifies his panic because he rarely calls me by my real name. He scans the scene before him, me on the floor with only a sheet covering my essentials and Jace thrashing around on my bed in pain for whatever reason. The calm washes back over Lane's face as he realizes there isn't a threat, although I'm still not convinced about that. Jace snuck into my room last night and I want to know why.

"Damn, dude. That does *not* look like fun," Lane says to Jace.

"Fuck, man, she just used her whole body to launch off my nuts," he says in a calmer, yet higher-pitched voice.

Lane sucks in a quick rush of air between his teeth, sympathizing with him. "I don't care what he did, Doll; that ain't right." He gestures toward Jace on the bed and leaves the room.

I kicked him . . . down there? Whoops. Jace still has his eyes closed as I cautiously approach him on the bed, thinking about all the times I've been taught what to do when approaching a wounded animal. I slowly sit on my knees beside him, the sheet clutched to my chest, while taking in his gorgeous body. If only I had known it was him, this wake-up could have gone so much better.

"You scared me," I whisper.

"Don't worry. I sure as hell learned my lesson." For the first time this morning, I'm finally gifted with the most striking blue eyes I've ever seen.

I had never seen the ocean until I moved to California. I remember the salty marine air hitting me the second I stepped out of the car, and it was unlike anything I had felt before. While walking through the parking lot, I was anxious to see what was causing those amazing roaring sounds. The second I stepped over the first mound of sand, I was finally able to see the breathtaking sight. The gorgeous, blue ocean immediately made me think of Jace's captivating eyes. He carries a vast amount of emotion and intelligence behind those baby blues, and just like the ocean, they appear never-ending. I wish I could stare into them for hours.

The rasp of his voice pulls me from my reflection. "Why are you looking at me like that?" he whispers.

"Because you're gorgeous," I reply truthfully. *Damn, my stupid mouth!* I feel my face flame up with embarrassment at my answer. I was too busy gawking at him and had no time to create a plausible defense. A smirk begins to pull up at the corner of his mouth, and I try to stop him before he can delve further into that admission. "Why are you here?" I demand.

"To be honest, I don't know . . ." he trails off. "After everything you said last night about . . . your dad, I just couldn't leave. I needed to be next to you. I needed to protect you."

"I don't need protection, Jace. If that's what I was looking for, then I already found it in Lane."

His fists clench together next to his hips, and I can tell my relationship with Lane is a sensitive area for him. "Audrey, if you ever need help, I would be there. I don't care what went down. I would have been there, even back then!" he says, lightly beating his chest with his closed fist.

His eyes are haunted with countless emotions, and I pray to God one of those is not guilt. I want to scream at how irate I am that he never came to me and asked what happened. I want to cry because of everything we could have had. Even after all that, I want to reassure him that he should never feel guilt, regardless of what he assumes my dad did. This is what Jace does to me. He makes me want to smack him and embrace him, all in the same beat of time.

"I don't need to be saved. I already saved myself."

"I can see that, and I'm having a fucking hard time with the thought that I should have been the one to do it. You shouldn't have had to deal with everything all by yourself. I should have been there . . . I was so stupid . . . I should have been there . . ." he rambles.

"Jace," I interject, "what are you saying right now?"

"Go on a date with me, Audrey," he responds without thought, and then quickly adds, "A real date. Just you and me. All the drama and bullshit set aside for now. Please."

I shake my head back and forth. "No."

His mouth drops open, obviously not expecting that answer. "You said you would talk to me. I need to know everything."

I scoot backward off the bed and stand in the middle of my room with the sheet wrapped tightly under my arms, shielding my naked body. I begin pacing the length of my room from one end to the next. There is nothing I've ever wanted more than to go on an actual date with Jace. I've dreamed about this moment for years. But at the same time, how can he ask that of me when he still believes so many horrible things?

He climbs off my bed, and the loud creaking and groaning of my futon makes him frown. I giggle at his frustration and he cocks an eyebrow at me.

"Your bed sucks," he declares, while air quoting the word *bed*.

I shrug my shoulders, because I think it's wonderful compared to the tiny loveseat I used to have to sleep on back home. His hands cup each side of my face, and then he moves them across my temples and over my hair, until they rest on the back of my neck. Completely surrounding me, he tilts my head back so I have nowhere else to look but up at him.

"I'm still so drawn to you. It's like nothing has changed in the past four years. You still feel like a breath of fresh air compared to every girl I've met before. I kept telling myself it was a good thing we didn't work out, that there was a reason for it. I kept telling myself there was someone better out there for you and for me," he says, never breaking eye contact. My hands clutch the sheet tighter, wanting to reach out for his amazing bare chest, which is only inches away and taunting me.

"But why, Audrey? How come even the smallest of things will make me think of you? How come whenever I catch a whiff of anything cherry-vanilla, I think of how your lips tasted that first day? How come anytime I have to write my phone number down, I recall sticking my fingers down your front pocket? How come every single long-legged brunette that walks by makes my stomach drop to the floor in hopes that it could be you?"

His words floor me. Literally. I should be lying on the hardwood under my feet and probably would be if his hands weren't holding me up. "How can you say that and still think so poorly of me?" I whisper.

"Well, first of all, Lane told me that I should talk to you."

Wrong answer. Why are men so freaking dumb? I shove off him and turn my back in frustration. That's a whole other subject in itself, so instead of trying to address it, I redirect. "Why did you yell at me last night, after what I said to you?"

"Don't change the subject, Aud—"

I interrupt him, "Why, Jace?"

With a sigh, he says, "Because you said that I got you out of my system."

"Didn't you?"

"Audrey, there aren't enough nights in a lifetime to get you out of my system."

I squeeze the sheet to my body again and pace the small area in front of him. "Then why did you say what you said after we . . . finished, that night in your car?" He gives me a confused look, so I continue, "Do you know how shitty that made me feel?" He stares at me and doesn't say a word. There's complete silence for seconds, which soon turn into minutes. Suddenly, I notice that the wheels are turning. He was drunk and doesn't remember, and now he's trying to scan back through the night. "Oh my God, you don't even remember! Do you even recall having sex with me?" My voice rises in mortification.

He reaches out and stills me by grabbing hold of my arms and pulling me closer to him. My sheet drops to the floor, but I don't even care. I couldn't be more humiliated at the moment anyway. His eyes dip to my chest for a fraction of a second and he immediately looks up at the ceiling. After a few deep breaths, he slowly lowers his amazing blues to look in my eyes, although I can tell it's a struggle for him to look only at my eyes. If I weren't so angry, I would laugh at his effort.

"I'm sorry. I'm so sorry. That night, I was on such a high that I don't remember whatever idiotic thing I said. I was drunk and I finally had you in my arms. And then I passed out so quickly afterward," he cries, and then tightens his grip on me to emphasize a point. "But don't you dare think for one second that I don't remember every single touch and feeling I had with you. I remember the way every inch of you felt under my fingers. I remember the way your skin tasted, and I sure as hell didn't forget the way I fit inside you so damn perfectly. It makes me physically ache at the loss."

JACE -

Just thinking about that night again is making me throb with need. She may have tried to kick my balls up into my stomach earlier, but that doesn't mean I'm out of the game. Especially with her standing practically naked in front of me. I want her to know that this conversation is imperative to me, but my eyes are straining from the effort of trying to keep them on her face. Damn peripheral vision is fucking with me, because I can see her gorgeous tits so close to my chest and I just want to taste them.

"Tell me what I said . . . please," I rasp out quietly.

She doesn't speak, just continues staring at me with her hypnotizing eyes that could suck a guy in and make him hand over whatever she wanted without a second thought. When her bottom lip sticks out a fraction, I press my body up against hers and kiss her deeply. Never mistake me for a man that doesn't strike when an opportunity arises. Her hands reach out to my chest and it feels as if she may push me away, but then she melts into me and her hands slide across my skin.

My fingers thread through her hair and I grip her scalp tightly as I walk her backward across the floor. When she bumps into the desk, I cup her from behind and lift her onto the edge of the smooth wood. Her little fingers run across my stomach and over my chest, all while her lips devour mine. I sit my ass down in the chair that's situated in front of her, and thankfully I'm tall enough to still be at the same level as her lips. But sadly, her fingers can't dance across my skin anymore.

I break the kiss and park my body in between her thighs, lifting one beautiful leg after another to rest each foot on the tops of my thighs. The view in front of me is fucking phenomenal. I want to consume her legs, since they are featured in about fifty percent of my dreams about her. I imagine her legs in the air, wrapped around my waist, intertwined with my legs, and my favorite, draped around my face.

My lips begin to trace an invisible line that stretches from her ankles up to her inner thighs. She grabs on to my head and tugs my hair. I shake my head back and forth without removing my lips or even looking at her, "Hands on the desk, Audrey." With a strangled moan, she immediately latches on to the desk. Audrey craves the surrender and I need the control; this is one of the many reasons why our bodies cry for each other.

I lift my eyelids and see that lust engulfs her. As my mouth lightly caresses the skin on her thighs, I watch short little breaths soar in and out of her lips, which form the shape of an *o*. Her fingers clamp down on the edge of the desk and her knuckles are turning white, a sure sign that she's barely containing herself. I smile against her soft skin at the tenacity of this woman.

Slowly my fingers catch up to my mouth and I rub across her sad excuse for panties. When she whimpers, I lift up so I'm at eye level with her and lick at the edges of her lips until she opens, and then cover her mouth with mine. Her body begins to rock against my fingers, so I slide the fabric over to feel how ready she is.

Groaning, I say, "God, I can't wait to be inside of you. It's been too damn long, but I remember *exactly* how you feel."

Her eyes continue to watch mine as I thrust two fingers inside, causing her to arch her back into me. She lets out a long, uninhibited moan and I'm on fire. It's taking every ounce of strength I have to keep this just about her at the moment. I'll have my turn.

"Quiet," I reprimand her, stilling my fingers. "Lane doesn't get to hear this. This is *mine*. Not a peep or I'll stop." *Yeah right, a fucking bulldozer couldn't stop me now.*

I watch as she bites down on her bottom lip to stop herself from letting any sound slip through. My fingers begin their ministrations again and her heels dig into my thighs, so I flex my legs to give her something steady to push off of. Slowly, I take her higher and higher with the slow, rhythmic, in-and-out movements. Her back begins to arch toward me again and I cup one of her breasts in my hand. She fits perfectly.

Right as her legs begin to shake, there's a loud bang on the opposite side of the door and she jumps an inch off the desktop. My fingers remain motionless inside of her, but my opposite hand holds her down so she doesn't bail. I forget how jumpy she can be.

Lane hollers through the door, "Doll, we've got class; hurry it up!" *Cock-blocking bastard.*

Her eyes are focused on the door and it's obvious she's lost her momentum, but my fingers aren't about to give up. Fuck the class. Why would anyone want to be anywhere else right now?

"Look at me, gorgeous," I direct softly.

Quickly, I stand and wrap my free hand around her head and tilt it up so I can completely surround all of her senses. The second her attention is back on me, I steal her lips with mine. The kiss becomes hungry and needy. I need more of her; I've always needed more of her. She quickly falls back into the moment as she grabs on to my shoulders, and it feels so damn good to have her nails in my back and her chest pressed up against mine. Skin-to-skin is a magical fucking thing. It doesn't take long to bring her to the brink again.

In the quiet of the room, she screams, "Jace!" and I feel her clutch my fingers harder and harder as her body crashes back down.

Through her heavy breathing, I kiss her lips softly. "I'll let that one slide, because how can I resist hearing you scream my name?"

She lets out a relieved sigh and I can't hold back any longer. As I step back to rip my boxers off, she hops off the desk. My body naturally follows her path.

"Damn, I needed that. Thanks, babe," she swiftly offers without any emotion. Then she reaches down, scoops up a shirt off the ground, and throws it over her head. She digs clothes out of her dresser and pulls a brush off of her nightstand, all while I'm standing here, shell-shocked.

What. The. Fuck? Did I just get used?

My face must convey what I can't find the words to say, because as she reaches for the doorknob, she throws over her shoulder, "That's what you said." Then she retreats out into the hallway before I can ask any questions.

I slump down into the seat and try to replay the reel of what the hell just happened. What did any of that just mean? When realization hits, I smack myself in the forehead. *Jace, you stupid idiot.* That's what I said to her after we had sex in my car last winter. How could I have done that to her? I thought *I* just felt used? What was she feeling when I barely said more than three sentences to her before I pulled her in the backseat and finished with a line like that? *Stupid, Stupid, Stupid.*

I pull on my shirt and jeans quickly, then shove my feet into my shoes and run out of her bedroom. When I get into the living room, everything is silent. The dog is lounging on the couch, wagging his tail and looking like he's about to take a midmorning siesta already. Lane and Audrey are gone. My stomach begins to hurt, and I get a sinking feeling that I just messed up another chance for us.

- EIGHT -

AUDREY -

As Lane and I leave class and walk to our last one of the day, my feet are dragging and my stomach is rumbling. I'm feeling sluggish and light-headed. I didn't have time to grab anything to eat this morning on our rush out the door. I barely had time to throw on my clothes while trying to escape Jace. We only have a ten-minute block between the two class periods, and I don't have enough time to hunt down a vending machine. I still don't know this campus very well, so I would more than likely end up lost.

"Lane, do you have any food in your bag?" I moan. He usually carries something edible around with him wherever he goes.

"I ate it all in class. Why?" he responds.

"I'm dragging. I don't know how I'm going to stay awake in this class."

"Well, guess you shouldn't have been getting another taste," he teases.

"There definitely won't be any more."

"Riiight," he says sarcastically.

We walk into our Accounting 582 class, Mergers and Acquisitions, which is bound to bore me to sleep. Unfortunately, a nap is unlikely in this small classroom, where professors are more likely to call me out than they were in the auditorium classrooms I'm used to. Despite this, the smaller rooms for the graduate programs are one thing I have actually learned to enjoy.

Lane and I have claimed two seats on the far left of the room, somewhat close to the front. By this time, everyone has already chosen the seats they will sit in for the semester, so I'm surprised when I see items that don't belong to me on my desk. Although there's no one in the seat, someone clearly left their to-go coffee cup and a bakery bag on my desk. It must be from a previous class. People are so rude sometimes. How hard is it to clean up your own mess?

When I reach for the trash, I notice that the cup is still warm, too warm to have been sitting here since the previous class. I set it back down and see my name written in black marker on the side in all capital letters. I step away from the desk and point at the cup as if it's insulting me.

"Lane . . . it has my name on it. What does that mean?"

He leans over my shoulder and studies the cup for a couple of seconds. I feel him shrug his shoulders and then he says, "Usually that means it's for you." I can hear the amusement in his voice.

I sit down in my seat and study what's in front of me. Who did this? A quick scan of the classroom proves what I already knew: I don't know anyone in here. So how could someone have left this for me on my desk?

"It won't bite you. Just drink it," Lane whispers from his spot directly behind me.

I pick it up and recognize the name of the coffeehouse that's printed in red ink on the side. I haven't tried that one out yet, although it's not far from my house. Hoping for more clues, I spin the cup around and then see extra script on the back.

I'm so sorry.
I'll make it up to you, I swear.
Please, don't write me off just yet.

I already know what the contents of the cup will be before I place it to my lips and swallow the warm, spicy mixture. A chai tea latte. The delicious drink makes me smile and laugh to myself at his gesture. I still don't have any idea how he knew what class I had today or even that I attend this school, but right now I'm grateful for the gift because this will be my saving grace for the next hour.

I lift the brown paper bakery bag next and unroll the folded top to peek inside. Lying on top is another note.

It's my fault you didn't get to eat before you left.
I'll make that up to you as well.
Go to dinner with me tonight?

He had written down his phone number at the bottom, and looking at the familiar area code, I'm almost certain that this is the same number he had four years ago. I still have that number programmed in my phone from the day he wrote it down on a piece of notebook paper for me. I have never had the guts to use it before.

Lane leans over my shoulder again, examining my goods. "Damn, he could have at least gotten me something. Douchebag." I elbow him back to his spot so I can enjoy this moment, even though I know he's just trying to have a good time with me.

When our instructor enters the room and begins the lecture immediately, I zone out, thinking about Jace. He's asking for a shot.

At least, I think that's what he's asking for. Or maybe he's just curious how the only story he's ever known could be any different. I would always regret it, though, if I didn't hear him out. Before I can change my mind, I pull out my phone and send a text to Jace.

I have to work tonight - A

Within seconds, my phone vibrates and his reply is displayed across my screen.

Sunday for lunch then. Please? I'll pick you up.

Sunday lunch? That doesn't sound like a date time. That sounds like an I'm-curious-about-your-story-but-nothing-else time. Not that I would have been able to do Saturday anyway, because I finally relented to Em's endless pursuit to go to the beach party tomorrow. Thankfully, Lane is going to tag along with me. I can't help wondering if Jace has a date tomorrow night, and that's why he suggested Sunday. *Forget it, Audrey, just get Sunday over with.* I quickly text back that I'd meet him and then put my phone away for the remainder of the class.

~

Tonight is my last night of training with Em. It's been a lot of fun, and this place will be kind of boring on the nights I have to work without her. She definitely keeps it interesting. Since I never really needed any training in the first place, we've been able to talk during our shifts, and I've slowly been telling her everything. Tonight, I finally just spit it all out. I told her all that's happened between Jace and me, starting from the moment I met him on the sidewalk in Texas, all the way up to this morning.

Her silent, stunned face has me cringing, so I turn to put away the last of the glasses. The bar is finally empty and Mark is sweeping under the pool tables, leaving Em and me to get everything squared away for tomorrow's shift. After several minutes pass, I glance back her way and see that she still hasn't moved from her spot. She's staring off into space, as if she's just been given some life-threatening news.

"All of that could not have happened to one person," she finally says.

"I wish I could say I made it up."

In a kindhearted tone, she says, "You weren't lying when you said you're a mess." She pouts her lip out in a sad expression. "But I think you're just a victim of circumstance."

I laugh and reply, "Yeah, the circumstance just so happens to be my life."

That makes her laugh and her mood immediately lightens. "Surely you've drawn the last chip out of the bad-luck jar. I mean, from here on out, I bet your life is gonna be fabulous."

I give her a look that clearly says, *Yeah, right . . .*

Then her face lights up and she claps her hands. "Jace! Oh my God, this is going to be so much fun! You and Jace!"

"Umm . . . I don't think you heard every roadblock I listed earlier. I wasn't kidding when I said the fates are not in our favor."

She shakes her head back and forth stubbornly, "Nope, this is happening. He sounds crazy about you. It all makes so much more sense now!"

She's getting way too excited about what will most likely amount to nothing. "What makes sense?" I ask.

"Wait, what happened last winter when I saw the two of you talking together in the store back in Texas?" she asks, avoiding my question altogether. "He said it was nothing and that you cornered him," she adds.

"Really now? *I* cornered him? Ugh . . . boys suck."

"So that's not what happened? I just remember that you weren't happy to see me either." She sticks out her bottom lip in a fake pout.

I shake my head back and forth in reply and laugh. "I felt like every time I saw you, Jace had his arm around your shoulders. Of course I wasn't happy to see you."

She giggles with me and says, "Okay, that I can understand."

"Remember that night I told you about, where we hooked up for the first time in his car?" She nods her head quickly, obviously loving the prospect of hearing some juicy gossip. I smile and continue, "Well, after he said what he did, I couldn't be there anymore. So once he passed out, I got out of the car and walked back to the hotel Lane and I were staying in."

Her mouth gapes open in shock. "Yep, he had the same reaction," I say with a laugh. "I've walked through that town more times than I can count, so it wasn't a big deal. But when he saw me at the store, *he* cornered me, demanding to know what happened to me and why I had left. He was spitting mad to learn that I had walked back. He went over every possible scenario he could think of as to what could have happened to me, but then that was when you came up and ended the conversation. I haven't talked to him again until we ran into each other last night. After which he snuck into *my* room, I might add."

"Oh, this is so good! He's totally into you. I do feel really bad for him and the huge mix-up from before. Now I finally understand the comments about how he's tired of being a twin and people getting them mixed up."

"Man, I wish I hadn't been such an idiot that first day I met them."

"Don't be so hard on yourself; it's hard to tell them apart at first. I got them mixed up too," she says. My head whips around to look at her in shock and she rushes to continue, "No, no. I didn't accidently sleep with Jace or anything. I just didn't know Jaxon had a twin brother either. The only way to really tell them apart at first is their . . ."

"Voices," we both say at the same time, giggling.

She sighs and whispers, "Jaxon's voice is so . . ."

"Irritating. Like nails on a chalkboard," I interrupt.

"What?! Girl, you're insane. That voice takes my panties off before his hands can do the job themselves."

I laugh out loud and redirect the conversation. "Anyway, even if by some miracle things did work out with Jace, I don't think he would ever be able to tell Jax."

"Well, he'll sure have to get over that now, won't he?"

I shrug my shoulders noncommittally.

As we walk toward the back to grab our purses, she says, "Hey, do you want to go with me and Quinn tomorrow to get pedicures?" Before I can turn her down, she says, "Don't worry about money. Quinn got all these gift certificates from someone she tutors, but they expire tomorrow so we have to use them."

"I don't know. The last time I saw Quinn . . . I'm pretty sure I heard her call me a she-devil."

She laughs out loud and covers her mouth to stifle it, but there's no holding back her amusement. "I'm sorry," she says between snorts, "I shouldn't laugh. That whole time was pretty outrageous. Quinn is loyal to a fault; it's one of the reasons I love her. And neither of us had ever heard of you until you showed up, so she didn't know your story either."

"Yeah, that makes sense. Doesn't make it any less nerve-racking to hang out with her, though," I say.

"I'll take care of it all. So be ready, because I'm picking you up tomorrow morning."

JACE -

With a nervousness I'm not accustomed to, I sit on the end of my bed and dial my mom's phone number. Calling her doesn't make me nervous, since we usually talk a couple of times a week at the very least. It's what I need to tell her that makes me uneasy.

After four rings I begin to wonder if she's home, but then I hear her familiar voice, which always makes me a little homesick.

"Hello, my favorite son," she says with her characteristic greeting, and I can hear the smile in her voice.

"Mom, it doesn't count if you say that to both of us."

"Damn, you caught me," she jokes. "But seeing as how I haven't heard from your brother since I left California a few weeks ago, you certainly are my favorite."

"Gee, thanks, Mom. I win on account of having no life."

"Is that why you're calling me on a Saturday evening?"

"No . . . there's actually a beach party tonight everyone's going to," I begin. I know she's staying quiet so I can tell her what I need to on my own. She's always had the patience of a saint. "Mom, I wanted to talk to you about premed . . ."

"What about it, sweetie?"

"I dropped it."

Without the sound of any surprise in her voice, she asks, "And what are your plans now?"

In one long breath, I say, "I've been double-majoring. Premed and business. But I don't want to be a doctor, Mom. I thought it sounded cool a long time ago, and Dad acted like it was the greatest thing ever. I tried to like it, I swear, but now it's my senior year and I'm so tired of doing both. Uncle Logan has been talking to me since last year, trying to convince me to come and take over when he's ready to retire."

"Go on . . ." she says.

Damn, she's more disappointed than I thought she would be. I know they are all excited to have this awesome doctor in the family, but do they not want me to do what I want to do? Especially something like taking over my dad's business? Well, at least Uncle Logan thinks it's a respectable idea.

"I want to do what Dad did. I want to join the Riley Group and keep it in the family. I know you're disappointed, but . . . I know it's what I need to do," I finish.

"All I have to say about this matter is . . . thank God!" she exclaims. "I'm so relieved you finally made this decision."

"What?" I reply, shocked.

"Jace, I never thought you wanted to be a doctor. I was surprised when you applied for the premed program. Of course, I wasn't surprised when you got in, but I always thought you were more interested in your dad's company than anything else. I remember you asking a million questions a day about his job. Any chance you had to go hang out at his office, you took. I know you'll do a fantastic job, and I couldn't be happier for you. I'm sad that you felt like you needed to impress us, though. What does Jaxon think about all of this?"

"Um . . ."

"Jace, you haven't told him?" she concludes, loudly and correctly.

"No. Jax is the worst when it comes to bragging about my major. How can I tell him?"

"Jace Riley, you need to stop being so concerned about your brother and what he thinks. He loves you and will support you through anything. No matter how distracted he is at the moment."

"That's the other reason why I haven't told him. He can't stay out of Em's mouth long enough to talk to me."

"Talk to your brother. Stop making excuses. I love you and you're doing a great job with school. You should know by now I'll always support your decisions."

"Love you too, Mom."

She keeps me on the phone for a while longer, updating me on everything happening back home, and even trying to get me to talk about any girls I'm dating. *Nice try, Mom.* She eases my fears about telling Jaxon and makes me realize that it really isn't as big a deal as I've been making it out to be.

When I finally disconnect, I realize that the beach party started an hour ago and I was supposed to be there with Quinn and Em. I rush to get dressed and run out the door.

I pull up in the parking lot at the same time Jax's truck is easing into a spot near the front.

"Dude, you're just getting here?" Jax calls when I step out of my car.

He and Cole are freshly showered from practice and looking a little beat. Coach must have run them hard today. He tends to do that at Saturday practices, because he likes to try and wear them out so they won't go out and party later that night. It usually doesn't work, though.

"Running behind. The girls here?" I ask, as I catch up to them.

"I sure as hell hope so, since they aren't answering their phones," Cole adds, sounding irritated.

"Ease up, jackasses. I'm sure they're at the party. Nobody carries a damn phone with them at these things," I explain.

I can hear the laughter and the hoots and hollers from the party. As we cross over the sand hill, I quickly spot our group standing around three lit fire pit rings. From what I've heard, some of these guys are out here several nights a week, just sitting around the fire. It does create a nice atmosphere, the way they've built the fires up as high as they can get them in the circular, concrete rings.

"There's Quinn," Cole says and walks away.

"It was nice seeing you too, man," I say to his retreating figure.

Cole shoots me the middle finger, and Jax wraps my neck in a headlock tightly.

"Aw, does my little brother need some attention?" he whines, mocking me. He knows how irritated I get when he calls me his little brother. A two-minute difference doesn't count in my book.

This asshole loves to pull the headlock move on me, and apparently he still hasn't learned his lesson yet. With my head restrained next to his armpit, I reach behind his back and lock his opposite arm against his chest and hold it there firmly. My feet bounce into position behind his, and then I move toward the ground, bringing his body with me. He falls to my side and I'm instantly released from his lock, which allows me to trap his legs underneath me.

He laughs and strains to kick me off of him, but I lean forward and use my forearm to hold his neck down. Eventually he's able to get his legs wrapped around my waist. He kicks them out, forcing me to release my hold on his neck, and then manages to get my head into an arm-triangle chokehold. We continue horsing around until we're both out of breath and slowing down significantly.

After I almost cause him to pass out because his stubborn ass won't tap out, we shove away from each other and lie back in the sand, laughing. This is how we've always been. If there's ever any bad blood or distance between us, we fight it out.

"God, this is better than porn," I hear a female voice say from above. Without moving my body, I turn my neck to see Tatum and Ashley, cheerleaders at our school, gazing down at us. "Can you reenact that, except this time can I lie in between you two?" Tatum asks, while giggling and nudging Ashley.

"Beat it," Quinn snaps, and the two onlookers grumble and stomp away.

"Thanks, Quinny," Jax says from the ground. "Have you seen my girl?"

"She's around," she states nonchalantly.

I stand up and pull Jax to his feet. I know by now he's dying to get his hands on Em, and I'd be lying if I said I didn't want to see her as well. It's surprising how Em has wiggled her way into our family without even trying. She's like a little sister to me now, and when she's not swapping spit with my brother, she's actually a ton of fun to be around.

She's always sending these short, crazy videos to my phone that she randomly films throughout the day. It's become a source of daily entertainment. Last week, she sent me a ten-second video of her and Quinn trying to rap to a song on the radio. But between the both of them, they only knew one word from the actual song, so the rest was them making up complete nonsense. Yesterday, she sent me a video of Jax singing and dancing in front of the bathroom mirror while getting ready. He obviously didn't know she was filming. And what kind of brother would I be if I didn't keep it for potential blackmail material?

We make a complete circle around the groups sitting by the fires without spotting Em. Jax begins walking at a faster clip and is about to make another round when I glance out at the waves and see two figures sitting side by side in the sand, the tide hitting their toes. When the person on the left throws her head back, laughing, I recognize the familiar blond hair.

I reach out, smack Jax on the chest with the back of my hand, and point out to the water. He glances over and releases a megawatt smile at the sight of her. We start walking out toward the two girls, and then I freeze, realizing who Em is talking *and* laughing with. How the hell did that happen?

"Jax, I think she's with Audrey."

He halts midstride. "What? That's not possible."

We hear the girls continue laughing, and then Em says Audrey's name out loud, confirming what I already knew. I'd recognize that body anywhere. They still have no idea we're no more than twenty feet behind them. While Jax is stressing that those two are talking, for some reason it makes me feel damn good inside to see them getting along so well. I can't even begin to explain how they got to this point, but I'm sure it's one heck of a story.

"What the hell do you think she's telling Emerson?" he grinds out and begins storming toward them. "Why is she here again?" he whispers under his breath.

I immediately reach out and stop him. "Chill out, Jax. Obviously Em's not upset. Don't go over there and ruin it by being a possessive asshole." He slows his charge, but continues forward. I can tell he's holding back his emotions when he squats down behind Em and kisses her on the cheek. Em turns her head into his kiss and smiles. Audrey startles backward and then immediately stands up. Her wide eyes are staring at Jaxon, most likely fearing what he may say, but she still hasn't spotted me yet. Slowly, she begins backing away.

"Em, I'll see you later, okay?" she says.

"You're not leaving, right? I mean, remember what we talked about?" she asks cryptically.

"Maybe. I don't know. I'll stay for a little while."

"Okay, well, I had fun today. Thanks for coming with us!" Em says with a smile. Jax sits down next to Em, facing the water, and she quickly gets up to sit in his lap, facing him. Audrey spins around to head back toward the party and accidently runs right into my arms. Or maybe I had planned it that way.

"Whoa, you're not gonna leave, are you?"

"Yeah, I'm hoping I can," she replies. Without letting her step out of my grasp, I reach out and tuck a wandering strand of hair behind her ear. In the dark, her eyes look as black as midnight when she gazes up at me. Slowly, I lean down so my mouth is level with her ear.

"We're still on for tomorrow, right?" I whisper. She nods her head up and down. With my face still close to hers, I run my lips lightly against her temple. From a few feet away, I catch Em watching us over Jax's shoulder. When she sees me looking at her, she smiles and gives me the thumbs-up signal behind his back. I stare at her, confused. Why is *she* happy about Audrey being here?

I lean away from Audrey and stand up straight before Jaxon catches on. I lead her back up the hill so we can rejoin the partygoers.

"Why doesn't Em want you to leave?" I ask.

"So I can talk to Jaxon," she says simply.

"What? You're going to tell him before me?"

"I don't really want to tell either of you anything anymore," she states in a hard tone. I grab her arms and stop her before we reach the crowd, then sit down in the sand, gesturing for her to join me. After a heavy sigh, she relents, but sits a good foot away from me. I don't understand why she's being cold all of a sudden. I take hold of her legs and pull her closer to me, her body leaving a trail in the sand as she reaches my side.

"Tell me what's wrong."

"Jace . . . let's not do this here."

"Where? Here, where no one can hear a word we say? Or did you actually mean, let's not do this ever? I think *here* is pretty damn perfect."

A fire ignites behind her eyes as she glares at me. "Yes, I actually meant let's not do this ever. You want to know why? Because none of y'all cared when it actually mattered. You heard a rumor and you believed it. You assumed and you ran with it. At what point did you come to me and ask if any of it was true? When, Jace?"

My mouth opens and shuts because I've got nothing to say to that. "Exactly," she huffs out in frustration and stands. "You don't deserve to know what happened in *my* life, because you never bothered before. Why are you here now? Why do you care *now*?" she yells.

As if he has an internal alarm for an upset Audrey or just supersonic hearing when she's distressed, Lane emerges from the crowd with a determined look on his face. When he spots her, he stalks forward.

"What's going on over here?" A voice I wasn't expecting makes my head pivot backward. Jax is standing behind me, taking in the scene. "Jace?" he asks.

Everyone is just staring at one another, and before I can even begin to formulate a response, Audrey says, "Jaxon, can I talk to you?"

- NINE -

AUDREY -

Jace has that deer-in-the-headlights look. I didn't mean to rip into him like that, but I am feeling overwhelmed by the situation. Em has just spent the better part of thirty minutes trying to convince me to talk to Jaxon. Then Jace comes along, acting like he's entitled to know anything and everything about me.

I'm so confused that I don't know which way is up and which way is down. Hell, right now I can't tell the difference between my right and my left. I know I need to get everything off my chest and come clean. But why can't it be on my own time? I feel like I'm always being forced to say and do things at everyone else's convenience.

As always, my protector hears my cries and stomps through the crowd to take down the threat to me. As I watch Lane's approach, I'm startled to hear Jaxon's voice behind me. So many people all at once, I'm beginning to feel claustrophobic. Lane can see the panic in my eyes, and I know he's two seconds away from dragging me out of here. Over his shoulder, if necessary.

Quickly, I blurt out, "Jaxon, can I talk to you?"

"Uh, yeah," he says in a less-than-sure tone.

Lane steps forward, ready to interject himself in this terrible scenario, but Em cuts him off and guides him toward the party. Jax's eyes follow their retreat. I can see the desire and need when he looks at her, but when his eyes transfer to Lane, they transform into a raging fire.

"He won't try anything with her," I reassure him. "He knows who she is and who she's with." He nods his head, and though he still appears confused, Jaxon seems to calm down a bit at my words. Jace stands up next to both of us and doesn't look as if he plans on leaving.

"Jace, what the hell's going on with you?" Jaxon asks.

Before Jace can create an excuse, I interrupt. "Forget it. Let's just get this over with, Jaxon." I turn to walk away from the crowd again, back toward the water, where worries are washed away with the calming waves.

I find the imprints where Em and I were just sitting moments ago. As I sit down, I reflect upon the day. Getting Quinn to warm up to the idea of my presence was easier said than done. But as Em had predicted, once we cracked through her loyal shell, she began to understand the circumstances. I don't see us trading friendship bracelets anytime soon, but we still managed to have a fun day together. I got my first manicure and pedicure, and I almost glued myself to that massage chair.

Jaxon clears his throat and I realize he's sitting down next to me, facing the ocean as well. Without looking at me, he says, "I'm supposed to be nice to you. If I'm not, my typically sweet girlfriend has threatened me with some pretty violent actions. Why is that, Audrey?"

His words make me laugh at Em's protectiveness. Once again, I'm shocked by her instant acceptance of me. "You got lucky with her, you know?"

A relieved sigh leaves his lungs. "I know. I feel like I'm just waiting for her to realize how much better she can do."

"From what she told me, she got lucky in finding you as well," I assure him.

"I think I was just more determined than all the others."

"I'm pretty sure there was a little more at play than determination, Jaxon. She really has brought out a good side in you. I'm glad you're happy," I say honestly.

He brings his knees up and wraps his arms around them. "We're talking like we used to. Like friends."

"*Were* we even friends?" I ask.

"Yes, of course we were." Finally, he looks toward me with a furrowed brow, obviously questioning my statement.

"We certainly didn't have a traditional relationship. We were using each other, Jaxon. You used me to get your family off your back, and I used you to get out of my house. It seemed to work for us. I'll admit, we shouldn't have continued to sleep together, but we were young and less than clever at the time."

"You act like you regret sleeping with me?" He feigns insult.

"I wanted someone else."

"Ouch." His hurt feelings don't last long as he laughs it off. "We were quite the pair."

"Yeah, until everything went to hell." Might as well get down to the hard stuff.

"Based on some indications I'm getting from Emerson, I'm beginning to think that maybe I was misinformed."

"You were the one that informed yourself, Jaxon."

"Audrey, you came to me one day and said you were pregnant. I tried to do the right thing and get married! You had so many opportunities to come clean."

My hands begin to shake as we start to get to the heart of our problems. The day I saw the "positive" sign on that little white stick,

I knew my world would never be the same. For some reason, I knew life was out to get me, and it was almost as if I had been waiting for this moment to happen. I was lost in a world full of pain and hate. I ran to Jaxon for help because I knew he would take responsibility, and I just needed someone to take care of me for once in my life.

"You guys okay?" Jace's anxious voice questions from behind.

"We're fine, dude, just clearing the air," Jaxon snaps.

"Then why were you just yelling at her?" Jace questions. I would hardly have called it yelling, but if Jace could hear him raising his voice, then he hadn't been too far away. It's clear that Jace wants to hear this story even more than Jaxon does, and I really don't feel like telling it for the fourth time in less than a week. Hell, we might as well bring over Cole and whoever else wants to hear.

"You might as well sit down and listen instead of eavesdropping, Jace," I call out, without looking behind me. With no shame or hesitation, he immediately sits down on my opposite side. He's far enough away that it's appropriate, but close enough that he can extend his fingers and touch the bare skin of my thighs without Jaxon seeing.

"Why are you being so nosy all of a sudden, Jace?" Jax asks from my other side.

"I was there when this all went down. I'm curious too," Jace says in defense.

"Who cares? The less I have to repeat this, the better." I wave off any further argument. Jace quickly squeezes my arm three times and smiles at me in support.

JACE -

The moon catches the natural highlights in her brown hair and lights up her silhouette as she sits in the sand. As I watch Audrey talk to my brother about everything that occurred between the two of them, I find a spot on the beach far enough back that they can't see me. It's not close enough to hear their words, but it's as far away as I can physically get right now. Everything about her is calling out to me. The distress in her eyes when everyone crowded around her had every cell in my body lighting up in defense.

The second I hear Jaxon raise his voice, I jump to my feet, but I decide to hang back and see if she can handle it on her own. Of course she can—she's strong. She's always been strong.

Leaning back on her hands in the sand, I notice that her hands and arms begin to tremble slightly at his shouting. If I hadn't been watching for it, I would have missed it. She won't ask for help; that's just not who she is. Hell, she doesn't even need my help. But damn it, I'm here now and I'm stepping in. After I interrupt and shamelessly claim the spot on the opposite side of her, I squeeze her arm while smiling at her. When she takes in a deep breath, I wrap my pinky around hers and give it a little tug to show my support.

"As you were . . ." I gesture with a flourish of my hand for them to continue.

Audrey clears her throat nervously and releases my pinky, clenching her hands together in her lap. "I'm sorry for making you believe that the . . . ba . . . that the pregnancy was yours." I watch as she looks up at him and he continues to stare out at the thrashing waves. "And I'm sorry that I let you go through with the marriage. I shouldn't have done that."

"Why did you, though? That's what I don't get," Jaxon questions softly.

"I just needed help from someone. Anyone. I shouldn't have done it, but you were the only person I knew that would actually help. You know I hated going home. I could have been on fire and no one there would have even given me a second glance." Her words are a knife to my heart. I should have been her someone, her anyone.

"It still seems a bit dramatic, Auds," Jax starts.

She quickly interrupts him, "Don't you dare start with that nickname. I hated it four years ago and I hate it now." Her strength and vitality shine through with her ability to make light of this dark moment.

"Sorry," he says with a small smile. "But it does seem that way. I'm sorry to say this, but girls from your school were getting pregnant all the time. That wasn't a reason to make me think the baby was mine and agree to marry me when I tried to be the good guy."

Audrey and Jaxon's past could have easily been portrayed on a late-morning soap opera. After the whirlwind way the two got together, they dated and appeared to be quite happy. Audrey was always over at our place or out with Jaxon, and I spent that time trying to make myself scarce. For about four months, I had to watch those two dance around, fucking merrily.

Then one day, Jaxon came home and told us that he and Audrey had eloped because she was pregnant. I'd never seen my mom turn as many shades of red as she did that day. I remember being glad that her fury was directed at Jaxon and not me. I, on the other hand, may or may not have punched multiple holes into the walls of my bedroom. When Mom demanded that he ask Audrey for a paternity test, she ended up admitting it wasn't his and it was actually her physics teacher's child.

After countless hours with a lawyer, my mom was able to get the marriage annulled due to fraudulent claims. Then Audrey slipped away quietly, never to be seen or heard from again. That is, until the day she showed up at our apartment last year, trying to talk to Jaxon. Although, according to Lane, she was attempting to talk to me.

"I'm so sorry, Jaxon. I should have never told you it was yours. I freaked, and I just needed someone to be on my side for a second. But I was young and stupid; I approached it all wrong. You're also right about the girls at my school getting pregnant all the time." Her hands begin to turn white as she grinds them against one another. Her fingers are threading in and out with those on the opposite hand, and I can tell she's squeezing them together as tightly as she can. Slowly, I reach out and gently rub my pinky against the outside of her thigh. I want to give her courage, anything that will help her get through whatever she is about to say.

After a deep inhale and a sluggish exhale, she continues. "But they weren't getting . . . raped by their physics teachers in the back storage room of the lab."

If it were possible to hear a heart breaking, then the sound of three shattering like glass right here in the sand off the Pacific would ring loud and clear. I hear the slight hitch in her throat, which clues me in to look up, just in time to see the tears falling from her dark eyes. It's as if a dam has broken and there's no stopping the flood pouring down her beautiful porcelain face. Screw my brother. I lean over and wrap her wilting body into my arms and push her face into my chest, hoping my shirt can soak up the tears and the pain.

Jaxon's face is buried in his hands, but I can see his chest heaving up and down and hear his strangled breaths. He's hurting. Now's not the time, but I want to tell him that he shouldn't feel as though he's to blame. None of this was either of their fault.

The loud crashes of the waves fill the painful silence and distract from their silent cries. Audrey's hands dig into my shirt, pulling my chest further into her face, and I can't seem to get her close enough. I just want to wrap her up and carry her away. I don't want to hear anything else. I know there's more for her to tell, but I don't think I can physically handle hearing any more of her painful past.

"Please tell me he's in jail, Audrey," Jaxon finally breaks the silence, his voice gravelly.

He doesn't lift his head. Instead, he turns to face us while still laying his head on the top of his knees. I haven't seen my brother cry since my dad passed away, and the image is gut-wrenching.

Audrey lifts her head from my shoulder, and I quickly wipe away the moisture in my eyes with the sleeve of my T-shirt. She sits back in her previous spot, but I can't remove my arm from around her. Thankfully, she doesn't shove me off. I gently squeeze her arm so she knows I'm here for her. Maybe it's four years too late, but I'm here now.

"I was eighteen, so they couldn't charge him with statutory rape, and no one believed my word against his. He was a teacher with a doctorate in physics, while I was the daughter of an alcoholic and a drug abuser. It all kind of . . . got pushed under the rug."

Jaxon shakes his head back and forth and repeats himself, each word spoken slowly and with conviction. "Please tell me he's in jail."

"He's not," she whispers.

"You should have told me, Audrey. I would have killed him. I'll still kill him," Jax says. Can't fault him there. I'm already trying to plan the perfect murder myself, something prolonged and painful.

"Jax . . ." she says and begins to shake her head back and forth. "There was so much I didn't tell you. I guess I figured that since you didn't seem to notice or care about all of the bruises I had, you might not be concerned about what had happened to me." When Jax looks at her in confusion, she continues, "From the day I met you, I had bruises on me at any given time. I understand now that I shouldn't have held that against you. You were young and going through so much already with your dad passing away. So I just didn't say anything to you. I couldn't stomach the idea of you not believing me, and I knew that if that was the case, your family wouldn't believe me either." She quickly eyes me and I drop my head in remorse.

A long, silent pause crawls by as Jaxon and I sit in deep thought. I can feel that we're both thinking the same thing right now. Would we have believed her? If we really think back to our eighteen-year-old selves, would we have trusted her word? It hurts to admit it, but I don't think we would have.

"I believe you now, Audrey," Jaxon whispers.

"Thank you," she replies with sadness still in her voice.

"I'm so sorry," he continues, sitting up straighter and clutching at his shirt. "I don't know how to say it any better than that. But from the deepest part of me, please know how sorry I am."

She nods her head slowly and says, "Thank you. The only reason I'm even telling you now is because I like Emerson. I like her a lot. I've never had a friend like her before, and I hope to stay friends with her. I hope that won't be weird for you." The way she says that makes me smirk on the inside. She isn't giving him the option to stop her friendship, and I love that about her.

Jax gives a small grin and says, "Yeah, she's something else."

Quickly, Audrey gathers herself and stands up in front of us, then readjusts her clothes and brushes off the sand. Both of us just gaze up at her, confused. "I think I'm gonna go find Lane and head out now."

"Wait," Jaxon says in a panic. "What happened after we broke up? What happened with the . . . pregnancy? Where did you go, and what did you mean about the bruises? Where did they come from?"

She shakes her head back and forth rapidly. "No, I can't do that right now. I think I've told you enough for tonight." Without another word, she hurries away. I still need to talk to Jaxon, but every inch of me is aching to follow her up the hill and hold her in my arms.

"I guess now is not the time to talk to you about my important news?" I ask.

"I don't know if I can take in anything else right now, man," he whispers, looking toward the ocean. "Do you know anything?"

"I don't know much, but she did tell me that her dad had something to do with the bruises."

He lies back in the sand with a huff. "I'm scum. I can't believe I let all of that get by me. What if something like that happened to Emerson?"

"Knock it off," I say quickly, before he goes on a rampage. "You aren't that guy anymore. You know every inch of Em, and you wouldn't let that happen."

"Do you think she knows Audrey's whole story now too?"

I give him an incredulous look. "Of course she knows. Em could get the leader of al-Qaeda to give her all of his secrets and any future plans he may have on a silver platter."

"God, I wonder what she thinks of me."

"She still thinks the world of you," Em interrupts, sitting on his lap. "She thinks you were young and an idiot, but that doesn't change who you are now." I'm glad Em interrupted when she did, because otherwise I would have told him how *I* feel. How can he be so concerned with what Em thinks when it's Audrey who went through a world of hurt? I realize that where Audrey is, that's exactly where I should be right now. Not here trying to console my brother. I stand up, kiss Em on the top of the head, and leave them to talk.

When I reach the party, I quickly spot Lane's tall frame in the middle of the crowd. He has a blonde and a redhead on either side of him, both vying for his attention. When he catches me looking over at him, he nods his head in my direction and begins looking around for Audrey, no doubt.

"I'll find her," I say, answering his silent question. "She couldn't have gotten far."

"What happened?" he demands harshly.

"She told us . . . about the teacher . . ." I grind out.

"What the fuck? Why?" he shouts and frantically searches through the crowd for her.

"Chill out. I'll find her and take her home."

He calms down at my words and nods his head. I add, "I'm gonna kill that teacher the second I get back to Texas, though."

"Don't worry about it. I met up with the guy on our trip out there last winter," he says cryptically. At the shock on my face, he continues. "Audrey doesn't know. And don't worry, I didn't actually kill him. I just delivered a *very* strong message," he states, with an almost unnatural ease and a shrug of his shoulders.

I reach out my fist and he bumps it in return. "I might need more info on him later. For now, I'm gonna go find her."

As I begin to walk away, Lane calls out, "Hey, one last thing. I might need to head out of town for about a week soon . . ."

"I've got Audrey covered now. She doesn't need her overbearing, protective big brother," I say in my retreat.

With a laugh, he shouts, "Let's not get carried away now."

- TEN -

JACE **-**

I don't have to scan the beach to know that Audrey has bailed. If she's not near Lane, then she's gone. I know her better than she thinks I do, and based on the fact that she's already slipped away from me once before, I'm betting that she's trying to walk home now.

I hop in the Camaro and gun it out of the parking lot. My best bet is to take the route toward her place. Not even two minutes away from the sand and surf, I see a dark silhouette walking down the sidewalk, passing all of the parked cars on the darkened street. I pull the car in behind another and jump out to catch up to her.

When I reach her retreating backside, I wrap my arms around her from behind and tuck my chin into her shoulder. She doesn't flinch or push me away, so we continue walking quietly forward while I'm wrapped around her body. Slowly, I turn in and kiss the side of her neck. Her breath shudders harshly from all the crying she's undoubtedly been doing, as well as her attempt to hike the five miles home.

As we continue walking forward, with me attached to her backside, I ask, "Can I take you somewhere?"

"I'm lousy company right now, Jace," she whispers.

"There isn't anything lousy about you, babe." I reluctantly let go of her body, walk around to the front of her, and with my back facing her, I crouch down. When she gives me a puzzled look, I laugh and say, "Hop on. It's called a piggyback ride."

Quickly she jumps up, wrapping her legs around my waist and her arms around my neck. "I know what a piggyback ride is." Then she nuzzles her face into the side of my neck and rests there. The combination of her cherry-vanilla lip balm and the salty-sand fragrance is surprisingly arousing coming off of her. But I can't think about her tempting body right now, especially not with the sudden gulp of breath she takes from crying so hard.

I carry her to the car and open the door to set her inside. After getting her situated, I swiftly hop into my seat and pull the Camaro away from the sidewalk. Audrey doesn't ask where we're going; instead, she lies down in the seat with her head on my leg. Her eyes drift close and the shuddering breaths that were ripping through her chest begin to subside. With my left hand on the steering wheel, I use my right to run my fingers through her soft hair.

This quiet moment is what I've always wanted with someone. Audrey can make me happy without saying a word or even without a touch. Just seeing her relaxed and sleeping next to me is a comfort after all of the horrible things I've just heard. I don't know how she's overcome the many obstacles she's faced. How can one person be put through as much as she has and still manage to wake up each morning, let alone smile and make others happy? Slowly, the weight of what has happened to her rests heavily on me, and I'm blown away by her durability and perseverance.

Thirty minutes later, we arrive at our destination. The loud rumble of the engine that lulled her to sleep shuts off and she begins to stir. Silently, I soak in this opportunity to freely watch her wake up. Her eyelashes flutter and the back of her hand moves across her forehead into a stretch.

I check my watch and say, "I hate to move you, but we don't have much time."

She pushes herself up and finally asks, "Where are we going?"

"You'll see."

We hike along the gravel path and continue through the trees and bushes. She doesn't complain about bugs, the itchy leaves striking our legs, or even our inability to see more than two feet in front of us. I try to shine the light from my cell phone near her feet so she doesn't trip, but she just holds on to my bicep and trudges blindly forward. She allows me to guide her, placing all of her trust in my unworthy hands. We finally push through the last bit of trees that open up into a clearing, and I pull her up the hill in front of us.

"Wow, it's beautiful out here," she says, looking straight up at the starlit sky as I tug her along.

"It's my escape from the city without having to go too far," I divulge.

"Is this a train track?"

"Yeah, and we only have ten more minutes until the 11:44 express runs through here," I reply.

"I still don't understand," she says, but there's a slight smile in her voice.

"Patience." I turn and kiss her on the forehead as we reach the top of the gravel hill that holds the steel tracks. I pull a penny out of my pocket, hold it up so she can see the copper-colored coin as it gleams in the light of the moon, and then place it on the center of a steel track. When I look back up at her, she still seems to be waiting for me to do something more. We leave the penny behind and head back down the hill.

Last month, I found this place and have slowly learned the train schedule. It's nice to get away from the lights and smog of LA. Trees surround us and the stars dance above our heads. The only sounds you'll hear out here are the crickets and the occasional train that blows all the trees in its course.

Once we're far enough that I know it's safe, I sit down in the dirt and face the tracks. She slowly lowers herself down between my legs and leans her back against my chest.

"Have you ever done this before?" I ask.

"Sat in the dirt at almost midnight? I'm sure at some point I've done it," she says. Her laugh is intoxicating and I hope I can always find ways to bring out that sound in her.

"No, not sit in the dirt, smart-ass," I say, laughing along with her. "Put a penny on a train track."

"No, I'm actually kind of worried you're about to derail a train," she nervously replies.

"That almost never happens," I say impudently. Her mouth drops open and she turns her face to look up at me. I throw my head back and laugh at her shocked expression. "Don't worry, babe. I've been doing this since I was little."

A cold wind whips past us and lashes her long, brown hair over my shoulder and then back in her face. Gently, I gather it all into my hand and twist the length around before tucking it in between our bodies. I then wrap my arms around her from behind and squeeze her into me as close as I can get her.

"I wish I could stay like this forever," I whisper into her ear. In the distance, I hear the train making its forward ascent.

"Me too."

She sighs when I run my nose along the edge of her neck, from her shoulder blade to her earlobe. "You smell so damn delicious. I know that the cherry-vanilla is from that lip balm I'll never forget. The salt and sand is from earlier, but you always have a hint of coconut on your skin that just makes me want to lick you from head to toe." Which is exactly what I hope to do later.

A shiver runs up her body as she says, "It's coconut oil. I use it for basically everything."

"I'm crazy about it. Almost as much as I am about you." Her hands squeeze my arms in closer to her and I continue, "I'm so sorry for everything . . ."

AUDREY -

I cut him off instantly. "Don't start that, Jace. Don't ruin this moment. What's done is done. We're here now."

"I want to be here for you from now on. I want to hold you safe all night and watch you wake up in the morning. I love how forgiving you are and I need that in my life every day."

I turn and look up at him again and say, "Jace, I've always wanted you and I've never pretended otherwise. No one has even come close to making me feel the way I do when I'm with you."

Then, right there for all of the trees and stars to see, Jace claims my mouth and takes what I've been begging to give since we last parted ways. The train finally barrels down the tracks, and for a split second I try to listen for the sound of metal being squashed beneath thousands of pounds of moving machine. But my thoughts are hopelessly filled with the gorgeous man holding me. The loud rumbling of the engine moving at a blaring speed suffocates all other sounds around us. For a moment there is only Jace, and I never want to go back. We don't break apart until long after my hair has blown wild in the wind from the passing train.

When it's gone and the tracks have cooled down, Jace stands and reaches for my hand. He pulls me up and asks me to stay where I am for a second. I watch as he jogs back up the rocky hill we had just climbed not long ago. He bends down, grabs his coin, and returns to my side.

He tenderly opens my hand and drops the warm metal into my palm. I feel the smoothness of the stretched-out penny.

"Wow, this is amazing."

"Yeah, my dad showed me how to do it when I was a kid," he responds. I close my hand tightly around the penny and think about how I'll always have this. Even if Jace and I don't work things out, I'll always have this little memento to bring out when I'm lonesome, remembering this night out under the stars. It's something I can tuck away in my pocket for only me to treasure.

"Let's head back," he says and crouches down in front of me again. Knowing what he's suggesting this time, I hop up onto his back and wrap my arms around his neck. He grips my thighs under his big hands and occasionally rubs them softly while we begin the trek back through the trees and shrubs.

"You're not really going to carry me all the way back to the car, are you?"

"I carried a backpack every day last year that was heavier than you," he replies, without a hitch in his breathing.

"Why isn't your backpack as heavy this year?" I ask.

"Well, aren't you perceptive?" he states with a laugh.

"I've spent my whole life observing."

"I was double-majoring up until this year," he reveals. "It was stupid of me."

"I'm sure it was anything but stupid, Jace. What were your two majors?"

"I was in premed because I thought that's what my dad wanted me to do. But I always wanted to take over his company, so I was also in business. I dropped premed." He says the last part quietly, almost as if he's ashamed.

"I'm glad you dropped it."

"Why?" he rasps out, sounding stunned.

"Because I always thought you would follow in your dad's footsteps. Even though we weren't together, Jace, I absorbed every piece of information I ever heard about you when Jax and I were together. I never saw you being happy as a doctor."

He continues quietly toward his car. I can tell he's surprised by my words. While being a doctor is a noble profession, he should always go after what he wants and not what others think that he should do. When I escaped my past by moving to California, I vowed I would never do something that made me unhappy. While accounting isn't the most exciting occupation in the world, I'm good at it and that makes me happy.

"I can't imagine working toward two separate degrees. Just the one I got was hard enough. I always thought Lane was crazy for coming back for a second bachelor's, and now he's getting a master's with me."

"Wow, I didn't realize you were so far ahead. No wonder I finally found you Friday morning in an advanced accounting class. So, Lane's older than us?"

"Yeah, he's twenty-eight. He already went to school once and graduated in the criminal justice field. He never talks about his past, not even to me, but I think something terrible happened. A long time ago, he mentioned that he flipped a one-eighty and tried to go in the exact opposite of his previous life. Criminal justice to accounting; doesn't get more diverse than that."

"Earlier he told me he might be going out of town for a week," Jace says.

I groan loudly and the sound vibrates from my chest into his back. "He does this every once in a while and never comes back happy. It usually takes another week before he's back to his cheerful self. I have no idea where he goes."

We reach his car finally and he says, "I don't mind keeping you company."

I slip down the backside of his body and my feet hit the ground. I watch as he pops the trunk of his car open, pulling out a small, black toolbox.

He extends his hand toward me with his palm up and says, "Penny, please." I squeeze it tighter in my fist. I wanted to keep it. It was supposed to be my trinket to always remember him by, not that I could ever forget.

When I continue staring at my closed hand, he laughs and says, "I promise to give it back." Those words are exactly what I need to hear.

When he picks the penny out of my palm, he leans over and kisses my lips with a soft peck. Then he starts to dig through the toolbox, although I'm not sure what he's looking for. I hop up onto the ledge of the open trunk and stare out into the dark distance. Jace tinkers away beside me and I soak in this simple time with him. Could it really all come together this easily? Could we finally get to be together? Was time all we needed? As two high school kids, it wasn't our time. But maybe now that we've become adults, could this be our time?

"How come you only drive Jaxon's car?" I ask to interrupt my confusing thoughts.

"Because it's my car now," he says, while continuing to work with his hands in the dark. "He gave it to me this past summer. I was always working on it and keeping it in shape anyway, but I never thought he would just hand over the keys like that. I love this car because it reminds me so much of my dad."

"Wow, that was nice of him," I say on an exhale.

"Yeah . . ." he sighs. "Just another reason why I feel so shitty about going behind his back like this. I'll tell him, I promise, Audrey. But you have to understand how hard it is. We always promised each other that we wouldn't date each other's girls, past or present. I just need to find the right way to tell him, but for now, I want to see where this goes." He gestures with his finger between the two of us.

So, what he's saying is that he wants to be with me, but he needs to keep it on the down-low. How do I feel about that? I would never let it be a permanent situation, but it doesn't sound like that's what he's asking. I can hold on just a little while longer. At least I can still have him in the meantime. That's what I've always wanted anyway. Jace. It's always been Jace.

I nod my head in agreement and then add, "But I'm not your girlfriend until I get a real first date."

"Damn, I was hoping I could give this to my girl tonight," he chuckles. Slowly, he lifts up his hand and a silver chain dangles from his fingers. My eyes follow the series of links until I see that my penny is suspended from the end of it. Somehow he's made a tiny hole in the metal and strung a chain through it.

"Wow, you just made me a necklace?" I ask incredulously.

His hands move the length of my hair aside and he drapes it over my shoulder. Then he wraps the chain around my neck, clasping the two ends together. I look down at the penny lying just above my breasts.

"I've walked past so many pennies in my life, never bothering to pick them up because none of them were ever appealing to me. Then one day, I literally crashed into the most gorgeous penny I'd ever seen, so I picked her up off the ground, wiped away her tears, and became mesmerized by her every movement. Stupidly, I let that penny get away from me, and I've regretted it ever since. You were my lucky penny, Audrey, and I've been dreaming about you for years."

I can probably count on one hand the number of times I remember crying in my life. Three of those times have been because of Jace, and two of them occurred today. Tears well up in my eyes at his sweet words. How many times have I secretly fantasized about Jace confessing his feelings for me? Never, not even in one of my dreams, did they come out like that.

"Babe, no more crying. You've reached your quota for the day," he says, as he once again wipes my eyes.

I laugh through my tears and insist, "These aren't sad ones."

I stand up on my toes, wrap my arms around his neck, and kiss him without warning. He is mine to take, whenever I want. Although a little voice in the back of my head annoyingly adds: *Yes, except when Jaxon is around.*

- ELEVEN -

JACE -

The futon bar pushes further into my ribcage as I begin to stir awake. Groaning, I shift to try and escape the evil bar that is determined to separate me from Audrey. I don't understand how it doesn't drive her fucking insane. Although I tossed and turned last night, I'd do it a thousand times more just to have her next to me all night long. Hopefully, I'll soon be taking her back to my bed.

Last night when I asked to stay the night, I didn't consider the true test of my willpower that would be required to resist her naked body beside me. Especially her begging-to-be-touched naked body. So much had happened last night, from the horrendous to the magnificent. I had witnessed her cry, twice in one evening. I felt as if there were too many raw emotions and it would be better for her to sleep on it all. Trust me, though, I was in pain all night long, and it wasn't just the metal bar in my back causing it.

I run my hand lightly down the length of her side. Her soft skin feels like silk against my fingertips. All I can feel is skin. My fingers don't have to detour across any clothing on her entire body. Audrey sleeps naked, well, except for my penny around her neck. She sleeps like this even when she's by herself. Incredibly, it's not to seduce a guy, but purely because that's what makes her comfortable. An unforeseen growl rolls through my chest at the idea of other guys in her bed. She begins to stir at my possessive motions.

Her back is tucked into my chest, but I peer over and watch her eyelashes as they begin to flutter open. She stretches her arms above her head and I run my hands up them to extend the stretch. One of her hands comes back down to her neck and I smile as she checks for the necklace. The act makes me kiss the back of her neck underneath her hairline.

Her back arches and it causes her ass to press into me. This time a groan rumbles past my lips at the fucking remarkable feeling of her unbelievable body against my willing and ready one.

"Please don't say you're planning to make me wait again . . ." she whispers in her sexy-as-hell hoarse morning voice.

"I couldn't even if I tried. If I don't get some relief from this body right here," I say in a low undertone, while cupping her breasts and grinding into her from behind, "I might explode. You're a tease even when you sleep."

"Sorry . . ." she says on a moan.

"Are you really?"

"No." she chuckles quietly. *That's my girl.* Slowly, while lying on our sides, we move against one another. It's a lot like the way we danced together last Thursday night, except now we're naked and alone. I'll take this with her any day. I reach behind my head and grab the waiting condom before putting it on.

I lift her top leg and hitch it up by holding the back of her knee. The closer contact makes her groan into her pillow.

"Do you want me?" I ask.

"More than air," she responds instantly, breathing out. Because I know she's ready from all the grinding, I slip inside of her, inch by inch. Pausing, I wait for her to adjust to my size. When I begin to move, she lets out a strangled cry and urges me to keep going. *Yes, ma'am.*

Hours. I could do this with her for fucking hours. Days. Months. Hell, probably even years. *Please just deliver my food and all other necessities to this bed, because if anyone wants me to leave, they will have to drag my ass out.*

For years my body has craved what I now hold in my hands. I tried to feed it with what I thought it needed, and yet there's something about finally letting your body have what it's always desired. You can try and create feelings, but you can't deny true attraction. Audrey feeds my soul with her strength and beauty.

"God, you feel amazing," I groan. My speed amps up, but it's still a slower pace than my usual. Lazy morning sex does have its perks. It's relaxing and slow versus the frantic kind you have at night in the backseat of a car after drinking too much. I pull her arms up and she bends them backward, grabbing on to my head. Her fingers scratch through my hair as she holds on. I bring her top leg up closer to her body so I can get farther in.

So many times I feel her get close, but then she calms down and doesn't let go. Damn, I'm so fucking close, but I can't do anything until she gets her release first. I feel her building back up as she squeezes around me and clenches my hair in her fists, but then she whimpers and holds it in.

In an instant, I have her flipped around so we're still lying on our sides, but now we're face-to-face. She appears shocked at the sudden movement. I push back inside of her and we both groan and cry out. I lay my hands on the top of her head so my forearms can craft a barrier around our faces. I use my arms to block out all other distractions around us and I look directly into her darkened eyes.

"You. Are. Killing. Me," I say, emphasizing each word. "What are you doing?"

"I just . . . don't want this to end. I want to delay it as long as possible."

I lean forward, kiss her perfect lips, and say, "Let go, baby. I'm not going anywhere. There will be so much more for us, I swear."

Relief encompasses her face at my words, and I feel like a complete jackass for not paying better attention. This is why I demand to be in control. When I release the reins a bit, her needs aren't being met like they should.

I continue surrounding her face while I kiss her lips hungrily. She matches my desire, kiss for kiss. A slight sheen of sweat covers both of our bodies, and together we find our release in the same moment. Mine is amplified by our closeness. She's directly in front of me, touching almost every inch of my body. The only thing I can see is her. The only thing I can smell is her. The only thing I can feel is . . . her. Hasn't it always been her? It should have been.

Slowly, I roll away and simultaneously pull her body partially on top of me. She hikes a leg over mine and lays her small hand over my stomach. Her face tucks in between my chin and shoulder and she snuggles in close. I lean toward her, drawing in the soft, clean scent of her hair.

For the next couple of hours, we fall in and out of a light sleep, as my fingers make small circles on her hipbone. Later when I wake up, the sun is much brighter than it was the first time I looked out the window. I stretch out my arms and feel the empty spaces on either side of me. She cannot be serious. I'd like to wake up just once where she hasn't either disappeared or kicked me in the nuts.

The door flies open and Audrey quickly tiptoes in, holding two steaming mugs. In only her bra, panties, and my penny necklace. Fumes have to be shooting out of my ears because I swear if Lane saw her, I'll lose my fucking mind.

She's distracted with the scalding hot mugs in her hands, so she just smiles and heads toward her desk to set them down. I sit up, scoot to the edge of the futon, and catch the door before it can close behind her.

"Lane! Are you gay?" I shout, loud enough so I can be heard throughout the entire apartment.

"Uh . . . not the last time I checked," he hollers, sounding confused. *Yeah, I didn't think so.* A slow growl rumbles up through my chest and then I hear Lane's deep laugh build louder and louder from his room. "Was she walking around naked again?" he yells. "Did I miss it?" he adds—to fuck with me, I'm sure.

"Audrey!" I shout and Lane's laugh becomes hysterical. Quickly, I slam the door and turn to look at her. Her eyes are wide because of my tone of voice. A look of terror splays across her face, but I quietly wait for it to pass. She needs to learn that there will be times that we'll yell, argue, and be upset with one another, but I would never, absolutely ever, hurt her. She quickly catches her error and wipes the fright away. *Good girl.* Now there's only shock on her face.

I scramble to my feet, trying to untangle myself from the sheets, and stalk toward her. She backs up into the desk and latches on to the edge. Frustration rolls off me in waves as I get a closer look at her tight little body that she just put on parade. Her eyes lick a slow path from my bare feet all the way up to my eyes. Every emotion that was on her face has been replaced with scorching lust.

"Don't look at me like that, Audrey. Now's not the time," I say in a deep, hushed tone. As I advance closer to her, she bites down on her bottom lip and pulls it into her mouth. "Stop, Audrey. I'm not happy with you right now."

The second the corner of her lip quirks up into a smirk, I'm a goner. What am I doing? Why am I mad? All I can focus on now is that plump lip being abused by her pearly white teeth. Her fingers run up my chest and wrap around my neck, and those big brown eyes gaze up at me with pure innocence.

Forty minutes later, Audrey crumples down onto my chest, panting and out of breath. Her legs are still straddling me on either side of my body, and my hands still have a death grip on her thighs.

"I hope you learned your lesson," I breathe out.

She chuckles against my skin and says, "Oh, I most definitely learned something." When I pinch her ass, she yelps and jolts off of my body, landing next to me.

My face becomes solemn and I turn to look at her. "I'm serious. I don't like you walking around like that for him to see."

"He's already seen ever—"

I instantly silence what she's about to say by swiftly putting my finger over her lips. "Babe, I suggest you not finish that sentence unless you *want* to see me go nuclear. No more," I say and quickly add, "Please?"

Her hands cup my face and she nods her head. "I promise."

I lean in and take her lips forcefully because it's still hitting me hard that she's mine. She doesn't mind, though, and she doles it out just as well as she takes it. After a few more minutes of making out like teenagers, she pulls back and releases an exaggerated breath.

"What are your plans for the day?" she asks.

"I seriously have to get to the gym today or Jaxon's going to be able to kick my ass soon." I laugh to myself before adding, "Nah, that won't ever happen, but I do need to get in there."

Her fingers outline my stomach muscles and she says, "Hmm . . . well, we wouldn't want to lose any of this, now would we?" Her voice is low and seductive and starting to amp me up again.

I grasp her fingers tightly. "We'll never get out of this bed today if you keep this up. Besides, I have to take this hot girl out on a date tonight. I'm kind of hoping she'll agree to be my girlfriend," I say, smirking at her.

A sexy blush creeps up her neck and dusts over her cheeks. "And what if she says no?" she challenges.

I lean in and whisper from her neck up to her ear. "Then she must not have heard me right, because I'm pretty sure she's just as crazy about me as I am about her."

With a quivering voice, she responds, "I don't blame the girl. Lucky bitch."

"If anyone's the fortunate one here, it's me, babe." Slowly, I push myself up to get out of bed, because if I don't, I'll end up lazing around all day with her in my arms. I'm not sure why that's a bad thing, though. "What are you up to today?" I ask.

"Not much. I have a few errands to run, and I think Em and Quinn wanted to meet up."

"You're seriously going to have to tell me how *that* friendship came about at some point. Don't get me wrong, I love Em to death, so I think it's fantastic. It's just not something I ever would have expected."

"Trust me, it's still a bit strange for me when I really think about it. Em was just . . . Em, you know? We hit it off."

"She is pretty great," I say, while searching for my clothes.

Her eyes narrow at me and I swear I see a hint of jealousy. "Did you ever have feelings for her? Honestly." *Bingo.* Nailed that one on the head.

"Babe, one of the first times I ever heard Em's name was out my brother's mouth, who had already practically proclaimed his undying love for this stranger. Which, by the way, was on our very first day in California. I never viewed her as anyone but my brother's girl. Sometimes I like to egg him on, but it has always been purely platonic between us."

"And what about me? Do you still see me as your brother's girl?" she asks quietly.

"Never. You were never his girl," I rush to say. She lets out a sigh of frustration, so I quickly continue. "Babe, I know I'm trying to lie low about us. Trust me, I want to scream it from the rooftops. But I just want to approach this in the right manner with Jax. We made promises to each other. I just need to figure out a way to bring it up without him feeling betrayed."

"I know you need time, Jace. I said I was willing to give that to you, but I won't wait long," she states confidently.

"And I won't make you wait long." I lean down and tug gently on her necklace while advancing toward her lips. I kiss her slowly, hoping I can convey how much I feel for her.

"I'll be back to get you at seven tonight, okay?" When she nods her approval, I head out the door, right after I shout my good-bye to Lane down the hall.

- TWELVE -

AUDREY -

The errands that I briefly mentioned to Jace earlier are a little bit more complicated than I let on. When I step into the shop, the sterile smell is what hits my nose first. I guess that's a good sign. The clean, black-and-white-checkered tile floor catches my eyes as my feet move up to the front counter. The deep blue walls are calming and the decor is tasteful. Definitely not what I expected to find. There are large leather couches and bulky portfolio books scattered on the tables in a waiting area. There aren't any designs on the walls to choose from like I've seen on television.

The receptionist is a tiny little thing with bright purple hair and metal or plastic jewelry in every conceivable place a person could get pierced above the neck. Although I'm initially shocked at her appearance, the closer I get to the counter, the more I'm blown away by how beautiful she is. The customers and the guys working here must love having her to greet everyone. Her smile lights up as I put my hands on the counter.

"Do you have an appointment?" she asks, rifling through the pages of a black notebook.

"No, sorry . . . I didn't even think about that . . ." I trail off. It took enough courage to walk in the door by myself. I almost asked Jace to come with me today, seeing as he now has a ton of tattoos covering his arms, shoulders, and ribs. He probably would have been able to show me the best place to go. I only chose this place because it's right next to where I work and it looked kind of fun from the outside. God, Lane would kill me if he heard me right now, choosing a tattoo shop because it looked *fun* from the outside.

"No worries. You might have to wait a bit, though. Since it's Sunday, most of them are about to get off, but I think . . ." she says, scanning the shop, "Jared should be done soon and he can help you out." As she pencils something in the notebook, she adds, "I'm Jinx, by the way."

When she lifts her head to look at me, she laughs at my open-mouthed expression. "Even your name is badass," I say, because it's the first thing that pops out of my mouth.

"Thanks," she says, chuckling. "It's just a nickname, though."

"I'm Audrey. I always liked my name, but now I'm finding it seriously lacking compared to yours."

"No way. Audrey, like Audrey Hepburn, the classic beauty!" She slips on some big, dark sunglasses and places a pen in her mouth as if it were a cigarette holder from the sixties. I giggle as she acts out the characteristic Holly Golightly pose. "See? Classic."

"Okay, you made me feel better," I say with a smile.

"I've got you checked in. Just sign these waivers and then you can wait on the couches for Jared."

"I got her," a deep voice says from close by. Jinx and I both turn to gaze at the person who's quickly approaching the counter. The man that advances is tall and has messy, jet-black hair. His black polo shirt barely contains his large, muscled chest and arms. *Poor shirt.* The first thing I notice besides his easy, handsome smile and eyes that promise trouble is the stranger's tanned, *un-tattooed* expanse of skin.

"Max, you're about to get off. Jared can get her," Jinx states.

"Yeah, I can get her!" I hear a shout from across the shop, and I'm assuming *that's* Jared. He pops his head up over his stall and winks at me.

"It's cool; I got her," Max repeats. "Besides, I'll bet you a hundred bucks, Jinxy, that she's got virgin skin. You know how I love poppin' cherries."

My mouth drops open at his blatant flirtation. "But . . . do you even have tattoos? How can I expect you to work on me when it looks like *you* don't even have any yourself?" I'm not sure why I can't keep my thoughts *inside* my head, where they should clearly stay. And why does having tattoos automatically qualify him as a tattoo artist in my mind?

Jinx begins to giggle and Max stares at me in fascination. Without missing a beat, he raises his black polo up by the hem and lifts it over his washboard abs and chiseled chest. Beautiful designs swirl and twist over and around his skin. Half a pair of stunning angel wings fill up the entire right side of his upper body, shoulder to waist. The wings are so finely detailed I want to touch them, just to see if they're real. Over his heart, the words "Even Angels Fall" are scripted into his skin.

It's amazing how businesslike he appears, but under his shirt is this amazing, beautiful artwork. I watch as he pushes up his sleeves and see that the tattoos continue over his shoulders.

"Impressive . . ." I whisper.

"I can keep going, if you'd like." He smirks devilishly and reaches for his zipper.

"No, no, keep your pants on, buddy," I rush to say. Jace would *not* be okay with this.

"I think I need to refresh my memory, though," Jinx cuts in, giggling.

Max ignores her and gestures toward his walled-off section. I walk in and sit in a chair that looks as though it belongs in a dentist office. His area is very neat, almost OCD clean, with everything lined up evenly and all labels facing outward. It looks as if there are about five other guys in this shop, and all of their areas clearly show their personalities. Pictures and drawings cover their walls, along with various metal-band music posters. But Max's area is a blank canvas. There are no personal belongings in sight, only the tools he needs to do his job.

"Do you have something in mind, or do you need time to search through the look books?" he asks.

I pull out a piece of paper and hand it to him. "These are the words I want. I'll leave it up to you how they're written."

He reads over the quotation and asks, "Damn, Jim Morrison? I like you even more now." He flashes me a smile, which showcases two dimples that are way too adorable to be on such a masculine face.

"The only thing I can thankfully say I got from my father was his good taste in music."

He nods his head in apparent understanding. "Where were you thinking of getting it?"

I point to the right side of my rib cage, and he smiles in agreement. "Perfect choice, babe. My favorite place to mark a girl up."

It takes him some time to draw up the stencil perfectly, and on paper it looks beautiful. I have to take my bra off, but he lets me keep my shirt on because it's loose-fitting and I can just push it up. After thoroughly sanitizing the area, he transfers the script onto my skin.

"Stand up and check it out in the mirror."

With my left hand, I continue to hold my shirt up and lift my right arm to view what he's done so far. I'm mesmerized by the way the curls on each letter flow into the next one, almost resembling a beautiful love letter. I could stare at it for hours. I can't wait to have it permanently etched into my skin.

He lays the chair down flat and gently drapes my right arm over my head. I stick earbuds from my iPod in and flick through my albums for the perfect, relaxing mix. Before I can hit Play, he taps me on the hand and I look at him to let him know that I can still hear him.

"The first few lines are pretty close to . . . your chest," he says. "I'll have to pull some areas tight and lean on you a bit at some point. I swear I'm not feeling you up, though!" He raises his hands in genuine innocence, and in this moment, I feel completely comfortable with his abilities and professionalism.

"Don't worry about me. Just do what you need to do," I say.

"All right, then, let's do this," he says, while pulling on black latex gloves. "It's gonna hurt at first, but usually it fades to a dull ache after a few minutes. Everyone is different."

I shrug my shoulders, push Play, and close my eyes. Throughout my years growing up, I've taught myself how to anticipate pain. When you know it's coming, you can prepare yourself and refocus your thoughts elsewhere. I'm an expert at this, thanks to my dad.

The second the vibrating needle hits my skin I love it. This is a good type of pain, the kind I can control, and it slowly becomes a pleasant feeling. I know what true pain is, and this isn't it. The humming noise of the machine can be heard over my music and it relaxes me, even more so than the massage chair from the pedicure.

I make it through one whole album when Max taps my side to let me know he needs to grab some more supplies, but that he'll be right back. At this point, I hope I can lie in this chair all day. *Tattoo to your heart's content, Max.*

JACE -

My workout was exactly what I needed. I was surprised to see that Lane attends the same boxing gym as I do. It was cool to spar with him a few rounds. He's crazy-ass good, though, and he got some good hits in on me. I'll definitely need to learn a few pointers from him.

As I'm heading out, I notice Max's brand-new pair of gloves lying outside of the ring. His can easily be identified by the tattoo-like drawings on the leather. The right one, in particular, has a pretty ferocious-looking tiger that extends all the way to where his knuckles would be.

Since his shop is right across the street, I decide to run them over to him. I try to sneak past Jinx as I enter the shop, but she spots me before I can get two steps in the door. Her face lights up as she calls out my name.

"Hey, Jinx, Max here?"

"He's with a client. I can help you, though," she says in a low voice. A few more rounds of "hey" call out from some of the guys in the shop, and I nod my head to all of them. Max walks out of his work space, so I excuse myself from Jinx's predatory gaze.

"Hey, man, you left these in the gym." He continues walking toward the storage room, so I follow behind.

"Shit, thanks. That's my new pair. It took me forever to draw that damn tiger."

"Yeah, forget the expensive-ass gloves; it's the tiger we're worried about," I mock.

He smirks while grabbing some ink from the shelves. "Dude, you have to check out this chick I'm working on right now." He sucks his lip in between his teeth and whistles. "I think I just found my wife."

"Wow, proposing already? That's fast, even for you." He jabs me in the side at my quip. "She covered in tats or something?"

"The exact opposite! Virgin skin. I'm totally poppin' her cherry. Get this, though—she's completely enjoying it. It's like it turns her on. She hasn't flinched at all, and when the needle touches her skin, she gets this almost serene-like look on her face."

"Damn, that does sound like your kind of girl," I reply.

"Walk over there and check her out. She's fucking gorgeous."

"I think I'm good, man. I got my own girl."

"What? When did that go down? Ah, forget it, you still need to see my future wife. She's got legs for days, and I know how you enjoy a good pair of legs." He pulls me across the shop floor, and just to appease him, I peer over the wall at the girl lying flat on her back with her eyes closed and music blasting through her earphones.

"What the fuck?" I say, a bit too loud.

"Nu-uh, back your predatory ass up. I don't like that look on your face. I already called dibs. You have your own girl, remember?" he quickly says, while walking into his area. Audrey doesn't budge from her relaxed state, and she still hasn't opened her eyes to see her audience.

"Back off, Max. *That's* my girl!" I point at her. His eyes widen and he looks back and forth between Audrey and me.

"Does she have a necklace on?" I ask.

"Yeah . . . it's got a pen—"

"A penny," I interrupt.

"Noooo," he whines. "This is *my* dream girl and you got her first?"

"Damn straight! And you better believe I don't plan on leaving her alone with you a second longer." I gaze at the work he's done so far. "Especially since you're practically working right on my girl's chest. Cop a feel and lose a finger. Got me?"

He grumbles and walks to the sink to wash his hands. After he slides new gloves on and sits back down beside her, I pull up a chair on her opposite side. Her milky white skin is now stamped with fresh ink, and I'm not sure how I feel about it. On the one hand, it looks pretty damn hot. But on the other hand, I loved her smooth, untouched skin. Mostly, I think it bothers me that she came here by herself.

Before Max begins, I grab her hand and kiss her knuckles lightly. Her whole body locks up and she immediately sits up ramrod-straight.

"Max!" she exclaims in anger.

I continue holding her hand while she looks at Max, who has his hands in the air in surrender. "Wasn't me! I sure as hell wish it was, but it wasn't me, babe."

With my empty hand, I reach out and swat at him, "Hey, she's not your babe, jackass."

"Jace?" She finally turns to look at where our hands are entwined together. I slowly lay her down while Max prepares the machine. I don't want her accidently flashing him with her shirt up like it is.

When she's flat on her back, I take out her earbud and whisper directly into her ear, "You have me now. No more doing this kind of stuff by yourself, 'kay? You're not alone. I want to be there for everything."

Tears well up in her eyes and she says, "How did you know I was here?"

"I came to see this douchebag. Max has done all my work that I've gotten in California. He's also my friend, but that's questionable now that I've heard how he feels about you." Her cheeks turn a nice shade of pink, and I kiss her lips lightly while squeezing her hand.

"Carry on, Maxi-pad." I gesture for him to resume.

"Asshole," he grumbles. I can sympathize with him, really I can. I know what it's like to learn that Audrey isn't actually going to be yours, but now she *is* mine, and he can just get over his little case of puppy love.

When he starts up the machine and touches it to her skin, I instantly see what he had been talking about. She does get an almost tranquil look on her face. Her music is blaring again and she's off in another world, giving me the opportunity to freely stare at her, uninterrupted. I've seen this look on her face after we've both satisfied each other for hours and we lay side by side, just trying to catch our breath.

Sitting here, staring at her satiated face, is beginning to be a major turn-on. I mean, how could it not? I know how to put that look on her face, and I damn sure want to know what she's thinking right now. It's fucking hard, though, because I know Max is sitting directly across from me seeing that same face, and probably feeling the same damn rush of hormones that I am.

When he wipes off an area of her skin, I watch his eyes quickly glance up at her.

"Stop looking at her face. I know what you see," I growl.

He turns his head and laughs into the crook of his arm. "Dude, it's kind of hard not to. Especially now that you've just confirmed that what I'm seeing is her 'I've just been fucked real good' face." He smiles to himself and gets back to work. I'd punch him right now, if I didn't think it would mess up Audrey's tattoo. I'll tune him up in the ring next time we're in the gym, though.

"I'll take care of you later," I warn.

"It'll be fucking worth it," he whispers back with a laugh.

After the longest thirty minutes of my life, he finally finishes without eliciting even a flinch from Audrey. She probably handled that better than I do. This whole time, I've been staring at her face and haven't stopped to read the script across her ribs. Max pats her hand to signal that he's finished. Her eyes blink open and readjust to the light. She begins to sit up, so I rush to hold her shirt against her chest.

She smiles and says, "I've got it."

I follow her to the mirror and check out the work he did. I've got to hand it to Max; he knocked it out of the park again. His art looks badass on her skin, yet also very feminine and sexy. I kneel down in front of her so I can look at it up close. My finger trails the outside of the tender letters without actually touching the ink as I take in what I see.

"Expose yourself to your deepest
fear; after that, fear has no power,
and the fear of freedom shrinks
and vanishes. You are free."

After thinking about what this means for her, I lean in and kiss a slow circle around the perimeter.

I look up into her eyes and ask, "What is your deepest fear?"

"Being alone," she whispers back. "I didn't realize how alone I used to be until I met Lane, and then I didn't fully accept it until I found you again. I've finally freed myself from that fear. I don't ever want to go back, but I know I can survive it." I lean in and kiss her side one more time before standing up and looking down at her beautiful face. I grasp her face on both sides and speak to her, hoping it reaches the deepest part of her.

"Never again, baby. I never want you to feel alone again," I express, and she stands on her toes to capture my mouth.

A groaning noise comes from behind us. "Damn it, knock it off. Doesn't anyone care that I'm heartbroken over here?" Max grumbles. He crooks his finger, signaling for Audrey to come over to him. He slathers on some ointment and covers the tattooed area. "If this asshole fucks up, please come find me. I'm ready to propose to you, run away with you, let you have my babies, kneel down and kiss your feet daily, babe."

It takes me about two point five seconds to reach him and then only another millisecond before I smack him upside the back of his head.

"Hmm . . . that's a tempting offer," she smarts off.

"Audrey . . ." I growl.

"Thanks again for the tattoo, Max. It's amazing. Better than I ever imagined," Audrey says, beaming.

After we go back and forth with each other at the counter over who is going to pay for the tattoo, she finally wins and swipes her card.

"You two know each other?" Jinx asks, looking bewildered by our exchange.

"Yup," I reply vaguely, not wanting to get into this with her right now.

Audrey gives me a confused expression and elaborates. "I guess he's my boyfriend . . . although he still hasn't taken me out on a date yet." Her smile widens and I can tell she's excited about tonight. Jinx's surprise is written all over her face as she gapes at me, and I inwardly cringe. Without a word, she hands Audrey her receipt, and we head out the door.

Audrey appears worried as she tries to interpret Jinx's behavior. When we reach my car, she says, "Did you ever date her?"

Slowly I inhale and exhale, trying to think of how to best approach this subject with her. I've never thought of Audrey as the jealous type, but you can never tell with girls. I've seen them flip a switch so fast it made my head spin.

"We did," I finally admit. "It was only a handful of times, but it didn't go anywhere. At least not for me. We were in no way compatible, although she thinks that something like that can just be fixed." The entire time I'm speaking, I watch her face for any reaction. A little crease forms on her forehead and I can see sadness behind her eyes, even though she tries to mask it.

Quickly, I rush to say, "We never slept together." I pull her in against my chest because I can't stand the distance between us any longer. "Please, don't be mad."

She jerks back and looks directly up into my eyes, "Jace, why would I be mad at you for dating someone? We weren't together."

"I don't know . . . some girls . . . they don't like to hear that kind of stuff. But I want to be completely honest with you."

"I'm only upset because *I* slept with you before even going out on a date with you. She got a *handful* of dates. I mean, how easy am I?" her little voice mumbles in my chest. I chuckle to myself, hoping she doesn't hear because I'm not making fun of her in any way.

"I'm so sorry, babe. I should have wined and dined you before putting my hands on you. It's just that I've never been so damn attracted to any girl in my whole life, like I am to you. It's so hard to keep my hands off of you." Slowly, I back her up against the side of the Camaro and lean in toward her mouth. "Even now, all I can think about is reenacting the first time we met, when I practically took you up against my truck."

She slowly pushes me back, but I can tell she's affected by my words as she says, "Date first; everything else later."

- THIRTEEN -

AUDREY -

It's crazy how if you aren't paying attention, an entire month can fly by in a breeze. An entire month of late-night talks with Jace on the phone or with him by my side. An entire month of becoming more and more consumed with each other. I think there have only been a few nights that Jace and I haven't slept in the same bed together.

Jaxon and Em have been MIA a lot lately. There has been speculation between Quinn and me that they went and rented another apartment together, one that they could escape to alone. Em hasn't admitted to it yet, because she knows that we would eventually follow her to find out where it's located.

For the most part, Quinn has been wrapped up with Cole, Em with Jax, and me with Jace. Lane disappears here and there as well, but for now he's back to his happy-go-lucky self. The downside is that a whole month has slipped by us without Jace telling Jaxon about our relationship.

A part of me is starting to think he likes the sneaky, espionage-type game we have created with each other. It really has been fun and exciting. With Jax and Em gone so much, I often slip into Jace's room at night and sleep in his giant, king-size bed. It's probably the most comfortable thing that has ever touched my body. Seriously, I think Jace is becoming a bit jealous of my love affair with his bed. But there's really no reason for one person to have that much bed all to himself anyway.

Em and Quinn have invited me to go see a movie with them today, and when I get to their place, I eventually find both of them down the hall in the guys' apartment. They're making food to take to Jaxon and Cole, who are both at football practice. I notice Jace's car is gone, so at least it won't be awkward for him to be here while I'm in his place with the girls. Even though they know everything.

"Do you mind if we drop this off for the guys before we go to the theater?" Em asks as I approach the kitchen counter.

"Sure, but y'all aren't even ready yet . . ." I gesture at their pajamas and wild hair.

"We're running a bit behind," Em mumbles, while stirring two pots at one time.

"Yeah, because Miss Chef over here burned the pasta!" Quinn states, pointing at Em and laughing.

"How do you burn pasta? It's in *water*," I say, laughing along with Quinn.

"Don't ask. I'm not even sure what happened," Em confesses.

"Audrey, do you mind scooping the food into Tupperware for us while we get ready?" Quinn asks. "Otherwise, if we don't hurry up, we'll miss the movie."

"Sure, go ahead." After the door closes behind them, it occurs to me that I'm in my boyfriend's apartment . . . alone. It's kind of a weird feeling, like I'm about to be caught doing something I shouldn't be doing.

As I scoop the newly cooked, unburned pasta into the plastic dish, a key turns in the lock. When whoever is coming in realizes

At the memory of our tryst in the fitting room, I grab his shirt and pull it over his head. Quickly, I reach for his belt buckle, not able to contain my need for him any longer. He halts my impatient hands and raises them above my head. Slowly, he urges both hands to grab on to the pantry shelf behind us. The level he wants me to hold on to is a bit taller than I can comfortably reach, so I have to stand on my tiptoes.

"Don't move your hands or I'll find something to restrain them with." I know from experience that he's resourceful enough to find something, even in the pitch-black dark. I can't decide if I'd prefer him to do just that or not.

Slowly, I let my heels drop back to the ground, causing my hands to slip. He catches them instantly above my head and, without a word, whips his belt off, wraps it around my wrists, and then ties it around one of the vertical support beams on the shelving unit. He doesn't pull it tight; it isn't meant to hurt.

"Better?" he whispers in my ear.

"Yes," I softly whisper. All the stress and pressure melt off of me like butter, as I allow Jace to make the decisions for me. Sex has never been this full-bodied affair for me until Jace. Before, it was always a blip on the radar. A short moment in time, but nothing ever memorable. Maybe it's the way he looks at me when he doesn't think I notice, or the way he seems to know exactly what I always need, but I can't imagine experiencing this any other way now, and hopefully never will with anyone else.

Slowly, he unbuttons my shirt down the middle and leaves it hanging open. I arch my back so my body can fuse against his. I need more friction and more of his naked skin. He reads my mind, like always, and I hear the telltale sign of his zipper being pulled down. I don't hear the rustle of clothing, so in my head I try to picture how he looks with his shirt off and jeans unzipped and open, just enough to free himself.

"I wish I could see you right now," I whisper.

"Then you would know when I'm about to do this . . ." he trails off and rubs two fingers down the apex between my legs. A sharp stream of air whistles past my teeth.

He works me up over and over, but never lets me fall over the crest. When I'm panting and begging Jace for more, we hear the front door open and close. My whole body freezes. Em and Quinn begin talking in the kitchen, and I vaguely hear one of them ask where I could be. At that very moment, Jace thrusts inside of me. A strangled cry escapes my throat, but apparently he was anticipating it, because one of his hands is already covering my mouth.

My body locks up, I clench my fists together, and my legs tighten to uncomfortable levels. Jace cups my face with both of his hands and begins to kiss me slowly, while moving in and out.

"Shh, be here with me, babe. Don't worry about them," he says into my ear.

"They could come in. They could see us," I nervously whisper back.

"Trust me." When I don't respond, he continues, "I can reach the door from here. If they try to come in, I'll hold it closed. Be. With. Me." The last thought is whispered so longingly I almost forget everything else around me. All of a sudden having the use of my hands sounds like a much better idea.

"I want to touch you," I gasp at his relentless rhythm.

He reaches up and begins to unwind the leather around my wrists. "I swear to God, if you go into your head and try to hold back, I'll keep you here all night."

"That's not much of a threat," I murmur, as my finally free hands run through his hair.

"Behave," he whispers threateningly into my ear.

The sad part is, the only reason we're doing this here and now is because he knows Jaxon is at practice and won't be home for another couple of hours. As much as I've tried to be patient with him, I'm getting tired of lying low. I push the thoughts back and teach myself to be in this moment with him like he commanded.

His hand grips one of my thighs and he pulls it up, hitching the leg around his waist. I stand on the tiptoe of my opposite leg and lean all of my weight into him. He picks up a relentless pounding pace that makes me forget to breathe. My back digs into the shelves behind me, but it's all a distant feeling with him in front of me. He's already so familiar with my body that he knows how to push me over the threshold and how to make me teeter along the edge. He reaches between our bodies and his finger circles exactly where I need it.

With my toe-curling, shooting release, I bite into his shoulder to muffle my cries. Surprisingly, he bites down into mine as well to dampen his own sounds of pleasure a few minutes later. Slowly we pull apart, panting heavily. I wish I could turn the light on in here. Jace's post-sex face is the most glorious sight to see, especially when he's staring right at me, letting me know he feels everything I am in that moment. I love knowing I'm not alone.

I feel him bend down and then a little tap on my foot indicates for me to lift it. Leisurely, he drags my panties back up my legs and secures them on to my hips. I stifle a chuckle as he tries to pull my skirt down lower and swears when he realizes my shirt isn't long enough now to cover my stomach. I feel him inch my skirt back up until it touches the edge of my shirt.

"You're killing me," he rasps into my ear.

"Well, maybe now you'll think about me all night," I tease quietly.

"That was already a fucking guarantee, babe," he grumbles.

"I hope I don't drop anything. Imagine if someone saw me bending over . . ."

I laugh as he growls. "That's it." I feel the leather of his belt as he grabs my wrists. "You're staying here."

"Jace, Jace!" I try to laugh quietly. "I'm kidding!"

I feel his hands touch the sides of my face and he speaks directly to me. I imagine his glacial blue eyes, even though I can't see them. "I know I'm a terrible boyfriend right now, but you're still mine."

"Just let me tell him," I whisper.

"Hell, no. I need to do it. I just can't ever catch the bastard long enough to have a conversation with him. I'm either spending the night with you, or he's off God-knows-where with Em." I nod my head and I know he feels it between his hands.

"Soon, I promise." He kisses me lightly and buttons his pants as I readjust my shirt. We both step up to the door and listen quietly for voices. "I haven't heard them for at least ten minutes. I think we're good," he whispers.

I turn and kiss him one more time before we're forced to play this silly game in front of everyone again. Gradually, I push the pantry door open, hoping it's not a creaky door. Jace holds on to my hips as I step out of the dark room. Instantly, I see Em and Quinn sitting at the dining room table, with their chins in their hands and huge shit-eating grins poised directly at us. Jace's hands fly off my hips and I sigh in frustration.

"Damn . . ." Quinn laughs.

"I bet that was awesome," Em adds. "Jax and I will have to try that one. Did you guys do it on the washing machine?" she boldly asks.

My head slightly shakes and Jace says, "I was just talking to her in there." The guilt drips off of each of his words.

"Riiight, just like you were 'talking' to her over winter break in the back of the Camaro, and just like you were 'talking' to her when you snuck in her bedroom," Em says defiantly. *Shit.* I didn't tell

Jace that they knew. His eyes bug out and he takes a step backward, almost as if he wants to go hide himself in the pantry until we leave.

"Jace, she's our friend. Newsflash: We're girls and we talk," Em says, before he has the chance to get upset.

"Fuck, Em. Let me talk to Jax before you open your mouth," he pleads.

"Well, seeing as I've known about this for a while now, I think your secret is safe with me. For now."

Jace nods his head, saying, "Stop dragging him off to your secret lair so I can actually have some time to explain everything." He drags his hands through his hair in frustration.

"Fine, why don't you talk to him tomorrow? Everyone's going to the beach for Mason's birthday," she explains.

His face contorts and he says, "I don't like Mason."

"Since when? You used to hang out with him all the time." Em is a freaking bulldog when she's on a mission. There's no stopping her either. Although in this case, where she's trying to push Jace to talk to his brother, I'll let her bully on.

"Since Audrey danced with him at the club, remember?" Quinn pipes in.

"They know about that too?" his voice rises and he quickly looks at me.

"Don't we have a movie to see?" I ask, trying to change the subject.

With a deep groan and a few labored breaths, Jace says, "Shit. Fine, I'll be there tomorrow night."

"Awesome!" Em claps her hands in victory and reaches for her purse. "Okay, now that it's settled, let's head out."

I file in behind them. As we make our way for the front door, Quinn exclaims, "Dang, girl, your wrists are red!"

"It's fine," I mumble and rub circles around them.

Out of the corner of my eye, I catch Jace whipping back around from his earlier retreat down the hallway. "Go on ahead. She'll catch up with you in a second," he says to Em and Quinn. When they walk out the door whispering to each other, he reaches for my hands. Tenderly, he kisses the reddened skin that rings my wrists. "I'm not gonna lie: It's pretty damn hot that you have to walk around with this all night, but I'm sorry if I hurt you."

"You'll really talk to Jaxon tomorrow night?" I ask, because I'm not concerned about my wrists. He nods his head in response, continuing his soft kisses. "And you didn't hurt me. I trust you." I hope he understands the double meaning behind my words.

He kisses me and wishes me a good night as I open the door. Before I can get two feet down the outer hallway, he calls out, "Don't forget, no bending over! That skirt is too fucking short."

I laugh at his possessive nature and give a little twirl that causes my navy-striped skirt to billow out, showing way more thigh than I would want anyone besides him to see.

- FOURTEEN -

AUDREY -

The bar is slow this afternoon, so I offer to finish the shift alone if Em wants to go hang out with Jax before he has practice tonight. Not even ten minutes after I suggest it, Jax comes strolling in the door with a wide grin on his face.

"You ready, Beautiful?" he calls out to Em.

"Babe, I was going to meet you. I have my car," she huffs.

"Let Audrey drive it. That way Lane won't have to come get her," he suggests.

"Do you mind, Audrey?" she asks.

"Not at all, but Lane will still come up here to make sure I get out okay. He's . . . overprotective. So if you want your car, you should take it."

"Huh, I heard Jace grumbling about that the other day," Jax says, appearing deep in thought. "Maybe he's got a crush on you. You're not trying to marry another Riley brother, are you?" His tone comes off as purely joking, but I freeze and hear Em gasp.

"That was rude, babe," Em says, while grabbing his arm and dragging him toward the door. Jax gives Em an apologetic face and begins to whisper to her on their way out. Before they exit, she turns and yells, "I'll see you tonight! Wear something hot!"

I clutch her car keys in my hand and wonder what would have happened if Jace had been standing here. More than likely he would have headed for the hills. I hope Jax doesn't say anything like that tonight. I never thought about him not handling it well, since there was never a reason for him to be upset about me dating someone else. I never considered the fact that he wouldn't want his brother dating *me*, though it makes sense after all of my history.

Tonight will be the true test. I just can't continue this charade any longer. It was fun at first, being sneaky and finding hidden places to rendezvous. But I want Jace all to myself now. I want to be able to hold his hand as we walk through the campus and I want other girls to know he's off limits. I don't think it's crazy for me to want Jace to want the same. His brother is going to be either mad about it or not, but it all comes down to how we handle it once it's all out there. I shouldn't have let this go on as long as I did. I know Jace is worried about hurting Jaxon, but how long does he plan to put his life on hold based on what his twin thinks?

Deep in thought, I begin scrubbing the bar top when a little blur runs past me and I look up to see a panicky-faced Quinn. She's looking around frantically for something or someone who's apparently not here.

"Em. Where's Emerson?" she breathes out in a rush.

I watch her as she paces back and forth with something clutched tightly in her grasp. Her hands are shaking and her eyes are rimmed in red. I wonder how she got here, since I have the car that she and Em usually share.

"She left early with Jax." I come around the bar and grab her shoulders to steady her frantic movements. "Are you okay?"

"No!" she yells and then begins to sob into my shoulder.

Slowly, I rub her back and whisper, "Sit down, Quinn. You can tell me what happened or I'll find a way to get Em back here." She steps up to sit on a bar stool, and I take the one next to her.

"Her phone is off. That's why I came here." She sniffles loudly into my shirt.

"Quinn, I promise I won't tell anybody, and I'll try my hardest to help. I know you want Em right now, but I just don't like seeing you like this. Should I call Cole?"

"Oh God, no. Please, no. He's the last person I need right now," she whimpers.

"Oh . . . kay . . ." I say, a bit confused.

Slowly, she brings her hands up to the bar and hesitantly slides the object in her hands toward me. It takes her a full minute to open them so I can see it. When she does, I gasp in recognition. I've seen this before. I've held this in my hands before.

While I *have* seen this exact item in the past, I was nowhere near the same place that she is. She has people who love her and would walk through fire for her. They will protect her and take care of any need she has.

"Quinn, it'll be okay," I say as calmly as I can.

"Cole won't think that."

"Guys usually don't, but Cole will come around. Eventually, he'll realize that the girl he loves more than anything in the world is carrying his baby. Soon, you'll be talking about if it's a boy or a girl." A tear escapes from my eye and I quickly swipe it away. "He'll start getting excited about teaching his son to play football or locking away his daughter from all the other boys."

Quinn finally lets a laugh bubble up out of her mouth and she furiously wipes away her own tears. "It's too early," she whispers.

I reach my hand out and place it over her flat stomach. "He or she doesn't think so." She picks up the white stick that clearly has the word PREGNANT written on the digital screen. She gazes at it for a few more minutes, and I imagine her thinking about all the positive things this could bring her and Cole. It's crazy and totally insane to have a child right now; we're all so young. Our lives are just about to begin. Soon, we're going to be shoved out into the wild and forced to survive on our own. And Cole and Quinn are about to be shoved out and required to take care of this little person.

I'm jealous. I'm absolutely jealous. I push those feelings into the back of my mind and try to ease Quinn's fears as much as I can. Fortunately, the bar is beyond slow today, so I'm able to sit and talk with her for the rest of my shift.

As we walk out to the car, I pass her the keys. "You should drive; it's your car. How did you get here anyway?" I ask.

"Taxi," she laughs. "I was kind of desperate."

"I'd say. I'm surprised Cole didn't see you flying out the door."

"I've kind of . . . been hiding from him today," she states shyly.

"When do you think you'll tell him?" I question, while sliding into the passenger side.

"Can I wait till I'm in labor? That way, I'll be in so much pain, there's no way he can get mad," she laughs uncomfortably. I quirk up an eyebrow at her and she quickly adds, "I know. I know. I'll tell him soon. Just not tonight. I need a second to let this soak in."

"That's understandable."

"I know I was searching for Em, but I'm glad I ran into you today, Audrey. Thanks for talking me down," she states with a smile.

"Em will freak. Prepare yourself." I begin to cringe at the thought of our friend's impending reaction.

"Oh, I know she will. I think I wanted someone to freak out with me. But that wouldn't really have been helpful. This isn't just going to go away."

"You and Cole are going to be amazing. I'm so happy for you guys."

"You get to be an aunt," she exclaims. "You'll be his or her aunt, right, Audrey? I mean, you're in our little family now. You have to be."

"I hope so . . ." I whisper. "We'll see."

"Jace will tell Jaxon, and it'll all be okay." She pats my knee from across the center console. "All three of them have been close their entire lives. They're the most honorable guys I've ever met. Especially Jace. It's hard for him to break a promise, but I think there's an exception to everything. Jaxon will understand."

I decide to get ready at her apartment with her, and we don't talk anymore about Jace or babies or the future. Although there are still some enormous elephants in the room, it's fun to just laugh with someone and not worry about what may or may not happen in the next couple of hours.

JACE -

Max, Danny, and I decide to get to the beach early so we can help Mason hold down our regular spot for tonight. I don't know why I'm helping out that douchebag, though.

"Chill out, man. It's not like he tried to hit on her after he found out she was yours," Danny says to my grumbling.

"His hands were all over her. You'd feel differently if you saw your girl getting groped."

"I touched her. You gonna hate me too? I pulled her shirt up and laid my arm across her chest. You gonna be a pussy toward me as well?" Max jests, making me remember Audrey's tattoo experience all over again.

"Max . . ." I caution.

"You're way too easy today, man," he laughs, while jabbing me in the arm.

The party begins to grow as more and more people arrive with coolers in tow. Last year, Mason's party was massive and they held it at the Sig Alpha house. Since they were expecting even more this year, they decided to hold it down here so they wouldn't have to turn anyone away.

As the sun slowly sets, I watch Max and Danny attempt to surf the few waves we're getting today. It's getting dark, but I've seen these two surf when there's a full moon, like there is tonight. The light of the moon will cast a glow across the water and we will be able to see the currents clearly.

I wish Jaxon was here now so we could get this over with, but the football team is practicing late again. They were three points shy of losing the game last week due to turnovers, so Coach has been drilling them hard all week. Which means I should probably keep an eye on Em and Quinn, in addition to Audrey.

I've parked myself down in the sand by the fire pit with a clear view of the parking lot. It's the perfect spot to catch the first glimpse of Quinn, Em, and Audrey coming down the hill toward us. All of the girls here are in bikinis, but I didn't really put two and two together that Audrey would wear one as well. Sure enough, I can tell that underneath that halter top she has on, she's wearing a light blue suit. My mouth is already drooling at the thought of what she looks like in it, while my eyes are scanning the area for anyone else who might be checking her out.

"Hey, Jace!" Em calls out excitedly to me.

"Hey, girls," I return. "Hey, babe," I say, while looking directly at the only girl who has been able to fully capture my attention. "You look amazing," I quietly express.

"Hi," she softly replies. An easy smile hits her lips, and all I want to do is pull her down onto my lap. Instead, I pat the ground next to me, but before she can make her way over, Max and Danny run up with surfboards in hand and dripping wet.

"What's up, ladies?" Danny interrupts, giving each one a ridiculous wink.

"Come out with us," Max says. "It's amazing out there at night."

"I can't," Quinn quickly replies.

"Jaxon would flip," Em says and shrugs her shoulder.

"Um . . ." Audrey nervously shifts from one foot to the other and glances at me quickly before turning back to them. "I think I'm good here."

"Come on; no one's stopping you," Max pleads, like the asshole he is.

A few others join the group to talk to us, and Max is still looking at Audrey while she looks everywhere else.

Em looks down at me, then turns to Audrey and says, "You should go."

"Yeah, the whole way here you were talking about getting in the water," Quinn urges.

"No, really, I'm good. I'm sure the water is freezing and I just . . . shouldn't," Audrey states.

"Not a good reason, babe." With that, Max crouches down and throws Audrey over his shoulder. He has his surfboard in his opposite arm and he walks out toward the water without looking back.

As I watch his hands touch her skin, my blood begins to boil. I jump to my feet and shout, "Put her the fuck down!"

Max spins around with Audrey's ass in the air and says, "And why's that?" The cocky bastard is trying to push all of my buttons. If it had just been our little group, I would have said it. If Jaxon were here, I would have shouted it from the rooftops. In this moment, I want to yell to everyone here that she's off limits. But Jaxon's not here and there are too many observers that would get the news to him in less than five minutes.

I stand there breathing harshly, with everyone looking at me with confused expressions. All I can think about is the fact that

Max still has his hand on the back of my girl's thighs. He must have decided that I'm taking too long because, with an annoying laugh, he turns around and heads toward the surf again.

When he begins walking into the water, I hear Audrey shout something at him and then he slowly lowers her back to her feet. She steps quickly out of the water and back onto the sand. My heart rate increases, thinking she's coming back up here to me. I don't deserve for her to come back, but I'm vibrating with need.

She steps away from the tide and my mouth drops open when she begins to take off her shorts and halter-top. What's left behind is mouth-watering. Her long legs are on full display under the light-blue bikini. Her porcelain skin glows in the moonlight, and I'd be an idiot to think that every other guy here isn't thinking the same damn thing.

Timidly, she steps back into the ice-cold water of the Pacific, standing on her tiptoes. I know how cold that bitch is. Although the water on this coast rarely heats to a warm temperature, it doesn't seem to stop people like Max and Danny. Max is straddling his board in the water, calling for her to move faster. She shakes her head back and forth, lifting her legs out of the water with each step. Slowly, he starts to paddle his arms back over toward her.

When I realize she isn't coming back anytime soon, I drop back down in the sand to watch them. I see people sitting down around me and I sigh when I realize that one of them is Lane. Em and Quinn join me on the opposite side.

"Go ahead, dude. Lay into me," I breathe out in a defeated tone.

Lane chuckles and says, "I think this is torture enough for you."

We all watch as Max reaches Audrey's side with a huge grin on his face. He's having way too much damn fun out there. He stretches out for her hand and she glances back to the beach. At us.

At me. A short beat later, she turns to look back at him and he pulls her onto his board to straddle it in front of him.

"She wanted you to say something." Em's brilliant observation rubs me the wrong way.

"No fucking kidding?" I grumble back.

"Watch it . . ." Lane warns. Why is he being protective over *her* now?

"I was going to say something. Shit, if Jax had been here, I would have. But I don't need the gossip crew to get to him first. He needs to hear it from me." I pull my knees up and put my head in my hands. "Why the hell has this been so hard for me to tell him?"

"Because you don't want to hurt your brother, Jace," Quinn says. I always knew she was my favorite. "Plus, Em hasn't been sharing well lately," she adds, giggling.

"I get it, I get it! I promise, I'll let him out to play more often," Em cries, throwing her hands up in mock defeat. "Jace, you know he'll understand," she adds.

Max tries to lay Audrey's back up against his chest, but she slips out of it and turns to face him. *Good girl.* The two look at each other while straddling the board and talk as if they're old friends. The girls beside me chat good-humoredly about all of the places Em and Jaxon have been sneaking off to, while Lane and I glare out at the water.

"Do you love her?" Lane asks out of the blue. If I hadn't already been sitting down, his question would have knocked me clear on my ass. I continue staring forward. "Okay, new question. Who was your last girlfriend?"

"Uh . . . Mandy," I reply.

"No, it wasn't. Mandy was before Claire," Quinn chimes in.

"Whatever, same difference. They were back-to-back," I say in a clipped tone.

"Hey, remember when Tatum was trying to rub her huge rack on your arm earlier tonight? What color was her shirt?" Lane asks.

"Tatum was trying to do what on my arm?" I am completely confused by his line of questioning.

While nodding his head, he continues, "You know when Audrey does that nasty ankle-popping thing?"

"Nasty? Dude, have you ever looked at her face when she's doing that? It's fucking adorable," I laugh.

"And there you have it, ladies and gentlemen. The man is hooked," Lane bellows out mockingly while clapping and whistling.

"Huh?" I reply. With wide eyes, I turn to frown at Quinn and Em, who are laughing their asses off.

"You're totally in love with her!" Em laughs.

"Dude, you're already forgetting about your exes; you don't even notice when a hot chick, annoying or not, rubs her tits on your freakin' arm. I'm gonna need your man card back for that one, by the way." He gestures with an open palm toward me. "And to top it off, you find Audrey's irritating quirks adorable. Besides crazy, there ain't any other word for it. You're in love," Lane states matter-of-factly. He pounds me on the back and grips my shoulder tightly. "Oh, and by the way, you break her heart, I'll break your neck. Welcome to the family, bro! Can't get rid of me now," he says in an annoyingly cheerful voice, all while I'm stunned to silence.

I've always wondered why guys go on the defensive when they're told this piece of news about themselves. If you feel it, own up to it! But I'm starting to realize the weight this kind of information can have on someone. No one wants to be surprised with the fact that they are now completely vulnerable to another person. Now, whether you like it or not, you have to trust that this person won't hand you your heart back in a million tiny, abused pieces.

I've always wanted to be here. I've watched my two best friends arrive at this very moment, the one where they realize that the girl they're with is *the one*. But now that I'm here, can I handle it? Can I hand myself over, raw and unguarded? But if I don't give my heart to Audrey, would there ever be anybody else worth it? Hell, no.

Quickly, I scramble up to my feet, grab Danny's discarded board, and head out to the chilly ocean. I remove my shirt along the way, leaving my black shorts on. Quinn, Em, and Lane clap, hoot, and holler behind me excitedly, but I leave all thoughts of them behind in the damn sand.

I have to get this off of my chest now. Audrey isn't the type of girl to wait around for anyone; she's strong and she makes her own happiness. If she wants a bouquet of roses, she's sure as hell not going to wait for me to give it to her. She'll go out and plant her own fucking garden.

The patience and tolerance she's shown by waiting for me to tell Jaxon have been astounding. She hasn't complained once, and I have no doubt that most girls would have nagged me daily, although sometimes I was so caught up in her that I honestly forgot about telling Jax, and maybe if she had nagged a little bit we wouldn't be here right now.

Walking across the sand, I watch her floating on Max's board with her head thrown back in laughter. I know she didn't come out here to make me jealous; that's just not how she is. She came to this party to have fun and she wasn't going to wait for her pussy boyfriend to man up. She went out and had her own fun. Damn it, it's true. I do love this girl.

When I hit the water, I cringe at the subzero temperature. I jump under the waves to get the initial shock over with and swim with the board toward my girl. She and Max have drifted down-shore a bit and Max is currently in the water, slowly kicking them back to where they started. Audrey has her feet on the board and she's hugging her knees while listening to him talk.

I feel uneasy about him taking her out into the water at night. I've heard that even the strongest swimmers can get thrown off by where the coast is and they can't see how far out they've gone. But Max is only a couple feet out and I can still touch the bottom. He spots me before she does, and the asshole smiles and nods his head in my direction. Audrey slowly turns, a curious look on her face, but when she see that it's me coming for her, her mouth drops open in a wide gape.

"Babe, you've gotta be freezing," I say when I reach them.

"It's not that bad, pansy," Max jests. "Just take my board; she's already on it."

"Thanks, man," I say, while switching over to the board Audrey is perched on top of. After I pass Danny's board to Max, I loop the leash around my wrist and secure it so I can't lose the board.

"We'll draw up that tattoo here pretty soon. I'll catch ya later, babe." He winks at her and quickly moves toward the shore before I can punch him for calling her "babe" again.

"Another tattoo?" I eye her questioningly. Then I lift my body up onto the board and she clenches the sides tightly to balance herself.

She shrugs her shoulders at my question and sheepishly replies, "I just wanted a little one right along here." I watch as she drags her finger lengthways on the collarbone of her left shoulder.

Slowly, I lean forward and kiss the line she just drew. "Mmm, I like it here," my voice vibrates into her skin.

"Jace . . ." she whispers breathlessly.

I lean back and look into her eyes. I'm fucking scared to death to tell her what I need to say. There's so much that could go wrong here. If she doesn't say it back, how will I handle that? Jax went months telling Em he loved her before she could say it in return. I never heard him complain, but I think the bastard was just thankful she agreed to date him exclusively.

With Audrey, it's different. She doesn't hold back her feelings. If she isn't able to reciprocate what I'm saying, it's because she truly doesn't feel it and that just sounds painful. My eyes search her face for the answer. I feel like it's written clear as day all over her gorgeous features, but maybe I'm misinterpreting what I see.

"Audrey, I need you to say it."

"Say what?" she asks slowly.

"Say what's written all over your face. Say what's on your fingers every time you touch me. Say what's in your eyes every morning that we wake up together. Say what your body feels every time I'm inside of you. Please . . . just say it." My voice is barely above a whisper, but judging by the expression on her face, she heard every word I said.

Her head begins to shake back and forth, and an emotion I'm not familiar with engulfs her eyes. My heart plummets because this is exactly what I was afraid of. I've already come too far, though, to go back now.

"No, Audrey," I say, a bit too harsh. "You love me. I know you do. I may have gone about this whole relationship all wrong with you and I know my life seems to be pulling me in a thousand different directions, but I *know*, with everything I have, that you feel it." I reach my hand out and cover her heart, feeling the rapid thumping. "Baby, I love you too."

Her eyes widen and she quickly looks back and forth between the people on the shore and me. Emotions are flying across her face, but no words are coming out her mouth.

I grab her chin gently and look into her golden brown eyes. "Focus on me, babe. Forget them." I reach out and squeeze her upper arm three times, and with each squeeze I say the words, "I. Love. You."

That must have been all she needed because before I can steady myself, she launches her body across the board into my chest.

Together, we crash into the water while holding on to one another tightly. Fortunately, we haven't drifted too far out because I can still stand in this depth.

She squeezes me with all of her strength, wrapping her arms around my neck and burying her head into the nook of my shoulder. I tuck her legs around my waist and laugh at her reaction.

"Okay, now I'm really confused," I say into her ear. Audrey pulls back from her death grip and looks me in the eye. Her smile steals the breath from my chest and I want to freeze this moment. No going forward, no going back. I want to stay right in this moment forever with her.

Her teeth begin to chatter from the cold, so with her clinging to my body, I slowly walk us back to the shore. Thankfully, the board is still attached to my wrist, or I'd have to go hunt it down. I step out of the water while holding her up. I don't have to work too hard because she's clinging to me as if I'm planning on going somewhere without her. I drag the board farther up the beach so it can't get washed away with the incoming tide and release the leash from my wrist.

With my hands holding her ass, I sit down in the sand with her on my lap. The second I hit the ground, her lips slam against mine in a hungry kiss. I grab hold of her head and enthusiastically return the ravishing. She lets a moan slip from deep inside and I eagerly search her mouth with my tongue.

We sink farther and farther until I'm lying on my back in the sand and she's perched on top of me. She pushes up, her hands on my chest, and I love seeing her breathing erratically with so much lust in her eyes. The full moon glowing behind her creates a halo effect, perfectly showcasing my angel.

"God, you're beautiful," I whisper. "I love you so much." My hands are still wrapped up in her hair and slowly I move them up to her scalp, so I can pull her back down to me.

She tugs back from my movement and whispers uncertainly, "You're the second person ever to tell me that."

Quickly, I flip her over on to her back and glare into her eyes. "Who the hell was the first? You're definitely the first girl I've ever said that to."

My stomach clenches. I don't know why it bothers me that she could have loved someone before me, but it does. We've talked about our past relationships, pretty much every single one of them, and I sure as hell don't remember her saying she loved any of those bastards. I hover over her, waiting for her answer.

She eyes me with nervousness and a little confusion. "Lane was the first."

We both stare at each other, trying to figure out what the other is thinking. Then it clicks, and I dread the question I need to ask. "Wait, are you talking about all kinds of love? You mean, even when you were a kid, no one told you they loved you?"

"Who would have done it?" she asks with an almost childlike innocence.

I'm struck speechless, because even after all of our late-night talks about our childhoods, I never put it together that no one loved this girl. The selfish part of me wonders if she'd had a different childhood, would she be here in my arms right now? But a bigger part of me would rather her have grown up feeling the love she deserved.

"You deserved it, baby. Just know that. You deserved someone to love you every single day," I say, while cupping her face. She stares deep into my eyes and I can see her searching for the words to say.

I try to let her off the hook and say the first thing that comes to mind. "You know, I watched Jax tell Em he loved her for months, never hearing a reply. I used to wonder how hard that was on him. How painful that must be. But now I understand that when you love someone, as much as you would kill to hear it back, you also just want them to know. I'll give you all the time you need, babe. I just need you to know how I feel about you," I say. And it's true. I don't feel pain or anger about not hearing it back. Just relief to finally have that out in the open.

Quickly, she pulls the back of my head toward her and says, "I don't need time, Jace. I've been crazy about you since the day you picked me up off the sidewalk. I think I've loved you since you gave me my penny." I watch as she clutches the copper coin dangling from her neck. "I love you too . . . so much."

The words are a choked bubble in my throat, so I mouth them to her while squeezing her. *I love you.*

She looks down at my hand that keeps gripping her arm. "You've done this three-squeeze-thing before. I remember you did it that night we hooked up in Texas. You also did it that night out on the beach when I told you and Jaxon what happened to me. What does it mean?"

"First of all, stop calling what we did a 'hookup.' It sounds too fleeting. Second of all, I honestly don't know where it came from. I just had all of these emotions toward you that I didn't know how to convey out loud. I guess it means I." *Squeeze.* "Love." *Squeeze.* "You." *Squeeze.*

"I'm not sure what I did to deserve you," she whispers.

"That's funny, because I've been wondering the same thing about myself."

She still has my face in between her soft hands, but I push forward to capture her lips. My hands slowly graze down her body, and when I feel more skin than clothing, I remember where we are. Out in public. Audrey is still wearing her skimpy bikini and I'm sure as hell tired of the admiring eyes.

Still holding her, I quickly stand up before setting her down on her bare feet. She whimpers when our lips part and I smirk at her eagerness.

"Soon, babe," I whisper on her lips. "But for now, you need clothes and I need to have that talk with my brother."

"My suit is still wet; I can't put my clothes on now," she replies.

We help each other dust the sand off of our backs. When I'm extra thorough wiping off her perfect ass, she giggles and shoves me away.

"If you're not putting any clothes on, then neither will I," I declare. Her eyes quickly scan my wet body, licking a trail of heat from my head to my toes. "I mean . . . you're practically naked. It's only fair . . ."

Slowly, I start to undo the top button of my shorts and her eyes widen. When I pull my zipper slowly down, her hand moves but she doesn't stop me or say anything. I hook my thumbs underneath my waistband and begin to drag my shorts deliberately down my hips. I wait for the moment she realizes I'm going commando, and that moment does *not* disappoint.

"Jace!" she gasps with bulging eyes, reaching for my waistband. Quickly, she pulls them back to my hips, and then hurriedly rehooks the button and yanks the zipper back into place. "You win! You win! I'll go grab my clothes."

I throw my head back, laughing, and smack her ass to get her moving. "Hurry. I'll meet you back at the fire pits."

She starts slowly running away and turns back to holler, "Love you!"

I smile like a damn Cheshire cat and call back, "Love you more."

- FIFTEEN -

AUDREY -

As I jog back to where I dropped my clothes earlier, I feel as if my feet are floating a few seconds longer in the air. My body feels lighter than it ever has before. I remember the first time Lane told me he loved me. To have that kind of connection with another person is a necessity in every human's life. I had no idea what I was missing until I was loved.

But to be loved by your significant other . . . to be loved on a soul-deep level is an amazing thing. To have someone cherish your mind and your body is beyond anything I ever imagined. Some people never find it and some walk right past it. We almost missed this opportunity, and what a shame that would have been. Hearing those words pass through his lips will forever be ingrained in my memory.

When I reach my clothes, I quickly pull my shorts up, put my shirt on, and tie the halter back around my neck. I catch sight of my phone in the sand, realizing it must have fallen out of my pocket. I dust it off and check the time. My heart beats wildly when I notice twenty-three missed calls. Why would anyone need to call me that many times?

Quickly, I unlock it and see that they are all from Cole, and all were made within the last twenty minutes. I slide my finger across his name and hold the phone up to my ear as I begin walking back toward the party.

"Please fucking tell me you're with everyone!" Cole shouts into the phone.

"I'm with everyone," I quickly say back. "Cole? What's going on?"

Jace is standing around talking to Lane, Quinn, and Em as I walk toward them, but I must have a frightened look on my face because he begins to quickly stride in my direction.

"It's Jaxon. Fuck!" Cole yells in a panicked tone through the phone. He continues yelling and mumbling, but I can't make out a word he's saying.

"What's going on? You need to slow down, Cole."

"Why doesn't anyone have their damn phones?" His voice hasn't calmed down and I'm slowly starting to panic at his tone.

"What. Is. Going. On?" I say loudly and as clearly as I possibly can.

"Jaxon got hurt at practice," he says, but it's difficult to hear because there's a lot of commotion and electronic beeping in the background of wherever he is. "I'm in the fucking ambulance with him, Audrey!" His speech begins to slow down and I hear a hitch in his breathing, almost as if he is crying or on the verge of it. "He's not waking up. They can't get him to wake up!"

My hand flies to my mouth to cover the gasp. "Oh God! Where are you, Cole?" I shout.

The second I yell his name I have everyone's full attention. I repeat Cole's words out loud, "UCLA Medical Center."

"The hospital?" Quinn asks in a confused tone. "What's wrong with Cole?" she cries in panic.

Cole continues yelling in my ear. I have four sets of eyes on me that want more information, and I still don't know what is going on.

"It's Jaxon," I whisper.

"Give me the phone, Audrey," Jace bites out harshly.

"Jaxon's hurt," I continue.

Em's whole body locks up and the red plastic cup she's holding slips from her hand, crashing to the ground and causing a wild splash at our feet. Jace lets out a string of curses and takes off at a dead sprint toward the parking lot. Sand flies out from under his feet in his hasty departure.

Once it clicks, the rest of us look at each other and start to run for our cars as well. At the same time we reach the parking lot, Jace's black Camaro is roaring out onto the main road.

"Girls. In my car. Now. None of you are driving," Lane calls toward us.

Thank God for him, because I don't think we even remember where we had parked, let alone how to start the car. We swiftly scramble into his black SUV, and Lane peels out in the same direction Jace is headed.

"Audrey, what did Cole say?" Em's small voice asks from the backseat.

"He didn't tell me much. I think we should wait until we get there to find out everything from a doctor," I respond, trying to delay her.

"I just need to know what he said."

I let out a sigh. "The only thing he told me was that Jaxon got hurt at practice and that . . . they couldn't get him to wake up . . ."

I turn back in time to see her flinch and grab on to Quinn's hand tightly. Lane softly curses and continues trying to drive as fast as he can without getting us pulled over. It takes thirty excruciatingly long minutes to get to the hospital. I can't even begin to imagine everything that is running through Em's head in that amount of time.

Lane pulls up to the drop-off to let us out, and I spot Jace's Camaro parked haphazardly in a fire lane near the emergency room entrance. Quinn, Em, and I hop out and they rush inside. Lane steps out and finds an employee staring in irritation at the Camaro. When he sees Lane begin to leave his car, he starts shaking his head and telling him he needs to move it immediately.

"Chill, I'm going inside. I'm gonna get my buddy's keys and I'll move both cars. Calm down," he says, in a tone that doesn't allow any argument.

I'm the last of my friends to enter the emergency room, and the scene is overwhelming to take in. I immediately spot my boyfriend's large frame towering over the receptionist. I can only imagine what she's thinking as he growls out commands at her. She probably doesn't know whether to cry or slip him her number for later.

Lane walks up and grabs Jace's keys from his pocket without even a sideways glance from him. Jace isn't paying attention to anything besides getting to where his brother is.

JACE -

"Jaxon Riley," I repeat for what feels like the hundredth time to the brainless girl at the front counter. "He's my brother. We look exactly alike. Can't miss him. He was brought in by . . . ambulance." I swallow the last word painfully.

"I'm not seeing a Jaxon here."

"Well try again, ma'am! Jaxon Riley. J-A-X-O-N . . ." I begin to spell harshly.

"Oh! Jaxon with an X. Well, that's different," she says nonchalantly and continues typing another million fucking words into her computer.

"Look, I hate to be a tyrant but I need to be back there. Like, yesterday. Just open those doors and I can find him on my own."

She continues typing away, ignoring my words. I'm sure she's heard this a thousand times before, but this time is different. This is my brother. This is my identical twin. The only person who has been through everything with me.

"Well, since you're family, I need you to fill out all of his medical information on this clipboard. Bring it back when you're done and I'll go see if they're allowing him to have visitors," she says, passing me a stack of papers.

"*Allowing* visitors?" I shout. "This isn't a prison! Look, I can fill out this paperwork back there with him. This is my brother we're talking about. I. Need. Back. There."

She ignores my rant and taps the clipboard infuriatingly. Before I can hurl the board across the fucking emergency room, Em squeezes in front of me and grabs it out of my hands.

"I can fill this out. If you could hurry and find out where he is, I would appreciate it." She smiles easily at the lady and I'm confounded by her calmness.

Em grabs on to my arm and digs her nails in deep. "My goal is to see Jaxon as soon as possible. I think we share a common goal here. I'm also pretty sure your mama taught you that you can catch more flies with honey. Quit being a bastard. If you piss her off and make me have to wait out here one second longer than I have to, so help me God, I *will* rip you limb from limb," she growls in a low voice to me and stomps off to fill out my brother's medical forms.

With nowhere else to go, I begin pacing the tile in front of the door that leads to the patients. If someone would just open this damn door, I could breathe a little easier. I pull out my phone and cringe at all of the missed calls from Cole. I can't believe I didn't have this on me. I tried calling him about fifteen times on my way over here, but he never answered.

My brother is somewhere back there, hurt or even worse . . . fuck, I can't think like that. He's back there and this fucking metal door is keeping me from seeing if he's okay. Small hands graze across my lower back and I flinch away from the touch. I'm strung too tightly and I can't handle soft words or pitying looks at the moment. Audrey calls out my name as I walk away in the opposite direction. Away from her. Shit, I can't think straight.

I lean my forehead against the wall and think about what I can do. Suddenly, the door opens and a nurse comes out. Evidently she's not new at this because she quickly shuts the door behind her. She glances around the room and does a double take when her eyes land on me. I can see the shock on her face and immediately know that she has to be Jaxon's nurse.

"Are you Jaxon Riley's brother?" she asks.

"Twin," I hastily spit out. The others quickly come over to join me.

"I can take you back there, but I can't let you see him yet. There's an additional waiting room for family members. That's as close as I can get you. You can wait there for a doctor to give you more information," she instructs. "Wow, you guys are a big group. I'm technically only allowed to let four of you in."

"I'll hang back here," Lane volunteers. Well, it sure as hell wasn't going to be me.

"Nice to hear you're claiming the twin-thing again, Jace. Not such a drag anymore, is it?" Em bites out at me as she pushes past to follow the nurse. *Ouch.* I'd take everything I said back if I could.

Quickly, we all file in behind her and my eyes dart to each door along the way, seeing if I can catch a glimpse of my brother.

We round a second corner at the end of the hall, where I see Cole sitting on the ground with his back against the wall and his face in his hands. My stomach plummets as I pick up my pace toward him.

From behind, I hear Quinn gasp, "Cole." Even though it was only a whisper, he was still able to hear her voice, and his head shoots up to look at us. I hate how fucking stressed he looks and how red his eyes are. What does that mean? How bad is this going to be?

"Wait right here in this room," the nurse says, pointing to the room next to Cole. "Ah, now there are five of you. I'll try to let you all stay, but they may send one of you out front."

"Your mom's on a flight already," Cole's ragged voice announces when we all enter the tiny prison they call a waiting room.

"That was fast," I say.

"No, it wasn't. I feel like I've been here for ten fucking years already," he mutters, while frantically running his hands through his hair.

Quinn finally reaches him and wraps her arms around his body, burying her face into his side. He grabs on to her tightly and hides his face in her hair. We all watch as he sucks in a deep breath. Em takes a seat, bouncing her legs uncontrollably while looking at the two of them. Out of the corner of my eye, I can see Audrey standing against the wall by the door. And I'm lost in the middle.

"Tell us," Em begs Cole.

"We were running a play. It was the last one before Coach was planning to dismiss us. At the snap, Jax shot down the side and cut to the middle just like he was supposed to. Fisher tossed a perfect spiral and it practically dropped out of thin air into Jaxon's arms. It was flawless. The only thing wrong was that the defenders were expecting it this time so they ran in front of him. Jax got blocked in, so he ran and tried to leap over them into the end zone. Midair someone clipped his legs and he spun at an odd angle headfirst into the ground." Cole grabs the bridge of his nose and shakes his head back and forth.

"It was awful. The second he hit the ground his whole body went limp. When I got to him, his eyes were closed. He was breathing but we just couldn't wake him. Coach broke out the smelling salts but nothing happened."

The room remains silent as everyone begins to let Cole's story soak in. I've seen Jax jump into the end zone more times than I can remember. He's leaped over defenders' heads and even done a flip or two to get the touchdown. We've all jumped and cheered watching him go to incredible lengths to get those extra points on the scoreboard. Except this time, one wrong hit and he crashes down on his head.

Everyone eventually finds a spot in the room as we sit to wait out the news. Em claims the chair closest to the door. She pulls her feet up and rests her chin on top of her knees. Her eyes never leave the door, almost as if they are trying to will the doctor to enter. Quinn fell asleep in Cole's lap—he was already stretched out across the length of three chairs—shortly after we arrived. Audrey parks herself next to the only window in the room and gazes outside the entire time. Her bathing suit is still wet and has soaked through her clothes. I catch her shivering slightly.

I alternate between pacing the room and sticking my head out the door, just to remind people that we are still here waiting for any piece of news. No one speaks and no one dares to leave the room. Hours pass, three to be exact, before a man in a white coat enters the waiting area and looks around at everyone.

When he finally sees me, he falters a step backward. "Wow, it's strange to see you after working on Jaxon for so long."

"Working on him?" I quickly inquire.

"I'm sorry. I'm Dr. Graham. You are related to Jaxon Riley, correct?"

"Yes, sir."

"Would you like to step out in the hall to speak?" he questions, while looking at all the eyes peering up at him.

I look down and see Em's anxious face and shake my head, "They're all here for him as well. You can say it here."

"All right, then. Your brother endured what appears to be a mild traumatic brain injury. We ran almost every test possible and I'm optimistic at his outcome. You need to know that he *is* comatose at the moment. The scans of his brain do show signs of mild swelling, so we need to just give him time to heal. I don't believe we need to take any drastic measures at the moment."

"Just give him time? That's all we can do?" I ask roughly.

"We'll continue to monitor him closely and let his body do the repairing," Dr. Graham calmly replies.

"How long could he be in a coma, Doctor?" Em requests from her chair, her hands gripping the armrests tightly.

"Everyone reacts differently to a brain injury, so I'm sorry to say we don't know at this point. He's rating average on the GCS . . ."

"GCS?" Cole asks.

"Glasgow Coma Scale," I answer quickly.

"Nice job. Are you in the medical field?" Dr. Graham questions.

"Not anymore. When can we see him?" I ask, not missing the slight gasp Em lets slip. Shit, I forgot I hadn't told her about dropping premed.

"We need to run a few more tests. His motor skills are responding to pain." When I flinch, he hastily adds, "That's a good sign. We'll make sure he doesn't have any additional discomfort, but it's part of assessing his brain activity. I just want you guys to prepare yourselves. Even though a coma simply means he's unconscious, he could be like this for a few more hours, days, weeks . . . if it goes further than that, we'll reevaluate our options. "

When no one says anything else, Dr. Graham continues, "He's breathing on his own and showing pupillary responses to light. Give him time; I have high hopes for him. From what I heard of the fall, it could have been much worse. He doesn't have any broken bones or damage to his spinal cord. We'll take this one day at a time. Just be there for him, but make sure you're still taking care of yourselves."

He leans over to shake my hand and lets me know he'll send in a nurse when we can go see Jax. I sink to floor beneath the weight of his words and cover my face with my hands. My brother is in a coma. Unconscious. Comatose.

- SIXTEEN -

AUDREY *-*

My heart breaks as I watch Jace's body gradually slide down the wall. His brother is beyond his best friend. He's spent almost every moment of his life with him. Seeing as I've spent my whole life craving to have just one person slightly care about me, I can't imagine what even a fraction of his sadness must feel like. But now I'm starting to see why Em tried to push people away from her. You can't miss what you never had.

I make my way toward Jace slowly and sink down next to him. He doesn't acknowledge me at all. I know I shouldn't be hurt by his coldness toward me, but after everything we've been through, I would have hoped he'd let me be here for him during hard times. I grab his thigh and he flinches but doesn't move. I squeeze three times, hoping he'll know what I mean and that I'm here for him. That I'll help him any way I can. He doesn't respond; instead he just lays his head on his knees and breathes in roughly.

The room is silent for a while until Cole's phone chimes, shaking us all from our individual thoughts. I watch as he pulls it out of his pocket and reads the screen.

"Jace, man, your mom grabbed a taxi. She should be here soon," he announces.

"We're pushing our limit of visitors. You should head home, Audrey," Jace says in a lifeless voice.

"I want to stay with you, babe. I need to be here for you," I whisper.

"Quinn and I can wait in the main lobby," Cole offers.

"Yeah, it's okay, Jace," Quinn adds.

"Please, just leave." Jace looks directly at me. "I don't want the drama right now. With you being here. With my mom and my brother. I can't deal with any of it," he replies coldly.

"Jace, I'm sure it'll be fine that she's here," Em interrupts in a flat tone. She doesn't even glance in our direction, just continues staring at the closed door.

"While I was playing in the ocean, my brother was riding in an ambulance. To the hospital, Audrey! I'd rather just be with my *family* right now."

His words slice through me like a knife, and it's as if I'm bleeding out right here for all of our friends to see. "Playing? Is that what we were doing?" I ask quietly.

"Don't twist my words," he cautions.

"I'm not twisting your words, Jace. I'm *repeating* them." I stand up and look down at where he sits on the floor. He's hurting. I can understand that, but this is just cruel.

Instantly, his arm swings back and he slams his closed fist into the wall behind him. "Leave!" His shout echoes throughout our little waiting room and I jolt a step away from him. Without another glance in his direction, I push through the door and launch myself out into the cold, dim hallway.

"Was that really the best fucking way you could have handled that?" Cole bellows out behind the closed door.

"I can't believe you just did that," I hear Quinn stammer.

When there's no answer, Cole continues, "I had no idea there was something going on between the two of you, but she didn't deserve that. I don't even know who the hell you are right now."

"If Jaxon doesn't make it through this, *I* won't even know who the hell I am!" Jace growls back.

"Shut up, Jace!" I hear Em yell. "Just shut up. Don't you dare say that again. *When* Jaxon makes it through this, *when*. There's no *if*. That's not an option," she says in an angry tone. Before she can even finish, I hear a loud thud against the wall and a frustrated groan follows. I decide to leave now before Jace punches holes in every wall of this hospital. As I quickly stride down the hallway, the nurse we met before steps out of a room and props the door open so she can wheel a cart out.

Inside, I can see Jaxon lying on a bed. He has cords, tubes, wires, and machines hooked up to him. He looks perfectly healthy, almost as if he were only taking a nap. Everyone in that waiting room down the hall is anxious to see him, and little do they know he's only two doors away.

Quinn pushes through the door and looks around frantically. When she spots me, she quickly advances in my direction. A second later, Cole pops his head out of the door and calls out to Quinn.

"I'll be right back," she calls, waving him off.

"Okay, babe. Just hurry, please," he says with desperation. "You okay, pretty girl?" he asks me. I shrug my shoulders noncommittally. "Hang in there," he adds before disappearing back into the waiting room.

I stay at Jaxon's door, staring into his room. Willing him to wake up. This group needs him. I just don't know how they would make it if they lost him. When Quinn reaches me, I hear her slight intake of breath.

"Oh, Jaxon . . ." she whispers with deep sadness.

"He looks perfectly fine, like he's just napping," I tell her. The nurse squeezes past us and I try to stop her before she leaves. "Excuse me, when can they see him? We've been here for hours, and I'm sure you can imagine how painful this is for his family not being able to be by his side."

She shucks off her gloves and cleans her hands with the sanitizer that's mounted outside of his door. "Well . . . technically I'm supposed to check a few more things, but I guess I can do that with them in here. I'm sure they're worrying."

"Thank you. We really appreciate it," I say with a smile.

"Thanks." Quinn squeezes my arm. "He'll realize what he just did. He needs you here." She points with her thumb back toward the room. I shake my head back and forth, not wanting to talk about the way Jace just delivered my shattered heart back to me on a silver platter.

"When do you plan on telling Cole he's going to be a daddy?" I ask, rubbing her stomach.

She sighs and replaces my hand with hers when I move away. "I was going to do it tonight after we went to bed, but I can't do it now. Hopefully this guy," she points at Jaxon, "plans on waking up soon so I can tell everyone."

"Understandable. Just know that I'm happy for you. You guys are going to be wonderful parents."

"Don't talk like that, Audrey. You're speaking as if we aren't going to see each other again. You aren't going anywhere. You two aren't done," she states adamantly, grabbing hold of my hand.

I don't know what is going to happen anymore. A few hours ago, I was so sure of everything. Now the wind has been taken out my sails. I can understand worrying and being in pain, but this was a side of Jace I've never seen before. And I hate that at the first sign of distress, he shoved me away. I squeeze Quinn's hand with a sad smirk and walk away without a word. There is nothing left to be said. Now all I can do is hope Jaxon makes it through this.

I race to the emergency room waiting area to try and beat the tears that are threatening to come. I just need to find Lane so I can go home. When I hit the double doors, I stumble out in my haste. Moving farther away from Jace is physically excruciating. I know he's in pain. All I want to do is hold his hand, but that's the last thing he wants from me. I can hardly breathe by the time I see Lane, who is sitting in a chair facing the doors. When he finally spots me, he charges toward me and catches me before I can crash to my knees.

"Doll?" he gasps. "No . . . no . . . is it Jaxon?"

"No, yes. No. He's alive. I just need to get out of here," I blurt out.

"I need you to tell me what's wrong first, love."

"Jace doesn't want me here."

His voice flattens and in a deadly calm tone he asks, "Why do you say that?"

"I just want to go home, Lane."

He wraps his arm around my shoulders and half-leads, half-carries me out of the ER. As we exit the sliding doors, I hear him mumble under his breath, "I'm going to kill that asshole . . ."

JACE -

When Quinn leaves the room shortly after Audrey, no one speaks to me. I don't blame them. But right now I could give a fuck because all I can think about right now is my brother. In the corner of my eye, I see Cole get up to comfort Em and ask if she needs anything. Em isn't talking to any of us, though—not unless it's about Jax.

I begin to pace the room. We're all getting antsy waiting in this stupid, depressing, cream-colored room. How can they ask people to sit in here for so long? It really is a prison, except that they know you won't leave, so bars aren't necessary. The door finally opens and all three of us immediately look to see who's coming in. When it's only Quinn, Em and I let out a deflated breath.

Cole rushes over to her and she squeezes him tightly, kisses his cheek, and then pushes off him.

"Audrey convinced the nurse to let us in to see him," she murmurs, while making her way back to the door.

"Oh, thank God. I knew I loved that girl." Em quickly rushes out into the hallway.

"Is she still out there?" I ask. At this point, I don't know if I'm asking because I don't want to see her or because I hope she didn't really leave.

Quinn rolls her eyes and pushes by me. "Don't worry, she followed your orders." *Ouch.* I shadow behind and with every step, my heart beats louder in my chest. What will he look like? I've never seen someone in a coma before. Will he look like he's hurt or sick? I'm not sure I can stomach the idea of seeing my brother like this.

Anytime he's sick, I'm always right there next to him, feeling all of the same symptoms. This whole night I've been waiting for our freaky twin vibe to kick in. Give me a headache or any kind of pain. Give me something that lets me feel connected to him. I feel nothing. Absolutely nothing. I feel as if I've lost him. I can't believe I ever complained about being a twin. I never wanted this.

Two doors away from the waiting room, we walk into Jaxon's large, noisy room. There are machines beeping and people talking. They all sound far away, as if I am standing at one end of a tunnel and my brother is lying unconscious at the other end. Em holds his hand and drapes herself across him with her head on his chest. He would like that. He would want her next to him as much as possible. Cole snags a chair, pulls Quinn onto his lap, and they both stare at him. I'm pretty sure we're all staring at him and thinking the same thing. *Wake up. Please man, just wake up. I'll give up everything I have, if you'll just wake up.*

My mom eventually comes barreling in the room, dragging her suitcase and bags. Shit, I should have gone and gotten her. She didn't need to lug all of her stuff around. But I don't even know where my car is at the moment. It probably got towed from the hospital entrance. And Jaxon's truck . . . is still at the stadium, where he left it. Fuck, I hate this shit.

"Oh, my poor baby," Mom cries from the doorway.

She rushes to Jaxon's bedside, across from where Em is sitting, and hugs him while patting Em on the back. Mom's little body can barely reach around his larger one, but she manages to squeeze as much of herself around him as possible. Not exactly easy since Em still hasn't moved her head from Jaxon's chest. I keep hearing her speak to him quietly, but I haven't been able to decipher what she's saying.

This can't be good for her, though. Em's reason for not letting anyone get close to her in the first place was due to the fact that she was afraid of them either cheating or dying. Just another reason Jaxon has to make it through this. He would be leaving behind too many unsalvageable pieces.

"Cole, bless your heart. Thank you for calling me, darling boy," Mom weeps and pulls him in for a smothering hug. Shortly after we got in here, Quinn passed out on his lap again. Cole tries to hold on to his girlfriend and hug my mom at the same time. Mom just pats her on the head and whispers a few more sentiments to him.

She makes her way back to the hospital bed and wraps herself around Em. "Oh, you poor soul. I'm so sorry this is happening to you." She runs her fingers through Em's golden hair and kisses her on the cheek. These two have gotten incredibly close this past year.

I often hear Em on the phone with her, and anytime I'm talking to Mom, she always asks about my dating life and then how Em is doing.

Without raising her head, I hear Em's upbeat voice pronounce, "It's fine. He's going to be fine. He wouldn't just leave like this. He just needs time. He's fine." There's something off about her tone. Something too cheery. It's almost as if she's trying to convince herself more than us.

Mom whispers in her ear and then turns and finally faces me. She opens her arms and says, "Come here, Jace. You aren't handling this well, are you?" I don't say anything because I can't cry in front of everyone. I just move into her arms and lift her up in a hug. "He'll be okay, love," she whispers in my ear.

~

The next three days float by like this, all of us just sitting around staring at Jaxon's eyelids. Coach comes by a couple of times each day to check on his progress. Players from his team filter in and out. Quinn and Cole decide to continue attending classes, so they come by before and after. I haven't spoken to Em and she hasn't said anything to me. I know my mom can feel the tension in the room, but thankfully she hasn't asked about it.

On Wednesday, Max knocks on the door and steps inside. Em doesn't even lift her head from Jaxon's chest. When she's up, she's unusually cheery and perky. She floats around the room, cleaning and straightening items that don't need it. I've yet to see her look upset, and she hasn't even cried. I'm not sure if that's healthy. Aren't girls supposed to cry at times like this? But pushing away the people you love isn't exactly healthy either. Audrey . . . fuck, I miss her.

"Hey, man, how's it going?" Max asks, while handing me two to-go bags from a local fast-food joint.

"Same," I pinch out.

"His scans are looking better. The swelling has gone down a bit," Mom elaborates for me.

"Damn, that's good news," he breathes out. He looks over at Em and offers a sympathetic look in her direction. "So, where's Audrey?" he asks me directly.

Fuck.

My mom's head whips around to look between Max and me. Quickly, she inquires, "Audrey Mills?"

Max's smile grows wide when he says, "That's the one. Your son is a lucky bastard."

I can feel her eyes boring into my skin and then she whips her head back around to look at Em, who hasn't moved a muscle.

"Audrey hasn't been with Jaxon in years. He's with Em now," she states in a confused tone.

"What? When the hell were Audrey and Jax together?" Max blurts out. "That's weird."

I stand up and clasp my hand firmly on Max's shoulder and steer him out the door. When we reach the hallway, I say, "Thanks for that, dude. You've got a big-ass mouth."

"Where is she?" he asks, completely ignoring my comment. I shrug my shoulders and glance down at my shoes. "You fucked it up, didn't you?" There's nothing I can say because he's right. I couldn't have messed this up any better. But right now I need to be here. My focus is Jaxon, no matter how often my mind drifts over to Audrey.

"I didn't tell anyone about our relationship. Jax used to date her back in high school, and that ended beyond fucked-up. I was going to tell Jax and then time got away from me . . ."

"You were a pussy," he seethes.

"Yeah, I was, okay? But I was finally going to tell him the night of the beach party."

"How convenient. I knew there was something weird going on, but I didn't realize you were keeping her hush-hush," he says.

I drag my fingers through my hair in frustration and breathe in and out raggedly. "It wasn't *her*, it was *us*. She understood."

"No, she didn't understand, but she's way too nice and trusting to say otherwise. Then you went and did something to mess it all up, didn't you?" His voice rises in anger but when he realizes his surroundings, he forces himself to calm down. He turns away and begins walking toward the elevator before swiveling around to glare at me again. "You'd better make this right, or watch someone else do it for you," he says in a calm but hard voice.

When he hits the button to call the elevator, I race toward him. "Max, what are you about to do?" I can't stomach the idea of him going to comfort her.

Steadily, he steps inside and looks me square in the eyes. "Maybe exactly what you should be doing."

The doors begin to close and I shout, "Max, what the hell?! Don't touch her; don't you dare touch her!" My fists bang on the metal door and I stop it before it can close on me.

He leans his head out and gets close to my face. "How the hell are you going to get all worked up over a girl you just tossed aside? You're my friend. I wouldn't touch her. All I'm saying is, there are others who are ready and waiting to offer her the world."

"I have to stay here with Jaxon," I say defensively.

He shrugs his shoulders and steps back inside. "Well, you'd better hope you're worth the wait. Oh, and by the way, you might want to fill Mama in on all of this. She looks mighty confused over there," he says, nodding his head behind me as the doors finally slide closed.

Slowly, I pivot around to see my mom standing casually outside of Jaxon's door, waiting for me to finish. She heard it all.

I raise my hands in surrender and rush to defend Audrey from all of the horrible things my mom must be remembering. "Mom, she's not who we thought she was. She's beautiful and amazing. She's kind and forgiving. Thank God for the forgiving part because, boy, did Jaxon and I need it."

"No girl wants to be kept a dirty little secret, son," she says, as I walk up next to her. Her line of thought immediately confuses me. She isn't thinking about the troublemaker we thought Audrey was. She's thinking about how I rudely kept her a secret from everyone I loved.

When she sees my wheels turning, she says, "I trust your judgment, Jace. I always have. If you say she's a good person, then I have to trust that."

"If Jaxon were awake, he could vouch for me. Em loves her. Quinn and Cole have become friends with her as well."

"Wow, Em loves her?" she asks in a surprised tone.

"Em bulldogged her into telling her the story of everything that happened. Shit, Mom, we had it all wrong. So very wrong."

"And then you shoved her out of here right before I arrived, correct?" she questions.

"How did you know?"

"Jace, your greatest weakness has always been caring too much about what others think of you. And I'm your mother; I can read you like a book."

I groan and lean my head against the wall outside of Jaxon's room. "Yeah, I yelled at her to leave. In front of everyone. I freaked out, Mom. Cole told me you were coming and she was trying to comfort me and . . . I just pushed her away."

She gasps and asks, "Jace, didn't you learn anything from Jaxon's mistake? At what point did I ever teach you two that it was okay to publicly embarrass girls? Especially the ones you supposedly love."

“We’re idiots.”

“You got that right,” she grumbles. When she disappears inside the room, I try to call Audrey. Three times. No answer.

- SEVENTEEN -

AUDREY -

Five days into my post-Jace life, I hit a groove. I've picked up all of Em's shifts at work while still working my own. Ed tried to convince me to give some to others, but I need the distraction. I've been doing schoolwork like a madwoman, and now I've almost completed all of my assignments for this semester.

I rarely sleep, and when it does come around, it's only for a few hours here and there. I feel as if I'm running on pure adrenaline, but I know eventually it will hit me and I'll crash hard. I've scrubbed down the apartment and even tried to hit the gym with Lane once. Going to a gym that has only men is not fun. I don't care how hot those guys are. I never want to be that self-conscious about the way I look while working out again.

I get off work early tonight because the customers actually clear out pretty quickly for once. Lane has bags under his eyes from the stress of trying to figure what he can do for me, but I don't need anyone's help. I'm handling this fine. I'm ready to get on with my life.

I realize that for five days I've kept Lane from sleeping a full night. So when I climb into bed, I force myself to stay and not roam the apartment. Just as I begin to calm down and think about the idea of sleep, my window slides open. I startle as I watch a pair of long legs slip through the window. Chuck gets up with a wagging tail to greet my intruder.

I can instantly tell by the size and build that it's Jace. I stay quiet and watch him navigate himself through my room. He steps out of his shoes, slips off his pants, and yanks his shirt over his head. Slowly, he crawls into my noisy bed and searches for me in the dark. He doesn't say a word, and I can't catch enough breath to formulate one.

When his hand reaches my body, he grabs hold of me and pulls me into the security of his arms. He's breathing heavily and he buries his face in my hair. His hands hold me tightly and it's hard to catch a breath from the amount of pressure he's placing on me, but I don't have the heart to pull away. He needs me.

"Jace . . ." I whisper in the dark. But he never responds, and when I wake up in the morning, I'm the one left all alone this time.

~

I bend down to pull out my newest batch of blueberry muffins. The apartment smells delicious, but I'm not sure what I'm going to do with all of these baked goods.

"Jesus Christ, Audrey. If you pull one more batch of carbs out of that oven, I'll go insane!" Lane grumbles from behind me.

"I think you're already there," I reply calmly.

"I don't like this. I don't like how you're acting. You're not dealing with this right. Shouldn't you be crying or bitching about him or eating a tub of ice cream?" he questions, while grabbing a chocolate muffin and taking a big bite.

I look around the kitchen at all of the pastries I've made this past week and a half. I don't know why I did it, except that it helps to keep my mind occupied. Unfortunately, I'm running out of ideas. Since sleep doesn't come and I can only work so many hours, baking is the next best thing.

He looks down at the muffin that he just mindlessly took a bite out of and growls loudly. He glares at me in frustration, as if he didn't realize he was eating the baked good, and harshly throws the remainder in the trash.

"See? I can't keep eating this junk! Make it go away."

"Shouldn't you be happy I'm not crying all over the place?" I ask, while wiping the countertop clean.

"No, because I know you're sad, but for some reason you're holding it all in. Pretend I'm a chick." He props his elbows up on the counter, rests his chin in his hands, and looks at me thoughtfully. *Brat.* "Seriously, doll, pour your little heart out. I'm here to listen."

"You're ridiculous," I reply, while searching for a container that can hold the blueberry muffins. I haven't told Lane about Jace's late-night visit a few evenings ago. I don't know what to think of it myself, so I can't say it out loud.

"Talk," he growls.

"No," I reply flatly.

"Talk."

"Where do you think we'll live after we graduate?" I ask, changing the subject.

"That's not what I wanted to talk about and you know it. But I figured I'd have to follow you to Texas."

"You would have done that?" I ask, surprised.

"Of course. You're my family."

I walk around the counter and hug him tightly. "Now you're just trying to make me cry."

"Did it work?" he laughs.

"No!" I laugh while pushing away from him.

"Well, just to humor you, let's go check out my hometown."

"New York?" I ask, surprised.

"Yeah. I haven't seen my mom in a while. I don't know if I'd ever want to live there again, but we can go look."

"This coming week?" I ask eagerly and then quickly add, "We can afford a break from school."

"Why are you jumping on this?" He seems unsure about my motives.

"I just want to plan a real future."

"Oooh-kay. I'll book it. Even though I think you need to give Jace some more time. Jax isn't even awake yet."

"Lane, he's never going to get over what others think I did. And I don't want to talk about him anymore." I finish packing up as many muffins and cookies as I can get into our plastic containers. "I'm going to take these up to Em and Quinn at the hospital."

"Might run into him," he speculates.

"Nah, Em said she'd come downstairs to get them."

"Just try to go and see him, doll. He was a fucking asshole—I'll give you that—but guys have no idea how to handle emotions. Don't you think that even if he can't admit it, he still needs you?"

"I'm going to get ready. I'll see you later tonight," I say with a smile, clearly not giving in to his probing.

I arrive at the hospital and decide to wait outside in the fresh air. Hospital air is stagnant and stuffy. I would kill to be in there holding Jace's hand, but since I can't do that, I'd rather not go in at all. My hands bounce the plastic containers around as I wait for Em to come down.

"Audrey?" I hear my name called from close by.

I turn toward the sound of my name and freeze when I spot Jace and Jaxon's mom coming around the outside corner of the hospital. She tosses down a cigarette and twists her foot on it slowly to extinguish the embers.

"Please, don't tell anyone about that. I only do it when I'm stressed," she says and gestures toward the white stick that's now crushed into the concrete.

"Secret's safe with me," I mumble.

I turn toward the revolving doors, hoping I can catch sight of Em. Julie Riley is the last person I wanted to see today. She walks closer toward me and I begin to bounce impatiently on my toes. I haven't seen her since the day Jaxon and I told her we had run off to get married. She was beyond furious with both of us. I never thought I would see her get so angry. I ran home that day. It was the only time I ever ran *to* my house and not *away* from it.

Em strolls out through the doors and smiles cheerfully at me. I don't understand this weird calmness she has about her. Her boyfriend is lying in a coma and she acts like there is finally world peace.

"Thank you so much for these," she calls out. I hand over the containers when she reaches me. "I want to thank you for taking over my shifts at work too."

"Please, don't even worry about it. You shouldn't have to think about work right now. Although I am going out of town next week, so Ed will probably have a coronary."

She laughs a bit too lightly, almost as if it's forced. In that moment, I can see the wall she's built. She's trying to protect herself from the hurt and the possibility of actually losing Jaxon. My heart breaks for her. Here I've been feeling sorry for myself, while Em has been going through genuine pain.

"Hey, Em." I reach out and grab her arm so I can pull her in close. I hope to speak to only her. "I left my textbook . . ." Lowering my voice to a whisper, I say, "In his room. Do you think there's any way I can get that?"

She smiles and replies, "Quinn's home. For some reason, she's been so tired lately. She can give you the key. Don't worry about running into . . . anyone." She quickly glances over toward Julie. "They're all here." I sigh with relief and thank her.

"They're about to start some physical therapy on him, so I don't want to miss that. He likes it when I talk to him." She smiles and walks back inside without any further conversation.

"He likes it when she talks to him?" I ask out loud, to no one in particular. I think Em is losing it.

"I'm really afraid of what this might be doing to her mental health," Julie echoes my thoughts. "She smiles all the time. She never leaves, but then again, neither does Jace. And she just lies there all day with him, talking about nothing in particular."

"She's just trying to protect herself." I attempt to think of a way I can end this uncomfortable conversation. I just can't do this right now, especially not with Mrs. Riley.

"I know about you and Jace," she says before I can escape. I immediately turn and face her, surprised. *Shit.* What does she think and how does she know? Before I can ask, she answers for me. "I'm his mom. I knew something was up." I give her a skeptical look, not believing that she has some kind of Mom ESP. She laughs, "Okay, fine. His friend, Max, ratted him out by accident." I nod my head while keeping silent. If Max knew what Jace had said to me, then he probably didn't take too kindly to that. I'm surprised I haven't heard from him already.

"I trust Jace's decisions."

"Would you say that even if I told you he pursued me before he found out that everything he thought was really a lie?" I ask. She falters a beat and nods her head. I consider leaving right this very second. I don't need to explain myself to one more person, especially this person. Jace and I are done. She won't be in my life. Why do I need to hash out this drama again? Because . . . whether I want to admit it or not, some small part of me still longs to have my name cleared.

Julie sits down on the curb and pats the spot next to her. Sitting right here on the concrete in front of the busy hospital, I pour my heart out to her. I don't cry this time. This story can flow out of my mouth now as if it knows it by heart, without any help from me. I tell her everything up until right after Jaxon and I broke up.

"How did I not know that you and Jace met first?" she says with a gasp. "I'm usually able to pick up on everything. I thought he had a crush on you . . . but this . . . this makes so much more sense."

Her words startle me and I ask, "Why would you say he had a crush on me?"

"He was always watching you guys. I just thought he missed his brother at first. After a while, I caught him specifically watching you. Not Jax, just you. You know those black-and-white photographs he has in his room?" I nod my head, thinking of them lined up above his bed. "You're in one of them."

My mouth drops open and I try to remember what they look like. I remember one of them is a picture of his dock back home that extends out over their favorite pond. Jaxon and I spent many hot afternoons jumping into that cold water. There are people in the distance in some of them, mostly silhouettes.

I think about the middle picture and how it has a person sitting on the dock with their feet hanging over the edge, dipping them into the water. The picture was taken so far off in the distance I wouldn't have been able to tell it was me. It's only the silhouette of a person. I sat on that dock numerous times, so it could have been any number of days.

I recall one time when Jax and Jace had been swimming and then went riding the truck through the mud. I had been waiting for

Jax to finish cleaning the truck off, so I decided to splash my feet in the pond. I thought Jace had gone home, but I guess he stuck around to snap some pictures out on the land. The rest of his pictures hanging on the wall are from around the property as well. My favorite is one of his mom taken from pretty far away while she was hanging sheets out to dry.

"Honey, what happened with the baby?" She interrupts my happy memories with a dreadful one. My stomach drops and I squeeze my fists together. "Please. Just talk about it. It'll help."

The first time I looked at the little white stick with its two pink lines, I cried my eyes out. I cried out of sadness, frustration, humiliation, and shock. I was scared. I cried because I didn't think I had anything to offer this child. Later, I gaze at the stick with hope. I can do this. I can love this baby and that's enough.

I know I need to move out of this house. Being around my dad just isn't okay anymore. I've never actually thought about it in that light before. It's amazing what even the prospect of being a parent can do for you. Before, my dad's aggression was just a phase that I needed to wait out. I would bear it. I would graduate and then I would leave Texas.

But now this tiny little plum-sized baby is my number-one priority. Now I realize that I can't allow my body to be harmed. I need to get out of here and find a safer home for the two of us.

As I pack my bags, I have a fleeting thought of seeing Jace one more time. I wish I could see those sea-blue eyes for just a second longer. In a way, if this baby had been Jaxon's, at least I could pretend it was part of Jace as well.

But it's not.

Mr. Howard stole that from me.

When he told me that I wouldn't pass if I didn't attend his after-school study session, I was confused. I thought I was doing well in his class. When I showed up and I was the only student present that should have been my first warning. But I was naive, so I followed him into his storage room to grab the supplies we supposedly needed. I'll never forget the echo the metal lock made when he slid it into place.

I chase away the bad memories by shoving more clothes into my backpack. One good thing about never really owning much is that I don't have a lot to carry out of here. I'm hoping that today at work I can talk to Nico about helping me find someplace to stay.

"Don't worry, little plum, I'll find somewhere safe for us," I whisper.

I quickly stash my loaded backpack underneath the couch and pull on my T-shirt for work. It's getting a bit snug and I'm sure people at work have noticed. I'm still in that awkward stage where others are probably wondering if I'm pregnant or just sneaking in a few too many of our famous breadsticks. Well, they'll all know soon enough.

I grab my purse and step out onto our front porch. My heart lurches when I see my dad coming up the stairs with a death stare focused directly on me.

His eyes flash to my stomach and back to my face, and then return to my stomach for one final perusal. I see the wheels turning and I pray I can just get to work without incident.

"What have you gone and done?" he growls in a low, threatening voice.

"Nothing. I need to get to work," I quickly say, stepping backward.

"You're just like your whore of a mother . . ."

I try to interrupt and tell him I am nothing like her, but he launches forward. His foot rises up and connects with my stomach. I feel the air rush past me, but I'm confused about what exactly is happening. When I feel the hard smack of concrete on my back and the coppery taste of blood in my mouth, my friend, darkness, returns.

Julie wipes away an escaping tear. She sits in silence for what feels like an eternity. Maybe she's giving me a chance to accept my words, but I've already done that. I can't let my father hold this over my head anymore.

"Audrey, it was never right for you to be there," she interrupts my thoughts. "I wish I would have known." I wave off her concern. There isn't anything that can be done now; we've all made our mistakes.

"I woke up in the hospital two days later, no longer pregnant."

"Did you stay?"

I shake my head and say, "I haven't seen my dad since. The boss I worked for let me sleep in the restaurant at night. The day I graduated, I hitchhiked out to California. Although before I left, I did go back and take our dog, Chuck."

"Hitchhiked?! Audrey, please tell me I just heard you wrong."

I laugh, thinking about all of the people I met on that trip. "I never told Jace that part."

"Don't you ever do that again, young lady," she scolds while hugging me. "Give Jace time."

"I feel like I've been giving people time my whole life."

"You know, Jace and Jaxon may be identical but they are nothing alike. Jaxon has always been my child that charges through life. He never thought about the consequences until he was grounded for two months for sinking his dad's boat to the bottom of the lake, amongst other crimes. Jace, on the other hand, is my thinker. He tries to reason through every scenario before he acts on it. He worries about what others think and he hates to make people upset. This type of situation, an unexpected one, throws him off. These moments don't show him in his best light. I know that doesn't excuse his behavior, but just give him some time."

I stand up to brush off my jeans and she follows. "I have to be at work in about ten minutes." The moment is awkward and I don't know what else to say.

Without warning, she hugs me tightly and whispers into my ear. "I know you don't want to hear apologies, but just know I wish I could go back and change the way things went down. You didn't deserve anything that was thrown at you, but you are strong and you've overcome it all on your own. Be proud of that."

With a nod, I walk out to the parking lot toward Lane's SUV. I've never actually thought about being proud of myself. I've always condemned myself for putting up with my dad's abuse and my mom's neglect. I should have done this or I could have done that. At the end of the day, isn't Julie right, though? I came out stronger, so I should be proud.

~

Work flies by, thankfully. We had a full house all night. There was a game on that all of the customers were watching intently, although I have no idea what game or even which sport. I moved around in a daze. Tonight, Em technically should have been on shift with me, so while the extra pair of hands would have been helpful, being busy kept my mind occupied.

Now I'm walking down the hallway toward Jace's apartment door at three in the morning, hoping my textbook is still lying next to his bed. I want to get in and out as quickly as possible. I don't want to see that giant, comfortable bed, his pictures on the wall, or even that darn pantry.

I had called Quinn from work earlier, asking her if she could keep their door unlocked since I would be coming by so late. I turn the knob and enter into the darkened living room. The familiar scent that I once found so comforting is unwelcome. I've been able to keep the sadness away, but being here is difficult.

I tiptoe down the hallway quietly and open Jace's door. Fortunately, even in the darkness I can make out my book lying next to his nightstand on the floor, right where I left it. Unfortunately, Jace is lying in his bed as well. He must have come in and passed out quickly. He's lying on top of his covers, still fully clothed. He has one hand sprawled out above his head and one draped across his chest.

I didn't even think to look for his car out front. Em told me that he's been sleeping in a chair in Jax's room. It's too dark to see his face, but he must be exhausted if he hasn't slept in a bed in over a week.

I reach down, grab my book, and turn for his door when a hand grabs me and tugs me down without missing a beat. I gasp at the sudden, unexpected movement. I still can't see his eyes in the darkness, but I can feel his lips move against mine. For a few seconds, I allow myself this.

The amazing part is touching him, feeling his body close to mine. I run my hands through his hair while his skim slowly up my back. Our lips meet hungrily, as if it has been another four years since they have touched and not a little over a week. He pulls me in more tightly and almost desperately.

The painful part is that this feels like a good-bye. A simple parting gift. My heart breaks a little at the idea of saying good-bye to him. I knew this would come, though. Jace and I are from two different worlds. I have my penny and my memories, and those should keep me company for at least a little while longer.

I shove away from him before the moment becomes even more agonizing, and I clamber out the door. When I escape into the hallway, I lean up against the wall. I will him to come out here and find me. I want him to tell me that he's not letting me go or that he just needs time until Jaxon wakes up. All of this I would understand, but I *need* him to *tell* me. I can't stand his silence and I can't assume what he's thinking, especially when it feels as if his lips just gave me a farewell kiss.

- EIGHTEEN -

***JACE** -*

After eight days, Em and I start to closely resemble the walking dead. At first we went home to shower and change, but now we just shower in the restroom here and have Quinn bring us fresh clothes when she visits. They had Jax in a unit where we were only allowed to visit for ten minutes every hour, but later they moved him to a neurological ICU. The nurses here have taken pity on us, allowing much longer visits, although we do still get kicked out a couple of hours each day during their "quiet times."

There isn't much activity with a coma patient, so Em sneaks into Jax's bed to catch some sleep while the nurses are out of the room. Only one nurse has caught her. She didn't say anything, though, when she realized Em wasn't disturbing his lines or tubes, but she still frowned about it. I, on the other hand, have been sleeping in a chair. I wake up multiple times a night with my head bobbing up and down and a strain in my neck. A few nights ago, I stumbled out of the hospital, and before I knew where I was going, I had pulled into Audrey's parking lot. I held her for as long as I could allow myself to stay and when it became too painful, I snuck back out to return to my chair.

Mom stays at the apartment so she can get a decent rest. There must be something to it because she has definitely been in a much better mood than the rest of us. Tonight, she finally kicked us out and demanded that we not return until we sleep in a real bed and shower for more than three minutes. It's a slow, sluggish walk out of the hospital for the two of us. We know we need to go, but wants and needs are two vastly different things.

Em keeps me awake on the drive home, talking about what I think Jaxon would like for her to read to him tomorrow. I want to shout, *He's in a damn coma for God's sake; he can't hear you!* But I've already been enough of an asshole to one girl this week. So I just ignore her for the remainder of the drive.

My feet are heavy as I traipse through the apartment. The second I see my bed, my heart sinks at the thought of the last time I slept here. Audrey was snuggled up with me, and I remember the sound of her contagious laughter as she tried to stealthily slip into my room that night. Jaxon and Em weren't even home, but she didn't have to know that. The second her head popped in through the door, she immediately dived under the covers with me. I also remember telling her how I'd never let her go, which is true—I haven't let her go—but I did fuck this whole situation up.

I should have let her comfort me. Hell, maybe I wouldn't have made it through this week ten pounds lighter if I had. I definitely wouldn't feel this homesick. I feel as if I've lost my home without her and Jaxon. I know Jaxon will make it through this, but will I have Audrey when it's all said and done?

I quickly realize that my body is only going to function for a couple more seconds. When I hit the pillow, I quickly succumb to my extreme exhaustion and fall into a deep sleep, without removing my shoes or jeans.

I dream about Audrey. I dream about her on the beach, in the back of my car, and at one point, I see her silhouette watching a train fly by. I also dream that she comes into my room in the middle of the night.

When I reach out for her, I magically feel her soft, smooth skin. I've missed her sweet face and her body touching mine. In my dream, I pull her on top of me and I don't even hesitate to touch my lips to hers. She comes willingly and, as always, with trust. I love this girl with everything I have. I can't believe she is letting me touch her after everything I've done. I'll always need her touch.

Too soon, she shoves off of my chest and moves away from me. The room is dark but I feel her hesitate right before she scrambles out. The only sound I hear is the click of the door. Dreaming about her only makes me ache more for her.

I want to chase her. Keep her next to me forever. I never should have let my stupid mouth speak before my brain could filter out the foolishness. But my body feels heavy and I slowly sink further into my mattress. I beg and plead for my legs to move, for my body to allow me to chase after her. I want keep her in my dreams all night. Instead, my eyes listlessly close and I crash harder into sleep, leaving only the faint taste of her lip balm on my lips.

~

A continuous buzzing rattles me out of the deepest sleep I think I've ever had. Apparently, sleeping upright for days on end can take a harder toll on your body than I thought. I reach out and slap my alarm clock, begging it to let me be. After all, if my brother can "sleep" for nine days, why can't I?

I know Dr. Graham said we could easily be looking at a couple of weeks, but for some reason I really thought he would pull out faster than this. All of his scans continuously come back showing signs of improvement, so why isn't he opening his eyes? I hope he doesn't think he can just lie there forever, because I won't have it. Not gonna happen. I need him to wake up.

When the buzzing doesn't stop, I lift up my heavy head and glare at the device causing my disturbance. The alarm clock is not flashing like it typically would, and it's then that I realize it's my cell phone that's actually going off. *Shit, sleeping in the hospital is really messing me up.* I reach and grab for the phone and without looking at my caller, I slide my finger across the screen and answer.

"Jace, it's your brother." My mom's voice kick-starts my heart, and I almost don't want to hear what she's going to say next. "He's awake. I need to tell Em, but I had to tell you first."

"Shit! For real?" I scramble up to my feet. "Shit, Mom."

"Yeah, he was fluttering his eyes all night, but the nurses told me that I shouldn't get my hopes up. That sometimes this happens. But about an hour ago, he started trying to open his eyes. They rolled him off to do a CT scan and EEG, but he should be back real soon. He wasn't fully awake or anything, and who knows what he'll be like when he comes back."

"What the fuck? Why didn't you call me *an hour ago*?" I yell.

"Excuse me, Jace . . . language," she replies sternly. "I've been running around signing paperwork and talking to doctors. They needed to run some tests, so none of us would have been able to see him anyway. Now you can come up here and be in the room before he gets back. I also need you to grab some clothes for him when you come."

"Mom, *a fucking hour ago*. How could you do this?" I roar.

Click.

Okay, maybe I deserved that. Put another check mark in my asshole box, but I still feel like she should have called a century ago. I knew coming back here to sleep was a bad idea.

I hurriedly change out of my dirty clothes. Rifling through my drawers, I grab articles of clothing that resemble a T-shirt and a pair of shorts, although I don't stop to check. Then I run out into the hallway, sprint into Jax's room, and throw items I think he will want into a bag. Em rushes into the apartment with wide, terrified eyes, wearing the same clothes she had on yesterday. She doesn't have to speak. We don't need words; instead we both run.

In true Southern California fashion, we get stuck in bumper-to-bumper traffic for an extra thirty minutes. I should have expected this. I don't know why I took the freaking highway. Em clutches her seat tightly and sways impatiently back and forth, but she doesn't say a word. She's been weird this week, like off-her-rocker weird. She smiles way too much, and I still haven't seen her get upset once about Jax's situation. She just repeats the phrase, "He'll be okay," over and over again.

When I pull up to the hospital, thankfully there is one open parking spot in the front row. I would have probably ended up illegally parking again, otherwise, because the parking garage is all the way behind the hospital. My tires squeal as I whip it in between the white lines and slam the gears into park. Em already had her door open before I was fully stopped, and I run to catch up with her on the sidewalk.

We quickly rush inside to the information desk so we can get our visitors' badges. Sheryl, a kind, elderly lady, smiles to acknowledge us, but when she sees the looks on our faces, she quickly tosses the badges to us and we continue running. I'll thank her later. I'd take the stairs, but it's probably not the best idea to run up six flights when I can't even remember the last time I ate.

Em's twitchy finger presses the correct floor number and we wait an eternity for the elevator to crawl up to where Jaxon is. Awake, hopefully. Em stands in a locked and unnatural position while I stand ready to peel the doors open, if need be. When it finally chimes to let us know we've reached our destination, we rush out. Passing by the vacant nurse's station, we make our way to the correct room.

My heart is pounding erratically and I'm not sure what I'm expecting to see when I enter his room. Right as I reach the door, I halt, causing Em to slam into my backside. I turn and grab her by the shoulders and she looks up at me with confusion.

"Jace, let's go in!" she says hurriedly.

"Hold up—let's breathe for one second," I reply.

Her terror is written all over her face. We were told he could have brain damage. Although the scans coming back have looked good, the doctors have repeatedly warned us that we wouldn't know much until he woke up and showed us his abilities. I can tell Em's as worried as I am about the possibilities.

"Whatever happens in there, I'm here for you and I'd do anything for you," I tell her.

She takes a deep breath in and slowly releases it. "Thank you, Jace. I love you."

"Love you too, munchkin," I jest, because of her height. She let's a sliver of a smile quirk up her lip, and then it quickly disappears when she glances back at his door. "Okay, let's do this."

I step inside first and I'm quickly relieved to see the only pair of eyes that match mine staring up at me. I let out a deep sigh of relief at seeing him awake and propped up, which is much different from the prone position I've seen him in for the past nine days.

"You look like hell," his raspy voice scratches out at me.

"Don't talk, Jaxon. You need to let your throat heal," Mom cautions, smiling brightly. I charge toward him and roughly wrap him up in a hug. My arms squeeze him tightly while he pats my back lazily.

"Don't ever do that again," I whisper, while trying not to get choked up.

"I'll do my best," he chuckles.

If there is any way to describe his voice, I would call it "expired." He hasn't used it in so long that it almost sounds painful for him to get the words out of his throat. When I pull back, I see that he's trying to look over my shoulder. I turn and see Em's small frame standing stock-still in the doorway. Her wide, frightened eyes are taking him in, almost as if she doesn't believe he's really conscious.

Jaxon stares at her adoringly for a long time, and then he finally opens his arms and whispers, "Beautiful." She lunges, the tears already pouring down her face before she can reach his bedside. See, *that's* a normal reaction. Not this weird smiley-robot thing she's had going on. Although Jaxon is extremely weak, he manages to scoop her up into the bed with him and nuzzle her neck.

"Thank you so much. Thank you so, so much, beautiful," he murmurs to her, over and over. I turn to give Mom a confused look and she shrugs her shoulders, equally perplexed. After a few minutes more of Em's sobbing, she finally composes herself enough to speak.

"Why are you thanking me?" she asks, while wiping her face.

"For always talking to me. For reading to me. For telling me so many times I lost count that you loved me and you would be here when I woke up." There's a collective gasp in the room as we all stare at him, shocked by his words.

"You . . . you heard me?" she stammers.

"For the most part, I could hear all of you. I was just at the end of a very long tunnel, but you stayed close. I just couldn't get my eyelids to lift. It felt like I had weights sitting on my face. I tried for hours to get them open, and they would for little spurts here and there, but y'all would be asleep or gone and I couldn't get my mouth to work past that damn tube down my throat."

"For days, I tried to will my hand to squeeze yours. It wouldn't listen. I think I managed it once, but no one noticed." He takes a deep breath after his little speech and his eyelids begin to droop in exhaustion. "It was so fucking terrifying, but you kept me sane, Emerson. I knew as long as I had you talking to me, I'd be okay."

His words are muddled and he takes a great deal of pauses, but we understand every word he utters. Even this short amount of conversing seems to be taking a toll on him already. He lays his head back against the pillow, but doesn't remove his eyes from his girlfriend. She runs her fingers through his hair slowly, and once again they disappear into their own little world. She whispers soft words into his ear, and as long as he's awake, I can stare at their mushy adoration all day.

Dr. Graham strolls into the room and smiles widely at Jax. He shakes hands with all of us and says, "It's nice to meet you with your eyes open, Mr. Riley." Jax gives a lazy grin and attempts to talk, but his body seems to be slowing back down, so he closes his mouth. Dr. Graham nods his head and says, "It's hard at first. I'm about to look over all of your scans, but I'm sure I'll be pleased with how everything is looking."

Mom clears her throat and asks, "How long do you think he'll be here?"

"He still has a ways to go. He's lost some muscle mass this past week and a half, so he'll absolutely need rehabilitation. We'll keep you up in this wing for a couple more days, just to make sure there is continual progress and no relapses."

"A week and a half?" Jax whispers roughly. Em stares into his eyes and nods her head. "I'm so sorry, babe," he apologizes.

"You've actually improved quicker than usual, so I feel good about your recovery." The doctor walks over to check his vitals, while trying not to disturb Em's intense grip on him.

Jaxon's eyes continue to droop and then they begin fluttering closed. My mom leans closer to him and I quickly walk to his side.

Em sits up ramrod-straight and clutches at his shoulders. "No, no, no. You just woke up. Please don't leave me again. Please!" she cries. A wave of pain crosses Jaxon's face, and I can tell he's trying his hardest to keep his eyes open—a battle he seems to be losing.

Dr. Graham gently pats her hand and in a soothing voice, he states, "It's okay. It's okay. Emerging from a comatose state is a slow process. He'll only be awake for a few hours at a time, if that, at first. This is sleeping, not unconsciousness."

Mom sits back in her chair and lets out a relieved sigh. My body deflates as the stress slowly dissipates. I sink to my knees on the cold, hard tile and lay my forehead on the edge of his bed. Em continues to watch his every inhale and exhale. I can tell she's still hoping he'll wake up and talk to us some more, as am I. It's a tease to have him up and then shortly after, I'm staring at the back of his eyelids again. Dr. Graham finishes up his exam and tells us he'll come back as soon as he has looked over Jaxon's scans.

Two intolerably long hours have gone by when Quinn and Cole burst through the door. I notice how let down they are when they see that Jaxon is still asleep. Quinn's eyes well up with tears and Cole pulls her into his chest.

"Quinny, he's awake from the coma. The doctor says he's just sleeping now," Em utters softly, while rubbing Jaxon's chest.

"Oh, thank God," Quinn sighs.

"Seriously?" Cole questions.

I stand up and point to my chair so Quinn can have it. She quickly claims it, pulls her knees up to her chest, and lays her head down. "Thank you," she says.

"How was he?" Cole asks.

"He seemed normal. His voice is shot to shit, but it just seemed like he was waking up after a long nap. It was so weird. Definitely not what I was expecting," I reply.

"He heard everything," Em whispers, without taking her eyes off Jax.

Quinn lets out a deep yawn and asks, "What do you mean he heard everything?"

"Well, turns out Em wasn't crazy after all. He thanked her for always talking and reading to him," I explain.

Mom reaches out, rubs Em's back, and smiles. "She pulled him through. He worked hard to wake up because of her," she says, and Em casually shrugs her shoulders. The room quiets down and another yawn rips through Quinn, which causes a tidal-wave effect of yawns around the room.

"Shit, babe, stop," Cole says through a yawn. "There is no way you can possibly be tired! You slept almost fourteen hours last night, and that was after you had a three-hour nap yesterday afternoon."

Quinn hugs her legs tighter and softly says, "I guess all this stress just wears me out."

"Well, he's awake now, so maybe you will be too," he grumbles.

"Damn, someone's grumpy 'cause he hasn't gotten laid," I jest.

"More than you, buddy," he stabs back.

"Touché," I whisper.

"I had a dream you and Audrey were together," Jaxon's raspy voice interrupts.

We all freeze and immediately turn toward him. There is a round of surprised exclamations, and everyone seems to move closer to his bed all at once.

Cole is the first to speak. "How are you feeling, man? Shit, I missed you."

"Um, I'm not sure," he croaks. "What day is it?"

"Monday," I reply.

"How did this happen?" he gestures at himself.

"You don't remember me telling you earlier?" Mom questions. When Jaxon shakes his head, she explains that he was hurt during practice.

"Well, at least it was practice and not a live game. I don't want to wind up on the highlight reel like Superstar over here did last year." He tries to laugh while pointing at Cole.

Last year, Cole got the wind knocked out of him in one of the first games of the season. It freaked us all out to see him lying motionless on the ground, but we can laugh about it now, especially every time they replay the hit on ESPN.

"Yeah, yeah, laugh it up," Cole groans.

"So my dream . . . you and Audrey. It was pretty cool," Jax says, looking directly at me.

"Nah, he fucked that one up," Cole's annoying voice states.

"It's real? I knew it! I totally knew you had a thing for her," Jax says with a smile.

"You would be okay with it?" I ask, shocked. "What about that promise we made to never date the other's girls? Past or present."

"That shit goes away when you've met 'the one.' I have Em now. I couldn't really care less about my ex-girlfriends. But that doesn't mean I'd ever want anything to happen to Audrey. She's been through enough. But what did you do?"

At the mention of her past, I want to dig a hole and throw myself inside. I was supposed to be the one person to treat her right, the one she could count on. "Shit, man . . . I pussied out and should have told you all of this over a month ago."

"I think I need to go get some coffee," Mom mutters. She gives Jax a kiss on the forehead and scurries out, obviously uncomfortable with the idea of hearing about her sons' sex lives.

"Over a month?" Jax raises his voice.

"Yeah."

"Don't beat around the bush, Jace," Em says and then turns to Jax. "Audrey was the girl Jace met—and kissed—back in high school, the same day you met Audrey at Cole's party. She was the girl Jace was gushing about meeting. She thought you were Jace, and then Jace didn't want her after she had been with you."

"Hey!" I quickly interrupt. "Don't say I didn't want her. I've always wanted that girl!" I pause and take a deep breath. "I just didn't realize how much until it was too late." Em shrugs her shoulders and snuggles in closer to Jax. He wraps her up in his arms and briefly kisses her lips.

"Wait . . . hold on, this is too much," Jax rasps out. "First of all, what the fuck, Jace? Why didn't you say something that night at Cole's party?"

"Because I thought she was mad at me about something. I thought she wanted you."

"Cole said you messed it up. What does that mean? What did you do?" Jax questions harshly.

"I freaked out, okay? I hadn't told anyone about us yet. You were in a damn coma! Mom was coming. I had so much to explain and I just needed to focus on you."

"Why? I wasn't going anywhere," he asserts with a smile.

"Not funny, man," I retort.

"So you chased her off?" he asks.

"Oh, more like threw a fucking fit until she left," Cole adds.

"Cut him some slack," Quinn chimes in.

"I yelled at her to leave . . ." I finally admit.

"In front of all of her friends?" Jax asks, and I shamefully nod my head. "You didn't learn from me?"

"Nope. I guess I needed to follow in your footsteps, big brother." I try to give him a snarky smile.

"Jackass." He lies back and seems to let me off the hook for a little while, but I have a feeling it won't be for long. "Quinn, wake up! Geez, I thought you'd be more excited to see me," he calls out.

She smiles lazily and gets up to hug him. "I did miss you. Don't do that again. I don't like the Em you leave behind," she says to him.

"She was perfect. I wouldn't have been able to pull through without her," he says, smiling down at her. Slowly, he pushes her up so he can look in her eyes. "Babe, seriously. You were amazing. I can't imagine going through this without you. Comas. Life. I want you to be mine."

"I am yours," she sniffles, showing him her palm.

Immediately, I can tell where this is going, and I thank the stars that I thought ahead. As he starts to speak her name, I rush to interrupt. "Dude, I grabbed something from your room."

"Freaky twin telepathy again," Cole groans.

Jaxon holds out his hand as I dig around in his gym bag for what he wants. When he has a hold of it, I see him start to contemplate something and I jump to stop him.

"Don't even think about getting up. Do it right there," I assert, pointing at his bed and pushing him back by his shoulder. He groans, but then stops when he looks up into Em's wide eyes. She cups his hand in between the two of hers and questions him with just a look.

"Beautiful, you charged into my life with barely any clothes on." He stops to wink at her and she rolls her eyes in return. "I was hooked from day one. I couldn't look at another girl from that point on. You ruined me, and I never want to be put back together. You molded yourself into my family so perfectly. I couldn't have asked for it to have gone any better." He stops and looks at the ground again, frustrated. "I wish I could do this on one knee, baby."

She quickly swipes at her eyes and laughs through the tears. "It's okay, it's okay! Keep going." She points to the box in his hand and he pops it open to show her the two-karat diamond I helped him pick out this past summer. Quinn and Em gasp at the same time when they see her ring.

"Emerson Moore, every day you find a new way to save me. Please, marry me. I love you and I promise to protect you for as long as I live."

"Yes, yes! Of course, yes," she cries. She grabs his face and plants her lips squarely on his. He sluggishly wraps one arm around her and straightens the other one out for me to bump knuckles with him.

When Em finally lets him breathe again, Jax turns to me and says, "Thanks for grabbing that for me, man." I shrug my shoulders because that's what we do. We all watch as Jaxon slides Em's new ring on to her left ring finger.

"Dude, you totally pulled the 'coma card' to get her to marry you!" Cole bursts out laughing.

We all join in and Jax smiles widely, "Hey, I had to convince her somehow."

Quinn bursts into sobs and runs to hug Em tightly. Girls are so damn weird. We all knew this was coming between Jax and Em, so why the tears?

"Jesus, the waterworks on this one lately . . ." Cole mutters, while pointing at Quinn with his thumb.

"You leave her alone," Em snaps, wiping her own tears away.

"Well, aren't pregnant girls supposed to be all emotional, though? And tired. You said she's been sleeping a lot," Jax says. The room goes completely silent. Cole's brow wrinkles, Em looks with confusion at Jaxon, and Quinn's mouth drops open wide. I have no idea what the hell just happened.

"Pregnant girl? Who the hell is pregnant?" I question, since everyone else has obviously been struck dumb.

Jax looks at Quinn in bewilderment. "Didn't you tell me . . ."

"You were in a coma! I didn't think you could actually hear me," she exclaims, trying to give him a dirty look.

"Oh shit, they don't know?" Jax rushes to ask.

"What?" Em yells. Quinn doesn't answer Em. She doesn't look at Jax or me. She just stares across the room at her white-as-a-ghost-boyfriend. Well, damn.

"Quinny?" Cole whispers.

"I . . . I just haven't found the time to talk to you yet . . ." she stutters. It takes Cole three long strides to cross the length of the room before he falls to his knees in front of Quinn. Immediately, he latches on to her hips and looks up at her from his position on the ground.

"Are you trying to tell me that my baby is in here?" he asks, his voice starting to sound as hoarse as Jaxon's. Quinn looks around the room uncomfortably. All eyes are on her and I feel for her.

"Well . . . I wanted to tell you privately," she stammers. "I found out the day Jaxon got hurt." She starts to fidget nervously. "I'm so sorry, Cole." He stares at Quinn's stomach as if he can actually see the baby growing inside. He gazes in awe, and I never thought I would be jealous of some guy who just found out he knocked up his girl unexpectedly.

"Don't be sorry. I'm sorry you've been carrying this around all by yourself all week. I mean, a baby . . ." A quick look of terror crosses his face as he stands up. "Shit . . . I don't know anything about babies. I mean, I literally know nothing. I'll be a terrible father. Oh my God, I asked you to pick up that heavy box the other night. Pregnant women can't pick up heavy stuff, right? Shit! No more getting your hair done, all those toxic chemicals and shit," he rambles while pacing the room.

Abruptly, he walks over to a side table and grabs her coffee cup. She protests as he slams it into the trashcan. "Caffeine, Quinn? No. I need books. I need to know everything. We need to find a store that can teach me about babies. God, I'm going to be the worst father ever!"

I grab on to his shoulder with one hand to try and calm him. "Okay, first of all dude, breathe. You just learned some pretty major news. Chill the hell out," I say. When Quinn walks his way, I pat him on the back and step aside. She stands on her tiptoes and wraps a hand behind his head, bringing his face toward hers and capturing his lips.

"Baby, I love you," she says against his mouth.

"I love you too. I'll try my best." He rubs her flat stomach and kisses her again.

"You'll be amazing," she reassures him.

"I want one!" Em calls out.

I look just in time to see Jaxon's face freeze with his own terror. "You want one what? You want a puppy? I can get one of those. You want a bigger ring, baby, I'll do that too. How about a nice long vacation—anywhere you want to go," he says, obviously trying to distract her.

"I want a baby," she begs.

"Whoa. Let's get married first, and then way off in the very faraway future, we can discuss the possibility," he states, but I can see the panic in his face.

"Dude, you've been following this chick around like a puppy for over a year, and now it's *you* that's afraid of the next step?" I laugh.

"We haven't graduated yet! We aren't even married," he squeaks. "I'm getting really tired," the bastard says, feigning drowsiness. "I'm getting a headache. I was just in a coma, guys, and this is all too much." I chuckle at his overdramatic show of drowsiness.

"You're not getting out of this," Em says sternly. Jax presses the button that calls the nurse to his room and she immediately pops her head in with a wide smile. She's shown Jax a little too much helpfulness, if you ask me.

"I have a headache," he whines to her.

"Of course you do, poor dear. I'll administer some more pain meds," Miss Overattentive Nurse says, rushing to his side.

I laugh when I see Em rolling her eyes. Then she leans down close to Jax and purposely juts out her chest. I can't help but stifle another laugh. This is classic Em. "Don't you worry. Soon you'll be home and naked in our bed again, giving your *fiancé* a baby," she loudly whispers, while winking seductively at him. Jaxon's mouth drops open in surprise and Em says, "Yeah, I still got it."

"Okay, okay, we're bringing the vixen out in her again," Quinn interrupts. "Oh, Jace, by the way, since you were home last night, did Audrey go by and grab her textbook? I know she really needed it."

"What?" I ask. "That wasn't a . . . she was really there?"

She looks at me with a confused expression. "I guess so. She left it in your room. I didn't know you'd be home, though, so I told her she could just go right in."

"Shit! I thought that was a dream!"

"Dude, what did you do to the poor girl now?" Jax asks sluggishly. The meds are really starting to hit him.

"Nothing. I need to find her, though. I gotta go," I say, reaching for the door.

"I'll be here . . ." he trails off.

"Oh, by the way, been meaning to tell you," I start and then, as quick as I can possibly get it out, I say, "Long story short, I dropped premed. I've been double-majoring in business. I'll be taking over Dad and Uncle Logan's company. Cole's joining and you should be there too. I know you never really had any interest in it, but it just wouldn't be the same without you. Okay? Just think about it, buddy. Love you, bro." With that last confession off my chest, I hurry out the door.

On the opposite side of the closed door, I hear Jax say, "Beautiful, you'll explain all of that to me when I wake up, right?"

"Just as soon as I figure it out myself, babe," she responds.

- NINETEEN -

JACE -

All day. I searched for her all day and found nothing. I'm embarrassed to admit the amount of times I have called her phone with no answer. With my head hanging low, I make my way back into Jaxon's hospital room. The second I step inside, I immediately step right back out.

I shouldn't even be surprised to see Em straddling Jax, but I guess I wasn't expecting it in a hospital bed. It looked like only her shirt was off at this point but I hightail it out, just in case. After some giggling and shuffling around, Jax calls for me to come back in. I step inside and smirk at the two guilty parties sitting casually on the white hospital bed with coy looks on their faces.

"You were just in coma. You remember that, right?" I ask.

"Hey, they told me to try and get back to normal. I've got a lot of muscle to build back up."

"I guess so," I say with a laugh.

"Where's Audrey?" Em asks, while flipping her hair upside down and scooping the length of it up into one of those colorful hair bands.

I groan and shrug, making my way toward the chair nearest to his bed. I empty out my pockets and say, "I was hoping you would know. I took cold coffee to all of her classes today. Well, it was warm for the first forty-five minutes I carried it around. She's not answering her phone, she's not at home, and I can't find Lane either."

"Sorry, the last time I talked to her was when she brought the muffins up here for you," she apologizes.

"What?" I gasp. "For me? She made those? You never told me that."

"Would you have really cared at the time? She just wanted to help you in some way."

"This really couldn't get any worse. You and Jax are getting married, and I couldn't be happier for you guys. You know that, right?" She nods her head and I continue, "Cole and Quinn are already starting their family. I'm just afraid I'll be moving back to Texas without Audrey and she'll disappear again, permanently." I run my fingers through my hair in frustration. "I just had this whole fantasy about marrying her and building a house with her. Am I completely off my rocker?"

Em shakes her head back and forth and Jax questions, "Do you really think you would let her get away? After all these wasted years, would you really let that happen again?"

"I would chase her to the ends of the earth," I reply emphatically.

"All right, then, case closed. You'll find your girl, but you better give her a second to forgive your sorry ass," he chuckles drowsily.

Em's phone begins to vibrate on the table next to her and I stare, willing it to be Audrey. She notices my intense gaze and shakes her head when she reads the screen, indicating that it's not who I want it to be. With a defeated sigh, I take the seat nearest the window.

"Hello?" Em asks. Whoever is on the other line is somewhere loud, because I can hear the roar of a party from her phone's speaker. I can't make out what's being said, though.

"Uh, no, sorry, I don't have that. Why . . .

"Well, check her phone. Obviously she would have it . . .

"Have you asked her . . .

"Shit."

Em's eyes dart to me and then quickly away. The hair on the back of my neck rises as I hear the one-sided conversation.

"Well, don't let her do that," she barks into the phone.

She looks at me again and asks, "You wouldn't happen to have Lane's number, would you?" Her smile is too wide, too fake.

"Who are you talking to?" I question.

"Do you have his number or not?" she demands. I shake my head with a negative.

"Where are you?" she asks her mystery caller. "Okay, I'll be there in like fifteen minutes." She hits the End Call button before I can yank it out of her hand.

"Where is she?" I growl.

"I think I should take care of it, Jace. She wouldn't want you to see her like this," Em says. I look to Jax for help because there's no way in hell he would let that fly.

"Sorry, babe, I have to side with Jace on this one. If someone had said that about you, I'd being going apeshit. Just let him go get his girl."

"Okay . . . fine . . ." she groans in irritation. "You'd better be nice to her!"

"I swear," I immediately respond, while shoving my wallet and phone back into my pockets.

"So that was Max, and he said that he showed up at the Sig Alpha party . . ." I groan, already not liking where this is going.

"Apparently, Garrett and Mason found out Audrey has never had alcohol before, so they convinced her to try some . . ." she trails off uncomfortably. Doesn't matter I'm already halfway down the hallway, heading toward the elevator. Oh, I'll be nice to Audrey, but I never promised anything about Garrett and Mason. Or Max. That asshole should have called *me*!

~

Frat row is lined with cars, and all the driveways are filled. Last year, we were on this street three or four times a week. I'm glad we all kind of backed off this year. Most of the parties are at the beach now, which keeps them somewhat under control. I pull up in front of the packed Sig Alpha house and park right on the grass of the front lawn. The music is pumping so loud I can feel my heart beating in sync with the tune already.

As I hop out, a little guy who looks a lot like a freshman comes barreling down the drive. "Hey, you can't park here; this is Sig property," he squeaks.

"I'll be out in ten minutes. I've got fifty bucks with your name on it if no one touches this car," I call out to him as I climb the porch steps.

"Deal," he cries with his hands up in surrender.

Max is perched at the top with his arms crossed and a smirk on his face. "I was hoping you would show up instead of Em."

The second I reach him, my hands shove his chest, forcing him to shuffle backward. "Next time, asshole, you call me," I demand.

He raises his hands and says, "She begged me not to."

"If it concerns her, it concerns me."

"Message received. Now go get her. Hopefully you'll have more luck than I did."

"Don't worry about that."

"Hey, if it means anything, I was hoping by calling Em I'd get you," he confides to my retreating back. I nod my head because that's all I can give him right now.

It takes some effort to push the front door open with the thick crowd on the opposite side. I shoulder my way in, searching for her. It's not hard to spot Audrey in this mass of bodies, and it's not because I practically have a homing device on this girl. It's because she's standing on the kitchen bar top with Mason, Garrett, and a few other girls I don't recognize, the five of them dancing wildly to the blaring music.

I may be pissed at the circumstances, but seeing her again is like a breath of fresh air. When Jaxon and I were kids, we used to go out to the lake near our house and swim all the way out to the very middle. Once we got out there, we would race down to the very bottom, touch it, and swim back to the top.

The only problem is that it was extremely deep. Our ears would begin to pop from the pressure by the time we were touching the cold sand. The worst part was swimming back up. I can't even remember the number of times I began to panic, thinking that this was going to be the time I wasn't swimming fast enough and needed air about three seconds ago. Each time the surface seemed a little bit farther away, but the second my arms would cut through the water into the open air, I would feel this moment of extreme euphoria.

Seeing Audrey again is like breaking through the water and taking that first gulp of air. Except this time, I didn't even realize how oxygen deprived I was. I can't let her get away from me again. If she doesn't go to Texas, I'll have to figure something else out, because I go where she goes. But first, time to get her away from these guys and get my girl back in *my* arms.

Garrett takes a swig from his beer bottle and tilts it toward her lips for her to take a drink. Audrey leans his way and takes in a mouthful. She covers her mouth to swallow and laughs out loud.

Mason moves up behind her and latches onto her hips. I begin to have déjà vu at this familiar scene. I yell for him to remove his hands, but the crowd is too loud and my voice is lost in the music. I'm charging forward when someone grabs a tight hold of my arm, halting my advance.

"Watch it," I growl and turn to face my captor. When I realize it's only Cole, I reel in my temper.

"Easy . . ." he cautions.

"What are you doing here?" I ask, still trying to get closer to Audrey.

"Jax called me in for backup. Good thing he did too." He gestures to my girl and whistles.

"I'm not gonna get in a fight . . ." I don't even believe the words that leave my mouth, so I know Cole's not going to fall for them.

"Right . . . seeing as how Mason is leaning in closer to her neck, I'm having a hard time believing that." His words cause my body to go rigid, and I instantly start shoving people out of my way. I'm fucking done trying to push through politely.

AUDREY -

My Auditing and Assurance class spent the day sitting in on one of Los Angeles's top accounting firms while they went through their clients' audits. The day could not have dragged by at a slower pace. Lane went to a different firm than I did, so I got to know Olivia, one of my classmates, really well today.

She's the reason I'm here now. I told her I needed to relieve some stress, when in actuality I just wanted to *feel*. Jace can't be the only person or thing that makes me feel alive. I realized this past week that I've been going through the motions, smiling when I thought appropriate, speaking when spoken to. The truth is I'll always love Jace. No matter how many times I think that maybe we're better off without each other, there's this part of me that won't let go. But I need to be able to breathe without him.

Olivia convinced me to wear these tiny shorts and this tight button-up sleeveless shirt. I was hesitant about the party at first. I never pictured myself as the type of girl to be pulled up onto a bar to dance and actually enjoy it. I should have never let Mason and Garrett know that I've never tried alcohol, because now I feel like I'm swimming in it. My stomach is full of liquid and I feel a buzzing sensation in my veins. My head is cloudy and my movements are sluggish, even though I feel like I'm moving at lightning speed.

I'm dancing with Olivia when Mason and Garrett decide to hop up and join us. I shouldn't be surprised, since I've been batting away Mason's advances all night. Earlier, Max popped in and asked where Lane was, but I just responded with a shrug of my shoulders. When I spotted him pulling out his phone, I shouted, "Don't you dare call Jace!"

So imagine my surprise when I see his handsome face charging through the crowd below. Cole follows closely after him and I realize that Max is behind this somehow, because these two look like they are on a mission. And I'm pretty sure that mission has something to do with me.

Jace reaches out, grabs Mason's leg, and growls, "You have three seconds."

Surprisingly, Mason actually considers his words before deciding not to argue it and jumping down. Garrett passes me another drink from his bottle and I quickly swallow the foul taste. Beer must be one of those drinks that has to grow on you, because I just don't understand how everyone here seems to enjoy drinking it.

"I'd stop doing that if I were you," Cole calls up to Garrett.

Meanwhile, Jace is still glaring at Mason. "She's *never* had a drink before, and this was your brilliant idea?" he hollers.

"Seems fine to me," Mason slurs. "Gotta start somewhere."

"Oh, yeah, and what did you plan on doing later when she's puking her guts out? Where did you plan on being then?"

"Hey, I would have had her upstairs and in my bed before she got to that point," Mason quips. Jace was already mid-swing halfway through his sentence. Mason didn't even have a chance. Jace may look a little skinnier than he was a little over a week ago, but that obviously hasn't affected his right hook. The crunch of bone hitting bone is loud, and I gasp at the sudden impact. Mason's body hits the floor, hard and fast.

"Jace!" I yell, but before my brain can catch up, my feet lose their battle with balance. I tilt away from the bar and all I can feel is the muggy air gusting around me.

"Shit!" Cole blurts out.

My body falls into a set of waiting arms and I smile when I look up into my favorite pair of eyes. No one can compete with them, not even Jaxon. While Jaxon's eyes are like ice and winter, Jace's look more like the ocean surrounding a tropical island. He's my personal paradise.

"Gotcha, babe," he whispers.

"That was fun," I breathe out through my rush of adrenaline. I cringe as I notice my slurring.

"Let's not do it again, okay?" he smiles softly. When he glances up, his grin instantly hardens into a look of murder. "You want to join him?" he calls up to Garrett, who steps away from the edge of the bar and shakes his head. I squeeze my arms around Jace's neck harder, hoping he doesn't plan on putting me down to deal with poor Garrett. "Don't ever touch her again. Better yet, don't even look at her again. You can relay that message to your buddy when he wakes up," Jace finishes. He doesn't put me down. Instead, he holds me tighter as he navigates the crowd toward the front door.

"Well, Jaxon's gonna kick my ass. Thanks, man; I was supposed to prevent all that from happening," Cole calls over Jace's shoulder.

"Not even Jaxon could have stopped that from happening. Mason had it coming."

When we reach the front porch, Cole squeezes his shoulder and smiles at me. "I'm gonna head back to my baby mama now."

"Oh, good!" I cry drunkenly, "You finally know!"

"How did *you* know?" Jace asks in amazement.

"I helped her down from the bridge," I reply, as if they should already understand this.

"Uh, what bridge, pretty girl?" Cole questions.

"The one she was gonna jump off of. She was pretty freaked out when she found out," I say, closing my eyes. The porch fan above us is making me dizzy, and there's already enough spinning going on without it.

"She was going to jump off a bridge?" Cole cries, interrupting my random thoughts.

"Not a real one," I whisper for dramatic effect. "You know, it's just a metamorphosis."

"I think she means a metaphor," Jace chuckles.

I lean forward and speak with my lips touching his. "That's what I said."

"Well, thanks for helping Quinn out," Cole says genuinely. "You're kind of cute when you're drunk." He chuckles and kisses my head before walking away.

"Jace, your car is on the lawn," I whisper, while looking around for who could have done this.

"You are pretty damn adorable," he laughs.

I wiggle out of his hold until my feet are planted firmly on the wooden porch. I reach out for his hand and pull him alongside me. I'm not sure where I'm going yet, but I'll show him how damn *adorable* I can be.

The side of the house is pitch black and, thankfully, deserted. When I find a spot hidden by the bushes, I push Jace up against the brick wall. He eyes me with confusion.

"Babe, I need to get you home before you realize how sick you're going to be later," he groans, as I slam my body and lips up against his.

"Shh . . ." I whisper, "You don't want someone to catch us, do you?"

"Catch us doing what?" he questions quietly.

Slowly, I begin to kneel down in front of him. The cold dirt cushions my knees softly and I look up to give him a devilish grin. Desire instantly begins swimming in his eyes and he tries to shake his head back and forth, but it's obvious he wants this too. I ignore him and reach for the waistband of his jeans. The button takes me a second, but I have the zipper down in no time. My eyes never leave his face.

"Baby, not here. Not while you're drunk." His hoarse words are barely audible.

"Shut it, Jace. You don't get to control this. You control everything and usually I like that, but not when it's to tell me to go away. It's my turn," I demand.

He groans and places his hands on each side of my face. "Audrey, I'm so . . ."

"Shh," I rush to say. I reach inside of his pants and pull him out, and he hisses as the air hits his naked skin. Or maybe it's because my hand immediately begins to pump up and down. I've missed him. And in this moment, I realize I'll never get enough of him. I'll never tire of him. I wet my lips and slowly slide him inside my impatient mouth. He moans as I move him in and out, with the rhythm of my hand sliding across his skin at the same time.

"Christ, Audrey." The words whistle past his teeth. He shifts on his feet and braces his hands against the wall. Without removing my mouth, I reach for his hands and bring them to my head. He groans as he receives my message. I guess I still need him to have some control. Slowly, he threads his fingers through my loose hair and grips my scalp, applying just enough pressure to bring a moan out of my throat that vibrates onto him.

I release more of my control and allow him to thrust in and out of my mouth. I stare up into his eyes and watch as he finds his pleasure with me. This is my favorite part of any act with Jace. Watching him claim what's his is the most euphoric sensation I could ever feel.

His mouth begins to open and close and he seems to be having trouble getting out the words he wants to say. His unspoken thoughts let me know he's close. I grab on to his thighs so I can feel his strong muscles working toward his release.

"Ahh . . ." he calls out loudly, and I smile around him at his shameless abandon. Knowing that anyone nearby could hear what I'm doing to him right now gives me a wanton feeling. When he's finished, he lays his head against the wall and looks up at the sky, breathing heavily. I gently place him back inside of his jeans and carefully zip them up. Slowly, I pull myself up and wobble a bit as the alcohol takes another hit at my balance.

Jace drops to his knees in the same moment and runs his hands down the length of my legs. I've never been more thankful for long legs than when I'm around him. He's undeniably a leg man. His roaming fingers reach my knees and he gently dusts the dirt off my skin. When he leans in to give each of my knees a gentle kiss, I run my fingers through his messy hair. With one more fleeting touch of my legs, he stands back up to his full height. He runs a hand down the side of my face, and I blink hard so I can focus past the fogginess in my vision.

"You're perfect," he whispers.

Just as I try to think of a snarky comment, the sky begins to spin and I suddenly don't feel as well as I did two minutes ago. I must have stood up too fast. I feel a clammy coldness engulf my skin. I push off of Jace and try to step as far away from him as possible. When I reach the opposite side of the large air-conditioning unit, my stomach heaves.

Jace is immediately behind me, scooping my hair out of my face and steadying me with one hand on my hip. Embarrassed, I remember one of the many reasons I've never had a drink. With my hair safely out of the disaster zone, he rubs my back gently.

Jace was right earlier. Who *was* going to help me when I reached this point? I'd be lying to myself if I thought Garrett or Mason would actually stand here and help me while I'm sick and humiliated.

Tears begin to squeeze out of my eyes, and Jace soothes my discomfort.

"Shh, it's okay. You're not alone. I'm here," he whispers. He doesn't rush or condemn me. He waits patiently for the moment when my stomach is finally empty and my body begins to sag in exhaustion. Gently he scoops me up into his arms and carries me away.

- TWENTY -

JACE -

If someone had asked me a year ago if I would ever lie on the cold, hard tile of my bathroom floor for a girl, I would have laughed in their face. But here I am with my cheek squashed into the freezing stone and with a little bit of my drool underneath. I push off the ground, wipe off my face, and rise to a sitting position.

I finally passed out last night after watching poor Audrey spend more than half the night hugging the toilet bowl. I'm almost positive that she'll never be doing that again. After she apologized to me for the hundredth time, I rubbed her back, slipped down to the floor, and made a pillow out of my towel, while she laid her head on my chest.

The bathroom isn't very big, but I still do a quick search to confirm that she's not in here. The sneaky escape artist strikes again, and I didn't get a chance to apologize or make anything right with her before she took off. Her newfound friendship with the porcelain god didn't exactly put her in the best position to have a serious talk.

Sluggishly, I make my way out to the kitchen, bypassing my bedroom altogether because I know she's not here. I spot a bright green sticky note affixed to the fridge when I round the counter. Sloppy handwriting is scribbled across the surface.

Here's my number for next time. Sorry we had to skip out. I tried to wake you but you sleep like a damn rock and I sure as hell wasn't about to carry your ass to bed, princess. —Lane

I pull my phone out of my jeans that I'm still wearing from last night and quickly call both Audrey's and Lane's numbers. Both go straight to voice mail. Typical.

If I want to graduate this year, I have to get my ass to class and beg for forgiveness for my missed days last week. I'm hoping the fact that I was so far ahead will help my case. I jump in and out of the shower quickly and rush over to the girls' apartment because our fridge is empty as hell. I knock twice and let myself in. I find Em sitting on the couch, looking better than I've seen her in days. Chuck rushes up to my legs and sits at my feet the way I taught him. Immediately, I begin walking around the apartment to look for her.

"She's not here," Em calls out.

"Then why is Chuck here?" I reach down and scratch him behind the ears.

"I forgot that I agreed to watch him while she and Lane went out of town," she says, grabbing for her cereal bowl.

"They went out of town? Together?" I ask, trying to keep the uneasiness out of my voice.

"I thought you were going to make everything better last night?"

"That was the plan. Obviously things changed."

"Last week, Audrey asked him if they could go check out New York to see if it was somewhere she'd want to move to . . . after graduation," she adds timidly.

"Hell, no. Hell, no. Over my dead body," I exclaim.

"I was hoping you'd say that. But since you're in the same boat as I am and can't afford to miss any more days of class, you'll have to wait here for her to come back." She smiles brightly as if that's the best fucking news she's heard all day.

"You're happy about this?" I ask incredulously.

"Hell, yeah, I want to see you grovel in person. Hearing it secondhand is never as much fun," she confides.

"You're lucky I have to love you," I tease.

"Hey, I have to make up for all those years I never had a brother."

"Funny, I never actually wanted a sister." And just like that we fall back into our normal banter and easy relationship. "Chuck's gonna stay with me, okay?"

"Go ahead. I guess he'll be your dog soon enough," she replies and pats him on the head.

"So how much longer do I have to suffer without my girl?"

"Shouldn't be more than a week," she replies with a smile.

I bite back a groan and say, "Well, shit. I might as well catch up on my sleep this week. I sure as hell don't plan on doing much of that when she finally gets back."

~

Once I told Uncle Logan I had Jax and Cole on board with me, his enthusiasm kicked into overdrive. Logan will keep the reins for another couple of years until we have the hang of everything, but I can tell he's itching to retire. Something about buying a cabin in the mountains, being able to spend his days with the wife, and catching fish.

Every day, I've had the damn UPS man at my door with another box of documents for me to get familiar with. I don't think Logan understands that I eventually have to move all of these boxes back to Texas. It's nice to get a head start on working there, though.

All of his paperwork is teaching me the groundwork of the company and what I should initially be expecting in our day-to-day operations. I've been trying to familiarize myself with our clients and their backgrounds. The last thing I want to do is show up and not know who the hell I'm protecting.

It all comes down to security, whether it's installing advanced systems on their properties or individual protection on their persons. The company itself is pretty well rounded, and I can't wait for the three amigos to jump in there and start taking care of business. Now I just need to get the third lady to permanently join this gang.

Luckily I convinced my professors to not drop me from their courses. A couple of them assigned an extra paper and one asked me to bring her a Diet Coke to every class until the end of the semester. The last one was a hard sale, but when I showed him that I have my entire business proposal that's due for our final already drawn up, he quickly turned a blind eye to my absences.

It's taken everything in me not to haul ass to New York and go all caveman on Audrey. While I would love to drag her back here, Em is right. It wouldn't do any of us any good if I get kicked out of school due to my deficient attendance record.

Jax is actually going to be able to come home any day now. He got up and walked the day after he woke up, but even though it wasn't anything spectacular, he was exhausted within seconds. He's continued to push through, and now he can get up and around on his own for short bursts here and there. Regardless of the progress he's made, he'll have to continue with outpatient rehab once he checks out.

I've hit the gym twice a day every day while Audrey's been away, and today is no exception. Chuck and I walk up to the double doors of the big red gym that I've been going to since last year. I've discovered that Chuck does not enjoy being by himself, or maybe it's because it's not actually his home. Either way, I've lost a pair of shoes because of his separation anxiety, and Jax has lost a pillow. He doesn't know about that yet. Chuck actually does really well sitting in the gym, though. When I hop in the ring to spar, he just sits and chills on the ground, watching the action and not bothering anyone.

However, the bastard makes me eat my words the second we enter the gym when he takes off running at full speed toward the boxing ring. He flies through the ropes and up onto the platform, and barrels into one of the guys currently handing his opponent his teeth.

"Chuck! You asshole." I hear Lane's deep baritone voice laughing out loud. My body freezes as I see Lane lying on his back with Chuck perched on top, licking his face. I didn't know Audrey was back! *What the hell?* They only left three days ago. Quickly, I jog toward the ring and whistle for Chuck. Just like I taught him, he immediately hops out and heels at my side, panting happily and looking up at me.

"Hey, asshole, hit the bags with me so I don't end up tuning your face up," Lane calls out. Chuck and I ran to the gym, but I'm still not warmed up enough to begin, so I head toward the heavy bags and grab a jump rope.

I extend the rope above my head to stretch my arms from side to side and ask, "Y'all are back?" With frustration, I pull the rope taut again and continue, "Man, I'm trying to be patient with her. I know I fucked up at the hospital and I need to apologize, but I can't do it if I can't find her anywhere! I call her phone and it's always off. I went to all of her classes on Monday and she wasn't there. I ran to a party because I heard she was there getting drunk! I take care of her all night and she's gone by morning. I'm about to go fucking crazy, Lane. Seriously, do me a solid and help me out a little."

"Chill for one second, princess," he groans dramatically.

With speed on my side, I reach out and jab him in the rib cage. Before he can retaliate, I step back and start jumping rope. "Cut the nickname."

"I had some stuff to take care of, so I came back early. She stayed."

"What the hell . . ." I drop my rope. "You left her alone?"

"Yeah, I left her all alone in a multimillion-dollar high-rise apartment in Manhattan with her cousin and her cousin's best friend."

"Ah, I forgot about Kennedy."

"By the way, she crushed her phone by accident the day she ran out of the hospital. She put it on top of the car and drove off. She wasn't in school because we worked in an accounting firm all day Monday and we had an early flight on Tuesday, which is why she was gone when you got up. Did you ever stop to think that maybe she's not avoiding you, that maybe she's just continuing on with her life?"

"No, I didn't think about that," I mumble.

"Well, start. Because if she's learned anything since I first met her, it's that she shouldn't wait for others to make her happy. Hence her spontaneous trip to New York. She wants a home, Jace, and she'll make it for herself if she has to. Well, actually, I'd make it for her, but she won't let me." He finishes and begins to punch the bag again.

"I'm gonna get her back . . ."

"You never lost her," he states, surprising the hell out of me. He sidesteps and lands three fast jabs before continuing. "You just need to get back on the same track as her. I'll let you know when she's coming back in town."

"I'm going to change her last name."

Lane's next punch comes in a fraction off, causing him to slip and miss the bag. Slowly, he leans his forehead against the leather and says, "I'm not ready for that. I'm not ready for her to be taken away from me."

"I want you to move to Texas. Come work for me. Audrey told me about your past in law enforcement. Join my security group."

"I just got a degree in accounting . . ." He trails off.

"Do you actually give a shit about accounting? Because I think it's some kind of distraction from whatever happened before you met Audrey."

"Audrey is my family. I'll go to Texas for her," he responds, avoiding my question.

We bump knuckles and I say, "I feel like I should ask your permission to marry her."

"You should," he replies, smirking, and starts to bounce around again before he resumes hitting the bag. *Bastard.* I shouldn't have mentioned anything.

"You know I'd never let anything happen to her, right?"

"That's not asking me," he replies in an annoying singsong.

"It would mean a lot to me if I had your blessing," I reply seriously.

He stops his routine and solemnly states, "Jace, I've known you were the one for her since before I met you. I couldn't be happier that this is going to actually work out. I know you'll take care of her. I also know you're too afraid of me not to," he finishes with a cocky grin.

"Aughhh," I let out a yell, partly in relief and partly out of frustration. "I'm going to go crazy waiting for her to come back."

"Well, I guess you've got plenty of time to get some muscle back on those bones. You're looking scrawny, dude."

"I wasn't going to mention it, but you're actually looking a little chunky. Guess you'll be doing a lot of cardio this week," I return. I take the bag next to him and start my first round. His body stills at my words. I have to bite my lip from laughing when I see him raise his arms so he can check out his own body. I knew that one would hit him hard.

"You know what? Now I'm really going to kick your sorry ass in the ring. Because this"—he gestures to his body—"is all your fault. Miss I'm-Going-to-Bake-Twelve-Batches-of-Muffins-a-Day because she doesn't know how to deal with emotions fattened me up this week. And did she eat any of those cookies or muffins? No! She didn't sleep either. She ran on adrenaline all week, baking, finishing up every last paper we've been assigned, and working double shifts."

I hang my head for a moment and take a deep breath, reminding myself once again that I still can't fly to New York right now. I know I haven't given Audrey everything she deserves. I haven't shouted from the rooftops that she's my girl. I haven't walked her to class with my arm around her shoulders. Max was right. I haven't treated her the way she should be treated. But somehow I'll make this right, because failure is *not* an option.

"For that, I'll let you get a few free hits in," I finally respond.

AUDREY -

The second I step through the revolving doors that lead to baggage claim, I see a crew of unexpected familiar faces. Em and Quinn smile brightly and wave enthusiastically. I'm shocked to see Jaxon sitting in a wheelchair with Cole holding the handles. Cole tries to wheel him forward, but Jax elbows him away and slowly pushes the wheels himself. Lane stands above all of them and darts toward me. I steady my rolling carry-on bag and brace for the impact. He scoops me up into a well-known hug that I will always associate with family.

"Missed you, doll," he says in his gruff voice.

"I missed all of you guys," I say to them over his shoulder. Curious, I look around for another face, one that I couldn't get out of my mind even if I tried.

"Don't worry, if he knew you were coming in today, he would have been here before any of us. He's been pacing circles around the living room since the second you left," Jax calls out.

"I thought you told him you would let him know when I was arriving?" I ask Lane, recalling the brief conversation he told me he had with Jace at the gym. "Not having a phone really sucks. Did you know that there aren't pay phones anymore? Like anywhere?" I complain.

"Don't worry. I plan to tell him," he says, smiling deviously.

"Uh-oh . . ." I groan and look to the others for elaboration.

"We don't know what the gorgeous hunk is up to," Em smiles at Lane.

"I'm still right here, babe," Jax grumbles.

"*We* don't call him a gorgeous hunk, by the way," Cole chimes in.

"I do," Quinn sighs.

Cole looks to Lane and deadpans, "We can't be friends with you anymore, dude."

Jax wheels over to nudge him in the shin with his foot, "Yeah. Sorry, but you're out."

Lane laughs out loud and wraps his arm around my shoulder. "Come on, ladies."

When we pull up in front of my job, I groan and look at Lane questioningly. "Don't worry, you're not working. It's just a fun night with friends."

I smile and begin to relax from my long day of traveling and an emotional few weeks. Being confined on a plane for hours on end is not how I like to spend my time, although being able to see my cousin again was totally worth the grueling flights. Kennedy has been the only family member to always make an effort to maintain a relationship with me. I know I have more blood relatives out there, but since they all hate my parents, I was unlucky enough to be grouped in with them.

Kennedy and I stayed with her best friend, Brynn, whose father owns a Fortune 500 company in Manhattan. Brynn doesn't have a limit to the amount of money she can spend, and she doesn't hesitate to spend it on her friends. Or her friend's cousin, as the case may be. I spent my time there in private, chauffeured cars, fancy restaurants that usually require a reservation months in advance, and swanky rooftop bars. It was fun for a week, but that whole lifestyle just seems exhausting to me. I don't know how Kennedy can keep up with her friends all year round.

After Em and I wave our hellos to some of the employees, we wind our way through the packed bar. Finally, we find a pool table in the back, and as we pull up some bar stools, I hear Lane on his phone speaking in hushed tones.

"Just come up here . . .

"You can do all that girly shopping shit later . . .

"You seriously need to have your man card revoked . . .

"See you in ten."

"Audrey, play a round with me," Em says, interrupting my eavesdropping, pointing to the table, and handing me a house stick.

I sink the eight ball before Em can even get her third shot in, and she tosses her cue to the table. Cole and Quinn look at me with wide, shocked eyes. Lane doesn't even bat an eye, since he's seen me play this game countless times before.

Jax laughs and says, "Yeah, I was wondering if you still had it."

"You knew she could do that?" Em cries.

"Oh yeah, she hustled me the first time we met," he replies.

"I want a try. I've never been beaten by a chick," Cole declares and grabs for Em's discarded cue. He swirls blue chalk on the tip and begins to rack the balls.

"Don't say we didn't warn you. I've never seen her lose." Lane laughs. He sits back on a bar stool with his arms folded tight. I keep quiet during the entire game, not wanting to break my concentration. It's a tight game, tighter than I feel comfortable with, but after all that talk, I can't let Cole beat me. We're both down to one ball each, not to mention the eight ball that sits there, daring me to knock it in before Cole does.

I lie across the table comfortably to get a hard-to-reach angle, aiming to put my last solid ball in the corner pocket. Just as I pull back, ready to tap the ball, big hands skim across my waist and a warm body lies across my back. "You're back. God, I've missed you," Jace's warm voice whispers in my ear. My hand slips and I knock the solid too hard, sinking the eight ball instead and losing the game.

Cole tosses his cue down and throws his knuckle out to fist-bump Jace. "That's what I call teamwork!" he shouts. When I turn in Jace's arms to see his handsome face, I forget the game, Cole, and even where we are and who we're with.

He gives me his signature cocky smile and says, "Sorry about that." I smile without saying a word and then flush when I think about the last time I saw him. I don't regret what I did on the side of the frat house, but I don't think I would have done that sober. I also threw up in front of him for the rest of the night, which I know I'll never be able to live down.

"I can't stop thinking about it either," he whispers in my ear, before trailing a kiss down my neck.

"I heard about that," Em laughs. "So hot." I gasp and cover my face in embarrassment. Please don't tell me that my entire group of friends knows about my drunken escapades.

"Shit, Emerson, there's a time for your mouth and there's a time for it to be closed. I thought you were trying to help me get her back?" Jace bites out.

"They know?" I whisper, with my hands still covering my flaming cheeks.

"I . . . it wasn't . . . shit . . ." Jace stammers.

"Don't blame Jace," Jaxon interrupts. "These two"—he gestures toward Em and Quinn—"are like a really small gang. Poor Jace didn't even see it coming when they pried it out of him."

"Okay, now there's another thing I need to apologize for. I just . . . shit, Lane, you threw me off with this surprise." Jace stumbles over his words nervously. "I had this whole apology planned out. Now I'm thrown."

"I think it was a damn good plan." Lane smiles widely. *Brat.*

Jace stares at me and I'm trying to see all the words in his head that he can't manage to get out. "Jace, you're flustered. What's wrong? This isn't like you," I say, loud enough for him to hear.

Out of nowhere, he drops to one knee and pulls out a small, red leather box with gold detailing around the edges. I watch as he clicks the gold latch and opens the box to face me. Without looking at the contents inside, I slam my eyes closed and reach out to snap the box shut between my fingers, lingering on the soft leather a moment longer.

"Jace, no!" I exclaim.

I wasn't thinking and now the gasps around us tell me that was the Snap Heard Round the Bar.

"Worse than being kicked in the balls . . ." Lane mutters.

Jace swallows roughly and says, "I deserved that."

"Jace, I don't know where we are. I was willing to give you time because that's what you needed. But you really hurt me when we were at the hospital. You didn't talk to me and then you rushed me out of there like some kind of dirty secret. I understand why you were upset, but . . ." He sticks the box back into his pocket, and my stomach drops at the idea of what I may have just ruined. His hands slide up my sides until they reach my face.

"I was wrong. The reasons I had at the time don't matter, and I was wrong. I'm so sorry. I can't seem to get my head on straight around you. From the very beginning, I should have stepped up and put you first. If you give me another chance, you'll always be first to me . . . I swear. Please forgive me," he adds, looking directly into my eyes.

"I think it's time for karaoke," Lane interrupts.

"That's a fucking great idea," Jaxon bellows.

"Apologize with your heart, man. Sing it out," Cole adds mockingly.

"Shit, can y'all keep to yourselves for one minute?" Jace asks, annoyed.

"Karaoke?" I ask, intrigued by the idea.

"Yep. You see, this week I convinced Ed he needed to add a karaoke night to the bar. Attract more customers and all that. Welcome to the first night!" Lane exclaims animatedly.

"Babe, can we go somewhere else?" Jace begs with both his words and his eyes.

"Are you scared?" Lane taunts, clamping a hand on his shoulder. I don't bother trying to respond. I've learned that when I'm hanging around these four large, loud guys, my voice gets lost in the crowd. They're a fun group, but it's hard to get a word in once they get started.

"He'll never do it," Jax says to egg his brother on.

"This was your plan all along, Lane?" I finally ask.

Lane nods his head with a huge grin, and Jace throws his hands up in defeat. He looks at me and I try to hide the grin on my face.

"You actually like this idea, babe?" he asks with surprise in his voice.

"I just can't imagine you doing it," I reply softly. He swivels on his toe and immediately starts toward the brand-new screens Ed apparently installed while I was gone. My mouth drops open in shock.

Everyone around me begins to whistle and Cole shouts, "Can I pick the song?" Jace throws a middle finger up in reply. Cassie, our newest bartender, mans the karaoke machine while Jace flips through the song title book. She gets on the microphone and welcomes everyone to Karaoke Night before announcing that it's time for the first victim.

"This hot thing right here is Jace," Cassie calls out, and there is a round of catcalls and whistles directed toward the small stage. Jace shakes his head and lets out a coy smile. This is totally not his thing. Despite the ribbing he was getting from the guys, I can tell he would never be up there if I hadn't expressed interest.

"Shit, he loves you something hard." Jax stands next to me while leaning his weight into the pool table.

"You think so?" I ask, trying to contain my excitement.

"Jace always needs to be able to control things and know what the outcome is going to be before his action. Singing in front a crowd?" He chuckles. "Yeah, he's totally burning up on the inside. This is good for him, though."

"I'm glad you're doing better, Jaxon. It wasn't a fun time with you down," I say sincerely.

"Thanks for picking up some of the stress for Em and still being here, even after Jace was an ass."

"It feels bizarre talking to you about me and Jace," I nervously admit.

"I couldn't be happier for the two of you. Lord knows y'all make more sense than we ever did. Don't feel weird," he says and pulls me in for a side hug.

"Lay off my girl," Jace's deep voice booms through the speakers. I smile adoringly up at the stage and move closer.

Cassie leans into the microphone and calls out to the crowd, "Jace is going entertain us with 'Whatever It Is' by Zac Brown Band. Get at it, hot stuff." The music intro begins and I get nervous butterflies in my stomach watching Jace up there all alone. He winks at me, but I can see that he's garnering his confidence.

"He's going to kill us later." Cole laughs while clapping for Jace.

"It'll be totally worth it," Lane agrees.

Jace belts out the first few words and the room falls silent. I am absolutely floored by his voice. How did I not know Jace could sing?

"Ho-ly shit!" Lane yells, while hooting with enthusiasm. "Well, that totally backfired on me!"

"I did not expect this . . ." Cole admits.

The third line in the song is fittingly about his lady's legs and heaven. Jace exaggerates the line and winks directly at me. I cover my huge smile and then begin clapping along with the beat.

Once he figures out how happy the song makes me, he really gets into it, strutting across the stage and pointing me out in the crowd. This doesn't stop the girls from dancing provocatively in front of his little stage, though. Seeing him up there in his faded blue jeans and button-up shirt, singing his heart out directly to me, is probably the most amazing thing I've ever experienced. Not even the sight of those girls could wipe this smile off my face. His eyes are focused only on me.

Anytime the line "I love you" comes across the screen, Jace clutches at his heart and sings to my soul. In this moment, I know how sorry he is for being cruel. I knew he was truly sorry earlier during his apology when I saw the real pain in his eyes. The song finishes with a few lasting chords, and Jace steps away from the edge of the stage. Everyone claps and calls out for an encore. Jace laughs and shakes his head.

"Thank you," he says into the microphone.

"Marry me!" an excited blonde yells at him.

"Sorry, I'm taken. Well . . . at least, I think I'm taken . . ." He looks out to where I'm at in the back of the bar.

"Very taken!" I yell back, and his smile lights up the room. A few groans are expressed from the crowd, and Jace shrugs his shoulders at them with a cute, bashful smile. He clears his throat and I freeze at the look in his eyes. I don't know why he isn't stepping down yet, but when he brings the microphone back to his mouth, my whole body locks up. I grip the edge of the pool table, my fingernails digging harshly into the green felt.

"That beautiful, tall brunette back there stole my heart a long time ago. We screwed it up and wasted a lot of years. But you know what?" he asks the crowd and then speaks directly to me, "I'd do it all over again, knowing that you were going to be there at the end. I'd walk through the sadness and the loneliness all over again for you. I truly was lonely, because you were always the one I wished I was with. I can't regret it, though. The journey was hard, yes, but falling in love with you was easy. I could never regret falling in love with you."

With everything we've been through, everything we've put ourselves through, all the pain we've endured, this act alone erases it all with one single swipe. The secrecy and sneaking around are instantly forgotten with Jace's very public display. He finally hops down, sets the microphone on the stage, and squeezes through his audience, his eyes never leaving mine.

When he reaches me, he once again drops to one knee and I cover the sob that rips through my chest. He reaches back into his pocket and pulls out the red leather box again. Then he looks up at me with a question in his eyes before he opens it. I nod my head up and down emphatically, letting him know it's okay.

"Audrey, you've been in my head since the moment I met you, and you've never left. Baby, I sure as hell don't deserve you, but I can't imagine anyone else being the mother of my children or being the hand I hold at the end of every day. You're my lucky penny, remember?" he asks. I dig my penny necklace out from under my shirt and squeeze it tightly. His eyes look moist when he sees that I'm still wearing it.

He hops off his knee and I frown up at him. He must have read my mind because he leans in quickly to kiss me and says, "It's coming, babe. I just remembered I wanted to give you something else first." He hands the red leather box back to Jax and my eyes follow it longingly. "Babe, I love you; it's coming. First"—he digs around in his pockets—"I made something for you while you were out of town." On top of the pool table, he dumps out a handful of tubes of lip balm. I grab one and he laughs. "Well, I didn't make these . . ."

"Yeah, I bought a ton of these for you. I never want you to run out. I also got all that coconut stuff you like. I cleared out my whole bathroom so you can have room for your things," he rambles on. I'm blown away by what he's saying and the amount of thought he's put into all of this.

He starts searching the other pocket and dumps out a ton of coins. They clank against each other on the table. I notice that they are all flattened pennies, each one a little different from the next.

"It took me a long time to get it just right, so I ended up making about sixteen of them, but this one turned out the best." He fumbles with the coins and I realize that I love this side of Jace. He's usually the confident intellect, but every once in a while, when he's around me, he turns into this clumsy fool. It makes me smile to think that I can make him as flustered as he seems to make me.

He reaches behind my neck and unclasps the necklace I'm wearing. "This one has the year we met, the year I picked up my lucky penny for the first time." Although the penny is smashed, I can clearly make out the year on it. "This one . . ."—he slides a second flattened penny on to my chain and it clinks next to the first—"says exactly how I feel." I pull the penny up close and read out loud the words that he's stamped into the metal.

Lucky to have found you.
Blessed to have you.

"Okay, that's seriously sweet," Em whispers from behind me.

"Jace . . ." I say warmly.

He drops to his knee for the third time tonight and grabs the box back from Jax. "I'm all over the place, I know. If I knew you were going to be here, I would have been more prepared . . ." he rambles on adorably.

"Jace, you're perfect," I whisper. The fact that he's actually been carrying all of this around with him makes me want to jump up onstage and sing *to him*. But I really hope he doesn't ask me to.

"Audrey, will you marry me?" he finally blurts out, and the audience enthusiastically starts clapping.

I can't contain my excitement any longer. I spring toward him and grab hold of his face. He catches my waist and pulls me in closer. I kiss his lips, his cheeks, his nose, and his eyes. I make my way back to his lips and devour them with need. I'm the one that's blessed to have him, and I'll never let him go again. I need him in my life always. I'll stand and fight for him, if need be.

The bar patrons filter back toward their tables. Jace and I remain on the floor, my lips still attached to his. There's nowhere I'd rather be, and he doesn't seem to be in any hurry for me to stop.

I don't know how much time passes while Jace and I make out like teenagers in the middle of the bar, but Lane eventually leans down and whispers, "Psst, so what's your answer, doll?"

Jace looks at me with confusion before he realizes what Lane is saying. "Hey, yeah, you never answered me."

I push Lane's face away with my hand and slide my fingers through Jace's messy hair. "Of course I'll marry you, Jace Riley."

- EPILOGUE -

JACE - One Year Later . . .

I toss my laptop into my bag and check my desk for any paperwork I need to take with me. When everything is in order, I take one more look at the view I'll never get tired of seeing. The windows behind my desk extend from floor to ceiling, and the Dallas skyline shines brightly all around. Uncle Logan works mainly from home now and is happy he's still on track to retire early since Jax, Cole, and I have been handling everything so well. Everything seems to have come full circle. My name is now on the same door my dad's name used to be on, Jax is working next to me just like my dad's twin did, and I'm finally marrying the girl I fell in love with so many years ago.

Right before I reach my office door, I turn back and scan my desk for anything I may need over the next week and a half. Ever since we moved back to Texas, I haven't gone a single day without setting foot in this building. The controlling side of me cringes at the idea of losing the ability to oversee all decisions for even a short period of time. Jaxon is always telling me to lighten up, but I feel as though I have some pretty big shoes to fill here.

"There isn't anything left for you to do. Seriously, time to go home," Josephine calls out from the open door.

"Josie, you'll call me—" I start to say before my secretary cuts me off.

"I'll call Jaxon first and then I'll call Cole. Not even then will I call you, because now I have Lane as well. If for some bizarre reason they can't solve the issue after a reasonable amount of time, then yes, I'll call you," she says, rolling her eyes.

"You're mocking me."

"You have a beautiful soon-to-be bride at home, but yet you're here . . ." she trails off while eyeing me.

The second the thought of Audrey enters my mind, I snap into action. My gorgeous fiancée is currently at our newly built house waiting for me to come home, and I couldn't be happier. Audrey is my peace at the end of a hard day or my excitement at the end of a boring one.

"You make a good point. I'll see you Saturday."

"Tell Audrey I'll be over bright and early!" she calls out, while turning off the office lights.

I pull into my four-car garage right next to Cole's Porsche. I don't know how long he's going to be able to keep driving that thing now that he has a baby. Quickly, I shuffle inside through the kitchen entrance and search for anyone who's home. All of their cars are here, but the house is dark and quiet. I navigate my way to a family room, where Quinn is lounging on the couch, reading a book.

"Hey, Jace," she whispers.

"Where's my baby?" I ask.

"She's sleeping," she warns sternly. Quinn should know by now that this never deters me. I push forward and make a direct line for the little pink-and-white bassinet sitting next to the couch.

"Please don't wake her, Jace. It just took Cole and me an hour to get her back to sleep," Quinn begs. As if I didn't hear anything,

I scoop up the prettiest baby girl I've ever laid eyes on. She looks exactly like Quinn but has Cole's blond hair. I can't believe how one little person can look so much like two different people. I'm yearning to see what my and Audrey's babies will look like. *Go ahead and take my man card; I don't care anymore.*

Right after Audrey accepted my proposal, Jax and I started planning our dream homes. Before we knew it, we had blueprints and contractors hired. We built on our family land, with Jaxon and Em's house backing right up to the pond they love so much. Right across the street we had paved is our house. Cole and Quinn were living in a house out near his family, but soon decided they wanted to live near us so that our children could grow up together. Their house should be done within the month, and meanwhile, they've been staying here.

I hold Chloe up to my nose and take in the smell only a baby can have. When her little blond eyelashes begin to move and she peers up at me with those forest-green eyes, I'm a goner.

"Jace! You're ridiculous. Now it's your job to get her back down," Quinn huffs.

"Hi, princess. Did you miss me today?" I whisper softly to her. She makes a little squeak as she stretches out and I hold her in closer.

"Oh, hell, no," Cole growls as he walks into the room. "Dude, do you know how long I had to pace this house with her?" I continue smiling down at her, not letting anyone talk me out of holding her after a long day.

"What am I going to do when you aren't here when I get home?" I coo at her.

"I'm gonna miss being here, man," Cole responds.

"I can see your house from my front windows," I laugh.

"I know, but I'm gonna miss having you and Audrey's help with Chloe. I'll miss Audrey's amazing cooking skills, and I also won't be able to hear the two of you have sex every night," the asshole says with a fake pout.

"Whoa, jackass! Don't listen to me and my girl," I scold.

"Hey, language in front of the little ears!" he laughs.

"Jace, I actually need to talk to you about Audrey," Quinn calls over.

"Where is she, by the way? I haven't seen her all day and I'm about to go crazy." I lean in and kiss Chloe's forehead and say, "I just needed to see you before I go to bed, little one."

"Audrey's already asleep. She went to that self-defense class today that you signed her up for."

"Shit, I forgot about that." I wrap Chloe in one arm and rub my temples with the other. I haven't been able to talk to Audrey much while I'm at the office because I get so caught up and side-tracked.

"Jace, I'm going to give you some tough love, so bear with me for a second, okay?" she asks and I nod my head. "I think you're working too much, and you need to realize it before everything you care about slips away without your even noticing." Her words catch my immediate attention and fill me with dread.

"What do you mean, Quinny? Where is this coming from? Did Audrey say she would leave me?" I rush to ask. I need to go see her. I need to stop whatever thoughts she may be having. This can't be happening.

"Calm down, Jace. It's nothing like that. I just don't want it to get to that point for you guys. I mean, how much have you really seen Audrey lately? How many times have you come home at"—she looks down at her watch—"ten thirty at night or later and had to wake her up?"

"I'm new to this company. I have a lot of grunt work to put in before I can pull back a bit," I rationalize. "Audrey understands this."

She nods her head and continues. "You're right, she does. But Cole and I have been talking, and you don't need to be there as much as you are. You can delegate. You have Jax, Cole, and now Lane, in addition to all of your many employees. Release the reins just a little, Jace."

"I can try, but y'all don't understand how much actually has to be done every single day . . ."

"Jace, you're missing out on crucial parts of Audrey's life, and this job has only just begun," Quinn says.

"I don't understand what you're saying . . ." I trail off.

"I went and picked up Audrey's gown from alterations today, and afterward, while she was out, I took it upstairs to hang it in her closest. How have you not noticed that she hasn't even unpacked her clothes?"

"She what . . . ?" I begin to panic.

"Jace, she's been living here for months and all of her clothes are still in suitcases. She wears them, washes them, and puts them back. She tiptoes around this house without touching a thing. If she has to use anything, she immediately washes it or stashes it away as if she were never there," Quinn adds.

"I really hope you're making this shit up. My heart is about to bust out of my chest," I say in alarm.

"She's lonely, Jace. Lane's been gone all the time. She won't go into town unless she absolutely has to, because she's too afraid of what people will remember about her from high school. Today she told me she was glad she finally found a job because she's running low on funds." With that, she eyes me and continues. "Now, I only know what Cole makes, but you have to be making more than that. So why is the girl running low on money?"

"What?!" I holler. When Chloe squirms away from the elevated sound of my voice, I immediately apologize and begin rocking her back and forth. "Quinn, I swear to God we have a joint account."

"Does she actually spend money out of that account?" Before she can ask another question, I wiggle my phone out of my back pocket and bring up our bank app on my screen. Swiftly I scroll through every transaction. Mine. Mine. Mine. I slump down onto the couch with Chloe snuggled into my chest.

"Wait, last week she bought something . . ." I say and then look at it further. "Dry cleaner. Shit, that was for me." How did I not know she wasn't even using our bank account? "She's going to leave me. She's absolutely going to leave me," I say in a defeated tone.

"No, she's not. That's not why I'm telling you this. I just think this has to do with how she grew up. You need to make her more comfortable. This house was *your* plans, *your* ideas, and you want her to spend *your* money . . ."

I quickly interrupt her. "*Our* money. If anything, it's hers. I don't want it without her."

She nods her head and softly says, "I'm glad to hear that. But you need to remember that she's never known a relationship like that. I'm done stressing you out. She'll kill me for saying something, but I figured you didn't even notice."

"Because I've been at the office every single day," I grumble.

"You need to at least have some rest days every week, Jace, or even *you* will burn out," Cole adds in. "What happens when you have a kid? Are you going to be that dad that's never around? I *had* that dad, and trust me, it sucked. Your dad took time away; you can too."

He has a point. My dad was home every day by dinner and all day during the weekends. I'll never forget the time he spent with us, building the Camaro with Jax and hitting the heavy bag with me in the barn. I look down at a now-sleeping Chloe and realize I can't become the guy I'm on track to become. I want to hear about Audrey's day over dinner, not a half-asleep conversation late at night. I want to wake up next to her on Saturday and Sunday mornings and be able to share the day with her.

"I'll fix this," I inform them, "and she doesn't need to go work for some random company. She can work at the office with me if she really wants to get a job."

"I knew you'd be reasonable about this," Quinn responds, while patting my leg. "But if I know Audrey, she's not going to take some pity job from you. She earned a graduate degree. Let her be an adult, Jace."

"I need to see my fiancée." I kiss each of Chloe's cheeks and stand slowly to walk her back over to her bassinet.

"Dude, seriously. Go make your own baby. This one is mine," Cole orders, while transferring his daughter to his arms. He looks down at her with awe and wonder, like he's done since the day she was born. He sits down on the couch and lays her little head on his chest. Yeah, she's got him wrapped around her finger.

"I plan to," I say, making my retreat. "Love you guys."

I hear their responses when I hit the first step of our large staircase. I take them two at a time until I reach the double doors that lead into our master suite. The knob turns slowly in my hands and I slip inside quietly. The bathroom light, which she leaves on for me every night, shines across her naked backside. The fact that she has to leave a light on for me should have been my first clue that I've been coming home too late.

I walk into my closet and discard my suit, leaving only my briefs on. Out of curiosity, I walk over and glance into Audrey's closet, where Quinn's observations are confirmed. It's a giant, empty space with three suitcases lying on the floor. There are empty wooden hangers lining the bars, and at the very back is a big white bag that holds her wedding gown. My fingers itch to unzip it and peek inside. I'm dying to know what she plans on wearing, but I hold back the urge, not wanting to ruin her surprise.

I can't wait for her to have my last name and someday soon carry my children. I stand in her empty closet and think back on the day she finally told me what happened with her pregnancy in high school. My jaw clenches at the murderous anger I have to suppress when I flash back to those thoughts. Since we've been back in Texas, I've tried to pay a visit to her dear ol' dad, but apparently he's been gone for a few years now. I'll find him, though, and when I do it won't be pretty.

I shake off the thoughts and quietly shuffle across the wood floor to our bed. Softly, I kneel on the bed beside Audrey's stunning body. She's lying on her stomach with her face turned away from me and her pillows pushed to the side. Her soft breaths move her back up and down. I take advantage of the position and reach into the nightstand. I hold the bottle of massage oil above her back and drizzle a line down her spine. When the liquid hits her skin, her eyes shoot open and she fidgets. I reach out and hold her in place.

"Shh . . . it's just me. Relax, gorgeous," I whisper into her ear. When she hears my voice, I feel her body loosen and begin to respond to my touch. She doesn't sleep as deeply as she used to, probably because I'm waking her up almost every night.

"Sorry, I fell asleep early," she mumbles with a sleepy voice. I spread the oil around and slowly start massaging her muscles. With deep, long pushes, I rub out her tension and soreness.

I signed her up for a pretty intense self-defense class by one of my buddies who just got out of the US Marines. He got all of his licenses and now runs a class. This isn't some basic class run by an off-duty police officer. It's extreme and tough. I wanted to go to the class with her, but it slipped my mind, and I hate that she has to go alone.

"You have nothing to be sorry about. I'm sorry I've been working so much. I'm going to change that; I promise," I say quietly.

With the oil still thick on her back, she lifts up and looks at me questioningly. "I know you're lonely, Audrey. I haven't been taking care of you and I'm sorry."

"Why are you saying this, Jace? What happened?" she asks, while nervously fidgeting her fingers. I unwind them slowly and run my hands up her arms, leaving a slick trail in their path. I can't help looking at her bare chest on the way up to her eyes.

"I want you to move in with me. I want to live with you. I want to live where you're going to be the happiest and if that's not here, I'll fix that," I say in a pleading tone.

She looks at me with confusion for a few beats, and then says, "You're scaring me. What do you mean 'move in'? Haven't I been living here with you?"

"Have you?" I ask. "Audrey, you haven't unpacked your clothes, and Quinn said you don't touch anything in the house," I say softly. Her body appears to deflate, and I can see her wheels begin spinning with what she should or should not say. If I could go a few rounds in the ring with myself right now, I would. How did I not notice this? I'm supposed to protect and care for her, not just provide for her. I promised to keep her first and in a way I thought I was by making sure she didn't want for anything, but I didn't take into account that most of all she just wants me. Not all this stuff I can buy her. Just me.

"Jace . . ." she sighs and looks up into my eyes. "I'm trying. I'm trying to beat these demons, but . . . it's a process. It took me a year to unpack my stuff when I moved in with Lane. You have to realize what my life was like. Before California, I had to hide all of my belongings in a backpack that I kept shoved under a couch. I've never felt like any place was actually mine. This house . . ." she pauses and seems to consider her next words carefully.

I finish for her by saying, "I made the plans for this house, and I had it filled with furniture before we moved in. I haven't let you make it yours. I thought I was helping the transition process, but I never considered how that would affect you."

"Jace, it'll be okay. I love this house. It's just going to take me some time to grow into it. I need you to know that I don't want to be anywhere else than in your house with you," she whispers.

"That's the thing, though. This is your house too, babe. Your name is on the deed right beside mine. I'll make this right," I assure her.

"I'll try to unpack. That closet is just way too big, though. Every time I open it, I'm intimidated. I yelled in it the other day and I could hear my own echo," she says in an awed tone.

"Move into mine, with me. Once you actually start buying clothes like other girls do, you'll probably fill yours up and take over mine anyway." I chuckle.

She gasps and says, "I could never have that much."

"And that's why I love you so much," I say, smiling at her unpretentiousness. I scoop her up into my arms and stride toward the bathroom. She squeals with laughter when my hands slip and slide from the oil that's smeared across her body. When we reach the glass shower, I reach in and turn it to a warm temperature, just how she likes it. With my girl in my arms, I carry her inside the soothing spray.

AUDREY –

Em, Quinn, Josie, and I had an early breakfast and nail appointments, so I snuck out of our bedroom without waking up Jace this morning. I can't even remember the last time I woke up before he did. He's usually out of the house before I even open my eyes every morning. He was sleeping so peacefully beside me, I didn't have the heart to wake him up for a good-bye.

With a wave, Quinn and I step out of Em's car and make our way up the front porch steps. If what Jace said last night is true, then I'll get to spend the whole day with him, and I couldn't be more excited.

"Jace has to be exhausted after being up all night," Quinn says from right beside me.

I stop and turn to face her, asking, "What do you mean? He didn't get home that late last night."

She looks at me, appearing unsure if she should say what she was just thinking. "Um . . . I had to get up with Chloe a couple times last night and each time I saw Jace pacing the halls while talking on his cell phone."

"Huh . . ." I reply, because I have no idea what he was up doing. I thought he had passed out next to me after our long shower together.

I push open the front door and step inside the house. After the first couple of feet, I realize my boot heels are creating an unfamiliar echo throughout the foyer. When I gaze around the house, I realize it's empty. Completely empty.

"What the hell?" Quinn questions.

"How long were we gone?!" I ask in a panicked tone. "Jace!" I cry out into the vacant house.

About ten feet from the front door, I find a piece of paper lying on the floor. I crouch down to scoop it up and recognize the small handwriting that flows across the page in black ink.

Dear Audrey,

There are furniture magazines in the kitchen. Circle what you want and Josie will have it all ordered and here before you return from your honeymoon. Fill me with furniture. Make me your own.

Love, Your House

P.S. Don't be mad at your soon-to-be husband. He loves you more than anything in the world and just wants you to feel at home.

I smile at his quirky-yet-sweet note. I should be mad at him for doing this the day before my wedding, but I just can't bring myself to find anger anywhere inside me. This is the new side of Jace I've learned to love. He tries to fix any problems between us immediately. After we realized how stupid we've been wasting so much time apart when we could have just talked out our issues, he won't let a second of misunderstanding pass without trying to resolve it.

"Me and my big mouth . . ." Quinn grumbles, reading the note over my shoulder.

"Do you hate me?" Jace's voice calls out from upstairs, and I look up to see his handsome face peeking around the corner.

I run up the stairs toward him and launch myself into his arms. "You big idiot—you have more money than sense!" I say into his neck, hoping that my words come off gentler than they sound.

"I want you to be happy in our home," he whispers into my ear, while pulling me into his arms tighter.

"As long as it's *ours*, I'm happy. I don't ever want you to think otherwise," I say, kissing a line along his neck.

A throat clears from behind us and we both turn to see Quinn stomping her foot in clear frustration. Jace chuckles under his breath before Quinn says, "And where exactly is my family?"

"Sorry, Quinny. I had to move you guys to Jax and Em's house. But you'll come back when the new furniture gets here," Jace explains.

"Well, if we're already over there, we should just stay until our house is done," she replies.

"No!" Jace and I say in unison.

When she gives us both a puzzled look, Jace says, "I want to see my baby as much as I possibly can before you guys have to move into your home. I'm gonna miss her."

When he juts out his plump bottom lip in a ridiculous pout, my heart beats faster at the idea of Jace being a dad someday. I know, without a doubt, that he'll be the best there has ever been.

~

That night after our rehearsal dinner, we all crowd in through Em and Jaxon's front door. Chloe is spending the night at her grandparents' house so that Cole and Quinn can stay out late tonight. Jaxon leads us all to his back porch where we can have a few more drinks and talk late into the night.

"Mom, you can't be mad at me forever," Jaxon complains, while trying to hold back a laugh.

"Yes, I can. Jace is my good son, having a nice, respectable wedding. But you! Not once, but twice now you've run away to elope!"

"Mom, it's been almost a year," Jaxon pleads. "How come you aren't mad at Em? She was there too, you know."

Em immediately whacks him in the stomach and says, "Thanks, traitor!"

"Because I know you tricked her into it somehow. I only have you to blame," Julie argues. This is an ongoing dispute between the two of them. We all know that Julie was over the moon when she found out Em was officially a Riley and honestly, I wasn't surprised to hear those two snuck off to Vegas. But his mom still likes to give him hell anytime there is wedding talk.

Cole and Quinn had a massive wedding right after she gave birth to Chloe this summer, with all of his father's political friends in attendance. It was more of a show-off affair for his dad's campaign and less about them, but we all had fun anyway. Jace and I are the next ones in our little group to get married, and I can't wait to finally ditch my father's name and lovingly add Riley in its place.

I walk out to the porch railing and gaze at the light from the moon bouncing off of Jax and Em's pond. Lane wraps his arm around my shoulders and squeezes me tightly into his side. Lane has been my rock for so many years that I can't believe our little era is coming to an end. I swipe away the tears that escape from my eyes.

"He'll take good care of you, doll," his raspy voice says from above me.

I look up to see the moisture in his eyes. "I'll be a sobbing mess in seconds if you start the waterworks too!"

He laughs softly and says, "I'm happy for you. I'll miss you like fucking crazy, but you deserve this more than you know."

"I can't wait to be in your wedding someday," I state, but he rolls his eyes. He doesn't like talking about falling in love or marriage when it pertains to himself. I give him a break and ask, "You're not upset about not being a groomsman, are you?"

"He doesn't even have groomsmen," he laughs. When Jace and I decided we wanted a very small and intimate wedding, we cut the idea of having a wedding party standing alongside us. Besides, if we had our close friends standing up next to us, we would lose half of our audience. "I would much rather walk you down the aisle any day, doll," he whispers.

"Thank you for saving a broken mess of a girl, Lane. I can't thank you enough. You'll never understand how much you helped me grow," I say, while hugging him around the waist.

"Damn, all this time I thought you were the one saving me," he chuckles, and I pinch his back, just like old times.

"You haven't finally realized what you're missing and trying to run away with my girl, are you?" Jace affectionately says from behind us.

I leave Lane's warm grasp to enter Jace's. I've never felt more at home than I do in this moment. It's almost as if there's been a light turned on for me, and I can finally see how blessed I am. And just like Jace said to me a year ago: I would walk through the sadness all over again if I knew I would be reaching this point.

Lane leaves Jace and me alone out on the porch to look out over the pond. When Jace wraps his arms around me from behind, I whisper, "You know, it's unheard of for a bride not to know where she's getting married."

He tucks his face into the nook between my chin and my shoulder and says, "I promise this is my last surprise. From then on out, we'll make joint decisions. This is a good one, though. I know you'll be happy with it."

I turn in his arms and grab the lapels of his suit coat. "I love your surprises, Jace. Quinn may have had a point about your work hours, but she failed to mention that you're great at surprises"—I rise up on my toes and whisper in his ear—"and at taking control."

A low rumble emerges from his chest and he growls, "Well, that's a damn good thing, babe, because there's no way in hell that'll ever change."

~

I never pictured myself standing outside on my wedding day, with my hair tightly pinned to my head and my long, white dress blowing in the cold breeze . . . blindfolded. When Em approached me as I was climbing into the limo with a light blue sash in her hands, I stared at her with apprehension.

"Your something blue," she says with a wicked chuckle.

"I already have something blue," I reply, gesturing to the thin, sterling silver bracelet with diamonds and turquoise gemstones that Jace had sent over while I was getting ready.

"He wanted you to have something else too," she says, shrugging her shoulders. That was the last thing I saw before she wrapped the sash around my eyes and helped me the rest of the way into the car.

Standing out in the breeze, completely blind to the world around me, I hear a familiar deep voice say, "Well, this is different. A blindfolded bride. I've heard that usually happens on the honeymoon, but not *before* the ceremony," Lane says, chuckling.

"Don't make fun of me. I have no idea where I am," I nervously confess.

His arm is instantly around me in a protective hold. "You look beautiful and you're going to love this." Shortly after, I hear a door open and close. "Well, doll, that's our cue. Should we bail and run away forever, or go inside?" he asks teasingly, although I know that if I asked him to, he would whisk me away in a heartbeat.

"I'm ready." And I am. I'm ready to marry my best friend and the one true love of my life.

"Good, because Jace has been pacing nervously all damn morning." When he feels my body lock up, he rushes to say, "Not that kind of nervous. More like, so-fucking-excited-to-see-you nervous."

I let out a deep breath and allow Lane to lead me inside to my mystery wedding. We step inside and I immediately feel relief at the warmer setting. My dress has a deep V-neck and my back is almost completely bare. Not the best choice for a wedding in the chill of November, but the second I put it on I knew Jace would love it. It feels classic and elegant, just like him.

Wherever we just stepped into has a very distinct yet recognizable aroma. It smells antiquated and musty. I scan through locations in my head that can produce this scent. When realization hits, I gasp and grab to pull my blindfold down. The first thing I see is Lane's brightly smiling face. I skim my surroundings and take in the beautiful old bookstore. The very same bookstore where I first crashed into Jace, right out front on the sidewalk. The store that I've spent countless hours in since we've been back. I don't like to come into town much, but this is the one place I make an exception for.

I stare up at the towering shelves full of old books with yellowing pages that contain beautiful love stories. Gorgeous white flower arrangements hang from the high ceilings. My family has strung tiny little lights between the books, and tea lights adorn the shelves to create a magical atmosphere. Strings of lightbulbs crisscross along the ceiling, giving off a romantic glow. I smile widely when I realize I'm going to say my vows in front of a bunch of love stories that have stood the test of time. I can't imagine a more perfect setting.

My eyes make their way down from the mesmerizing shelves and finally land on my handsome fiancé. The breath is stolen straight out of my chest when I catch the look on his face. Tears are streaming freely and shamelessly down his face, and I can feel his deep love with just that look alone.

Jace stands at the end of a long center aisle, with our closest friends and family sitting in front of him. Before I realize it, Lane has walked me all the way down the aisle and placed my hand in my soon-to-be husband's comforting one.

Nothing else matters. No one else matters. It's only Jace. Jace, with his gorgeous gray suit and copper-colored tie that perfectly matches the pennies strung around my neck.

"It's not fair that every time I see you, you look even more delicious than the last," he whispers into my hand, right before he gives it a soft kiss.

"You can't keep using the same lines on me," I softly say back.

"I'm sorry, but you really shouldn't be allowed to look this beautiful," he expresses, while leaning in toward my neck.

A couple of throats clear from behind us, and Jace freezes. "Vows first, you guys," I hear Jaxon chuckle.

We behave for the remainder of the ceremony, repeating each vow after the priest prompts us. Sniffles are heard from our audience, but my eyes are still glued to the man in front of me. His eyes are equally spellbound as he looks at me. We are all alone in this magical bubble. Although I'm aware of the eyes boring into us, the only ones I care to look at right now are Jace's.

Jace surprises me yet again with a beautiful, sparkling wedding band. Tiny little diamonds surround the platinum ring, and the lights above us cause it to glisten and glow.

I realize that the priest has finished his speech and that the room is completely quiet. I look up to Jace for clarification, because I don't remember what we are supposed to do now. I hear a few chuckles and then Jace gives me a drop-dead-sexy smirk, right before he scoops me into his arms and lands me with a breath-stealing kiss. Instantly, I remember what I'm supposed to be doing, so I thread my fingers through his soft hair and return his kiss with equal passion.

After a few more beats, Jace pulls back and gazes down at me. "I love you, Mrs. Riley."

"It's about time you changed my name," I whisper breathlessly up at him.

"I couldn't agree more," he says and smiles lovingly.

Before he can dip down for another kiss, I stand up on my tiptoes, deciding it's finally my turn to give him a surprise. When my lips brush the edge of his ear, I let him know the news he's been begging to hear from me. I overhear the catch in his breath, and his grip on my arms squeezes a bit tighter.

In front of our clapping and cheering audience, he leans back to look at me with tears running down his face for the second time today and with questions in his eyes. He needs me to confirm it for him.

"You're going to be a dad, Mr. Riley."

ABOUT THE AUTHOR

Kimberly Lauren is the bestselling author of *Beautiful Broken Rules*, *Beautiful Broken Mess*, and *Beautiful Broken Promises*. Kimberly lives in Texas with her husband, son, and their three dogs. She is a wanderer, an adventurer, and a traveler. She hasn't seen it all, but it's all on her list. Lately, if she's not traveling or chasing a toddler, she gets some time to write a book.